BLOOD OF THE THIRD

Heralds of the Culling

Book 2

MJ Stewart

Other works from M.J. Stewart

Heralds of the Culling (Vampire action/horror)
>*Heir of Darkness*
>*Blood of the Third*

Displacement (Time Travel Sci-Fi)
>*Displacement: The Long Sleep*

Kingdom of Lorr Novels (Epic Fantasy)
>*The Kingdom of Lorr: WorldGate Crossing*
>*The Kingdom of Lorr: The Return*
>*Demon of Lorr*
>*Key Quest*

Previews and purchasing information at:

https://majorstewart.com/

Andre's Story

*– Takes place before the events chronicled in
Heir of Darkness –*

Sam did not believe in God until he embraced Satan. He did so happily, eagerly, in fact.

Born into slavery on a plantation in southeastern Texas when Texas was still a republic, his life was a hazy memory of physical and psychological brutality.

He was told his mother died in childbirth and his father was sold to a plantation in Louisiana, so he might as well forget about anyone giving a damn about him, ever. According to his overseers, there were only two kinds of niggers: working ones and dead ones. Any transgression meant a back striped bloody by the lash. Sometimes mere boredom on the part of a sadistic overseer meant the same.

Life was worse for Sam prior to his teenage years. The males and females who were not related by blood or marriage were kept in different quarters at night. As a boy, Sam was often considered pretty, almost as pretty as a girl. He found to his horror how much of a curse that was when some of the older male slaves used him at night when the women were not available. That went on until he grew old enough and strong enough to stop it. The last man who tried him died of a crushed skull and a crushed larynx, the latter a result of a savage human bite.

Sam very nearly followed his assailant into death. The killing of another slave was a worse offense than escape. A healthy slave was worth money at auction. With a runaway slave there was at least a chance of capture. A dead one was a financial loss that had no chance of being recovered.

As punishment, Sam was forced to wear a muzzle, chained to the hanging tree, given just enough food and water to survive and beaten into unconsciousness daily. Only two things kept him from being hung: the monetary loss of yet another slave; and the plantation owner, claiming to be a pious man, took into consideration the fact that Sam killed the other in defense of his manhood.

Sam grew up picking cotton and corn. He was not a big man but he was broad-shouldered and strong. His aversion to the lash made him a hard worker and obedient to his overseers. Those traits eventually earned him what passed for favored status from his captors.

In his late teens he was even allowed to stud. His favored status, however, did not spare him from the lash. An occasional drunken overseer might want to impress his drunken friends by thrashing a strong young nigger buck. It did, however, minimize the frequency of his beatings.

While he was quiet and reserved on the outside, Sam murdered them all in his mind every single day, both those who enslaved him and those who shared his enslavement.

He loathed overseers for obvious reasons. Their cruelty and their disdain for anyone that did not share their skin complexion placed them beneath Sam's contempt. Many of the other slaves disgusted him nearly as much as their slavers. Those sitting in timid acceptance of their horrific circumstances…Sam found them repugnant.

Once, when he was a boy, a small coalition of would-be runaways conspired to escape. They made the mistake of recruiting one conspirator too many. That one informed the overseers of the escape plans in an attempt to gain favor. Sam and all of the other children were forced to watch six slaves hung. Six more were randomly selected and severely beaten on the off chance that they had known about the conspirators.

That abject lesson did not teach Sam fear as the slavers intended. It taught him to hate them more. It taught him that trust was for fools. As the years passed and he grew into manhood he formed his own escape plan. Chances came and went during his teenage years but Sam stayed. Escape for him would not be enough. He had to find a way to leave some corpses in his wake.

The lead overseers had to die. The plantation owner had to die. The slaves who would sacrifice others to gain the approval of their masters had to die.

But most of all, the God-fearing slaves had to die, the meek that accepted their forced servitude as "God's will." They humbly submitted to degradation, torture, rape and murder with the belief that they would be rewarded with an eternity in some mythical paradise after death. As far as Sam was concerned they were nothing but cowards looking for a way to justify their cowardice. The slavers encouraged religion. It made them peaceful, more pliable slaves. The greatest portion of Sam's wrath was reserved for them.

Sam knew he would need to read and write. As much as he despised the religious folk, Sam used them. The overseers allowed them to gather in the horse barn every Sunday for church service. Sam suffered through weekly sermons delivered by Reverend for over ten years in order to endear himself to the man.

Sam's unerring attendance to the makeshift church over the first few years made Reverend comfortable enough with Sam to allow him to attend his small, secret reading and writing sessions. The plantation owner gave the churchgoers slightly more latitude than the other slaves. As a result, Sam got to move around with minimal supervision.

By the time he was in his mid twenties, Sam knew the plantation and the land surrounding it for miles like the back of his hand. He had scouted multiple routes for escape. He had even mapped out the path and sequence he would use to silently and swiftly move around the estate and kill a handful of slaves and several overseers.

There was a tree on same side of the house as the master's second floor bedroom window. The tree had sturdy branches that Sam knew he could use to get into that bedroom in the dead of night. His last task before he escaped would be to cut the throats of the master and his wife and set the house on fire.

Sam tested that path and sequence every few nights. He waited until well after midnight but well before dawn, when even the night patrols stole brief naps. He used his path to go from person to person. Sometimes he would sidle right up to drowsing slaves and overseers alike, barefoot, in complete silence, just to see if he could. He even climbed the tree to peer into the master's window and spy on him and his wife as they slept. Sam's knives had been picked out long ago and were well hidden in different locations along his path. They would be there when he was ready.

It occurred to Sam more than once that what he had been doing was bat shit crazy. He did not care. To him, it would have been crazier *not* to do it. Hope for vengeance and escape were the only things that kept him going.

One still night, buffeted by the soothing music of cicadas and the song of hooting owls and croaking frogs at a nearby creek, Sam once again walked his kill path. A sky full of twinkling stars and a crescent moon lit his way. He realized the time for his escape was near when he could almost walk the path with his eyes closed. He crept back toward his quarters that night full of nervous excitement.

Before the new moon, Sam would walk his kill path one last time, collecting and using his knives all along the way.

"It will never work, you know."

Sam jumped and nearly cried out with fear at the sound of the unfamiliar voice behind him. He turned to face the speaker, prepared to recite the well-rehearsed lie he had concocted in the event that an overseer caught him wandering the plantation after curfew.

The man he saw, however, was no overseer. The stranger crouched atop a slender fencepost as easily as Sam stood upon the ground.

Not only was he not an overseer, he was not a white man. He had the facial features and wore the clothes of men who lived across the southwestern border of Texas. His English was thick with a Mexican accent. The man's complexion, however, seemed too pale. Sam assumed it was an effect of the darkness and the pale moonlight.

Sam noticed one other thing. The night had gone deathly still. A profound hush had fallen over them, as though the mere presence of the stranger had startled every nocturnal creature into silence.

As if the newcomer's arrival was not peculiar enough, he spoke as if he knew what Sam had been doing. Taken aback by every aspect of the situation and lacking a better idea, Sam proceeded with his prepared speech.

"I don't know what you mean, sir," Sam began, careful to remain respectful. "I heard coyotes nearby and got scared for the chickens and cattle. I was checkin' on 'em."

The stranger chuckled. "Coyote's eh? I doubt you saw any coyotes in the master's bedroom." He nodded with satisfaction when Sam's eyes widened. "Yes, I've watched your nighttime excursions for weeks.

"I was going to take you when first I saw you. You made it so easy, with your prowling around alone in the dead of night. But then I grew curious. I cannot see what is in a man's mind as others of my kind can. I see what is in a man's heart. You mean to kill many and then escape."

Sam remained silent. *Others of my kind?*

"Your plan intrigues me," the stranger complimented. "It shows cunning and great patience, yet it will never work."

Sam had trained himself to be a good listener at a young age to better avoid the lash. While he had heard and understood every word the stranger said, he could not help but go back to one thing in particular.

"You was gonna *take* me, sir?"

"You have seen death on this plantation, I am sure," the stranger went on, ignoring Sam's question. "You have murder in your heart but you have not yet killed in the way you have planned. That is why your plan will not work. You expect the killing to be easy, a sharp, silent knife across the throat of your prey."

"I…" Sam stammered. "I don't…"

The stranger shook his head. "It will not go as you would like. Not all prey die quietly when you cut their throat. Many fight or thrash. Some gag and cough and choke on their own blood. They make noise. This you do not know, for you have never seen a man's throat cut, no?"

The stranger's grin widened, displaying feral canines at the corners of his smile. "But I have cut throats," he said in an ominous whisper. "I have cut the throats of many, with blades and teeth."

"Who are you?" Sam asked. "*What* are you?"

"*Me llamo Del Sol. Manuel Del Sol. Es muy irónico, no? Soy un vampiro.*"

Sam did not understand Spanish so most of Del Sol's words were lost on him. He did, however, understand two very pertinent parts. He recognized "Manuel Del Sol" as a name.

The last word Del Sol uttered sounded frighteningly familiar. "Vampire?" Sam breathed, shaking his head in denial. "No such thing. Vampires are demons from hell and there ain't no hell. Ain't no heaven either."

Del Sol cocked his head curiously. "You do not believe?" A dim crimson light began to shimmer in the stranger's eyes.

Sam inhaled sharply and held his breath. The hair on his arms and on the back of his neck stood on end. He blinked slowly, refusing to believe what he was seeing.

When his eyes opened a fraction of a second later Del Sol was gone. Sam spun in a slow circle, expecting to see the man sprinting off into the shadows. Del Sol was nowhere to be seen.

The night creatures' music began again.

"I done lost my mind," Sam whispered to himself as he continued his trek back to his quarters. "Seein' things…"

It was easy for him to convince himself that what he saw was not real. There were no such things as vampires. No one could have known about Sam's plan because he had not mentioned any part of it to anyone. Sam was perhaps starting to feel guilty about what he intended to do. There was no question that he was afraid.

His anger and hunger for vengeance, however, far exceeded his fear and guilt. He would follow through no matter what. If he died as a result, at least he would die fighting for his freedom, and he will have sent at least some of his tormentors to death before him.

Back in one of the men's sleeping quarters, soft knocking at the front door roused a teen from a comfortable sleep. "Who the hell…" he muttered, rising to a sitting position on his pallet on the packed earth floor.

He looked around at the other four bedrolls and saw that Sam's was empty. Again. Sam thought no one knew about his late night excursions but the boy slept lightly. He saw Sam every time he woke, dressed and slipped quietly out the door. He watched Sam slip quietly back in, undress and ease back into his bedroll.

Why was he knocking on the door this time?

The youngster assumed Sam was meeting a woman. Why else would a man sneak around the plantation in the middle of the night?

"That man gonna get himself killed…" the teen mumbled as he climbed groggily to his feet. He stepped over to the door and opened it. The man on the other side was not Sam. It was a Mexican man with unusually pale skin, wearing a fancy riding cloak and boots.

"Yes, sir?" the teen asked in a nervous whisper.

The stranger nodded politely and responded in the same low whisper. "Good evening. Boss Sadler sent me to fetch you. May I come in while you dress?"

"What he want with me this late at night?" the boy asked suspiciously. "Why ain't I ever seen you before?"

The stranger's polite tone turned cold. "I'm sure I do not know why he sent for you." His glare darkened in a way that sent an icy chill down the teen's spine. Were those pinpoints of red light in his pupils?

A threatening snarl crept into the stranger's voice that was made even more sinister by his thick accent.

"And I'm sure your master will *not* be happy at your questioning his command. Now, I will ask you again. May I come in while you dress?" It did not sound like a question.

"Yes, sir."

The stranger smiled. Wolf-like fangs protruded from blackened gums. The red points of light in his eyes flared.

Manuel Del Sol was on the boy before he could scream out a warning to the others.

Five minutes later, Sam slipped back into the quarters he shared with four other males, two older and two younger. The quarters consisted of a two-room house, not much more than a shed. One room was the main area where the five of them slept on bedrolls spaced around the floor. There was a smaller back room where they bathed.

Sam first peeked in the window to make sure the others were sleeping soundly. The moon hung low in the sky on the windowless backside of the shed, so the room was almost completely submerged opaque shadow. There was just enough starlight to satisfy Sam that the men and boys were not moving. He slid over to the entrance, opened the door slowly, and stepped into the room without making a sound.

Sam stood there for a long moment to allow his eyes to adjust to the deeper darkness. He did not want to trip over anything on his way back to his bedroll.

His vision grew sharper as his gaze went from one sleeper to the next. If he found one of them awake and looking back at him, he would lie and say he had been to the shitter out back. He could only hope they had not been awake long enough to know how long he had been out. No eyes were open, but for the second time that night, Sam's hair stood on end.

The others were unnaturally still. Sam could not even detect the rise and fall of their chests to indicate breathing.

To a man, their threadbare sheets were pulled right up under their chins. None of them usually slept that way.

And then the smell hit him. The stench of human waste permeated the room from every direction.

Sam frowned and tipped carefully over to Seth, the youngest of the housemates. The smell intensified with every step. He got close enough to extend his leg and nudge Seth with his foot. He knew the boy to be the lightest sleeper of everyone in the house, but Seth did not respond.

Sam hooked his foot under Seth's shoulder and lifted it a few inches off the floor and then pulled his foot away. Seth dropped stiffly back to the floor with a thump that echoed through the room. The movement threw a wave of stench at Sam that made him cough involuntarily. He feared the noise would wake everyone in the room.

No one stirred, not even Seth.

With a chill that slithered from the base of his spine to the base of his skull, Sam knelt down and slowly pulled the sheet from Seth's chin. Sam jumped to his feet and backpedaled so quickly that he completely lost his footing and fell heavily to his backside. Gasping for breath and using his hands and feet to scramble further away, he could not tear his eyes from the deep, ragged bite marks torn into the side of Seth's neck.

He did not stop backing away until he bumped roughly into Lucas, the oldest of the housemates. Like Seth, Lucas did not make the slightest move in response to the contact.

Still struggling to breathe, Sam turned slowly to look at Lucas's face. His eyes were closed but his mouth was frozen in pained grimace. Sam debated whether or not to pull the almost translucent sheet from under Lucas's chin.

"Do not bother," advised the now-familiar accented voice from the doorway to the back room. "All of these men shared the same fate."

Sam was back on his feet in an instant and turned to bolt out the front door. He stopped in his tracks when Del Sol stepped into that threshold. Faint starlight turned his form into a dim silhouette that left none of his features visible, with the exception of the demonic blood red glow of his eyes.

"Now, do you believe, Sam?"

Sam was too horrified to respond, to even ask how Del Sol knew his name, so he simply nodded.

Del Sol nodded back. "I thought you would, *mi amigo*. This is how you kill silently and swiftly. I took these four in minutes and you did not hear the slightest noise. Of course, you would have heard if you had the ears *del vampiro*."

"Why ain't you killed me, too?" Sam asked.

"Curiosity," Del Sol reminded. "The patience and cunning of your schemes have impressed me. Tell me, Sam, do you wish to have my power?"

Sam felt his heart beating in his ears. His vision wavered and his entire body trembled. Yet even through the raw terror he felt a morbid fascination stoked by Del Sol's words and actions. He forced himself to look at the death surrounding him. If this much killing could be done in less than five minutes, what would Sam be able to accomplish in an hour?

"You'd give this power to me?"

"I would if you chose it."

"But...why me?"

"I'm a traveler," Del Sol explained, "and a scholar. As I said before, I know men's hearts. I think you have the potential to be the catalyst for the culling and I wish to see if I'm correct. I want to observe what you would do, what you would become if you accept my gift."

The culling? Sam had no idea what that was. "What if I say no? Will do me like you did them?"

Del Sol thought for a moment, considering the question.

"No. If you refuse my offer I will leave. You'll have to escape tonight, before these bodies are found. You'll have your freedom but not your vengeance, and when they set the hounds on you I doubt you'll get far. Accept my gift and they will never find you... unless you want them to."

Sam's knees got so weak they could no longer hold him. He sat on the floor and hugged his knees to his chest in a futile attempt to stop their shaking. His thoughts raced too swiftly to follow. He imagined the surrounding corpses were watching him, waiting expectantly for him to speak.

"What say you, Sam? Will you choose petty mortal freedom or immortality and blood?"

Sam buried his head in his folded arms and took a deep steadying breath. He reflected on his life, what it had been, what it would be if he refused this power and what it could be if he accepted it.

He did not believe in God before that night, but then he met the *vampiro*. If vampires existed, then so did the devil. If the devil existed, then God had to exist, too. And since God existed, it was obvious that God hated him. He met Del Sol's crimson gaze.

"I choose blood."

The vampire's fangs were in Sam's neck the instant he finished his sentence. Sam never even saw him move.

Stabbing pain just to the right of his throat made him gasp. Two claw-like hands gripped his shoulders so forcefully that Sam feared his bones would break. His heart pounded like a sledgehammer against his ribs. The blood in his veins felt like liquid fire as it pulsed out of his ruptured jugular into Del Sol's gluttonous mouth.

The night-shrouded room wavered in Sam's vision. A dull gray pall began crept inward from the edges of his sight. The pain from the vampire's clutch and bite then ebbed until Sam was completely numb. He felt weightless as the ashen shroud closed in on his vision. Comforting warmth accompanied his failing vision. It washed away the numbness and replaced it with a serenity he had never experienced.

His heartbeat slowed to its normal pace, and then continued to slow and weaken until he could not feel it at all. Sam knew at once what he was feeling. It was the welcoming embrace of death. He forced his lips apart in order to take one last breath and something bitter and metallic dropped onto his tongue. It burned like smoldering pebbles of coal. The searing pain shocked him out of his contented haze and brought his vision back into glaring focus.

Del Sol kneeled above Sam, who was lying flat on his back with no memory of lying down. He had been so close to death that he did not notice when Del Sol released him. What he did notice was Del Sol's wrist hovering just above his face. A long slit was open across the vampire's vein and his black blood dripped onto Sam's lips and into his mouth.

The last vestiges of human instinct implored him to spit out the foul liquid. His body refused to listen and he swallowed involuntarily. The blood hit the back of his throat and threatened to burn completely through his flesh. Fresh agony exploded in his brain and spread through every inch of him. Sweltering ecstasy immediately followed that agony.

He knew that no one lit a lantern or a fire in the room yet the night brightened in his vision so intensely it pained his eyes. And then came oblivion.

When he rose at sundown that evening he knew he was changed. He awoke with primal scream. It felt as if his body had been completely hollowed out and filled with fire. The greatest pain was concentrated in his belly. It was wracked with sweltering convulsions that folded him into a fetal position and seemed to last for hours.

When the anguish finally subsided enough for him to move, Del Sol was there. He lifted the new vampire to his feet, helped him climb out of the underground storage shelter of an abandoned barn. They stepped out into the night and Sam looked at a world that was both familiar and completely alien at the same time.

To his vampire's eyes, the moonlight and starlight lit the night like a frigid silver sun. The volume of nocturnal creatures' music that he had so often and so easily relegated to background noise had become deafening. The sound of an opossum's beating heart resounded like a bass drum. He could identify the light thrum of a spider creeping along a strand of its web. None of those sounds were nearby. The animals that would usually occupy the immediate area gave a wide berth to the two monsters surveying their domain.

The smells were overwhelming. Sam's nose detected and stored the scent of every creature that had passed nearby for days. He could even smell the fear of the creatures cowering in the distance.

Del Sol looked at his protégé with satisfaction.

And then he took him hunting. The night flashed by in a shadowy blur as the two vampires nearly flew through the forest. In his hungry and weakened state Sam was barely able to keep sight of Del Sol zigzagging around trees and hurtling over thickets and soaring over streams.

"When you are strong enough, we will fly," Del Sol promised. "Not all of our kind can, but you and I will not be tethered to the ground."

Even earthbound, they covered a distance of several miles in fewer minutes. It was not long before the plantation spread out before them.

Sam's first intended victim was Reverend. He swept silently up to the preacher's door but was stopped violently by an invisible wall of energy. A repulsive wave struck him and sent a flare of nausea through his belly. It combined with his burning hunger and brought him to his knees.

He looked back up at the door, wondering what had happened. When his eyes fell upon the wooden crucifix hanging on Reverend's door, a spike of pain drove into his eyes and burst into his brain. The vampire whimpered and scampered backward like a wounded pup until the pain finally subsided.

"There sleeps a man of great faith," whispered Del Sol from a few feet behind Sam. "If you are silent enough, we can clear this plantation without waking him. We can then trap him inside and burn him."

Sam nodded and struggled to his feet. "I know just where to start."

Within seconds Sam and Del Sol travelled nearly a quarter mile from the slave quarters to the plantation owner's bedroom. They entered through the window so swiftly that the breeze of their passing followed them a second later. Del Sol stood on Boss Sadler's side of the bed while Sam loomed over Mary, the master's wife.

The slight disturbance of air woke Mary, who inhaled violently to scream at the sight of the stranger and the slave in her bedroom. Sam's hand clamped down painfully over her mouth before the scream could escape. The resulting movement of the bed brought her husband out of his slumber. Del Sol clutched the man's throat with unnatural strength and held him down.

Sadler was a tall and powerfully built man but he could not budge the slender man's hand. He watched as his slave held one hand over his wife's mouth and pinned the heavy woman to the bed with his other hand pushing down on her bosom. Sadler tried to scream as Sam knelt beside the bed, grinning with a mouthful of sharp, jagged teeth.

Boss Sadler renewed his struggle, as did his wife. They both battered their attackers, punching and scratching as they squirmed to free themselves. All of their efforts were to no avail. Their blows were ignored and their scratches healed seconds after they were made.

Sadler's eyes bulged with confusion and dread when Sam bit savagely into his wife's neck.

Sam went lightheaded the instant the woman's blood touched his tongue. It was sweeter than Del Sol's, and much more satisfying. He felt her blood as it coursed down his throat and into his stomach. It immediately soothed his belly's searing spasms to a dull ache. The relief he felt in his core spread slowly out to the rest of his body.

The fiery pain that had weakened his limbs since he came out of his death sleep cooled to a warm tingle that hinted at unspeakable strength. That sensation flowed to all of his nerve endings. He felt it in the tips of his fingers and toes, even in his loins, where it exploded with shuddering, orgasmic pleasure.

Mary fought savagely for several seconds more before she went still. Her eyelids fluttered but never closed. The whole time she stared at her husband, her gaze pleading helplessly. Boss Sadler's tears streamed down onto his pillow. Even though Mary's eyes were still open, he knew it the moment her life ended. She exhaled a long, rattling breath and never inhaled again.

Sam stood tall and licked his lips. "You can have him," he offered Del Sol. "Let me watch him die from here."

Two men armed with shotguns and hunting knives and riding horses led another man who trailed behind them on foot. The walker held tight to three leashes, each connected to the collar around the neck of a bloodhound. A half moon shone down on them through the trees.

One of the riders spit a wad of snuff onto the ground and frowned. "If we ain't found them after three days, Cletus," he began, "I reckon we ain't gonna find them at all."

Cletus hawked and spit a gob of phlegm before replying. "That may be, Roscoe, but I ain't gonna be the one to tell that to Boss Sadler. Just keep your fool mouth shut and keep hunting until he tells us to quit." Cletus looked over his shoulder at the dog handler. "Easy money, I say. Ain't that right Mackie?"

"It ain't natural," Mackie said, shaking his head with frustration. "We know damn well them black bastards ran off sometime Friday night. We set the dogs out after them at first light and they lost the trail just after less than a mile. Five niggers gone and not one scent after a mile? It's like they up and fucking flew away."

Roscoe shrugged. "Well, hell, we've been hunting them for three days since. How are we supposed to find them with no scent."

"I know how," Cletus said. "We'll gear up for a longer hunt. Boss Sadler won't mind. It'll be cheaper to pay us to find them than it will be to lose them, I'll tell you what."

"And that fucking Sam," Roscoe snarled. "Should of known he was planning something. He was too goddamned quiet, too goddamned well behaved. He tried to hide it by looking at the ground all the damned time but if you caught him quick enough you could see that uppity look in his eyes. Boss Sadler should of let me beat that nigger to death way back when he crushed Homer's skull."

"Hell no," Mackie disagreed. "He should of let *me* feed him to the hounds."

Cletus sniffed. "Fellas, y'all smell something burning?"

They spurred their horses to a trot, leaving Mackie behind cursing and struggling with his hounds. The dogs started whining, tails between their legs, trying to go any direction but forward. They had not gone far along the wooded path when they approached a clearing at the top of a gentle slope. An orange glow shimmered from somewhere below the slope that both men knew at once was fire.

Cletus rode a half-length ahead of the others. "That's Boss Sadler's down there." He looked over his shoulder. "Do you see that Ros –"

A blur of shadow burst from the right and barreled into Cletus with an audible crunch of bone, tearing him from his mount and sweeping him into the brush bordering the path.

Roscoe's horse skidded to a stop so abruptly that Roscoe went flying over the horse's head. He flipped head over heels before slamming to the ground on his back. Dazed and breathless, Roscoe took a moment to gather himself. Once he regained his senses and his wind, he rose unsteadily to his feet and drew his six- shooter.

"Cletus!" Roscoe called.

His only answer was a strangled scream that sent a chill up Roscoe's spine. The scream ended in a gurgling whimper but Roscoe did not hear it. He was already sprinting back to where they left Mackie. The sounds of his own panting and rapid footfalls were the only things he could hear.

It took Roscoe little more than a minute to find Mackie and he was immediately sorry he had. The dogs were gone. The hounds' handler lay sprawled on the ground with a dark figure crouched over him, cradling Mackie's head in his arms and worrying at his neck like a ravenous wolf.

Roscoe cried out something he did not even understand and opened fire. Three bullets struck Mackie's attacker in the chest and shoulders and sent him scuttling a few feet back. Instead of falling from the assault, he stood to his full height and fixed Roscoe with a glowing, blood red glare.

"Sam?" Roscoe gasped.

He fired again, hitting Sam in the chest with the three remaining shots and drove him back a step. He favored Roscoe with a terrible smile. His nose, mouth and chin were slathered with Mackie's blood. His teeth were accented with long, curved, and pointed canines. When Sam spoke, his voice was more of a bestial growl than a human voice.

"You were right. Your boss *should of* let you beat me to death back then."

Roscoe tried to reload his revolver but his shaking hands made the bullets slip through his fingers. He turned to run and Sam was already there. Sam's hand darted out and Roscoe jerked violently. When Sam pulled his hand back it was as bloody as his face.

"Now you *can't* kill me," Sam taunted.

A short tube dripping with dark liquid was clutched in Sam's fingers. He held his hand up close to Roscoe's face to show the man his own windpipe. That was the last thing Roscoe saw before he fell dead.

Sam brought the disconnected throat to his mouth and pressed the tip of his tongue to it. The cooling blood tasted foul. He spat it out disgustedly.

"There is no substitute for hot blood straight from the vein, is there?" Del Sol asked as he stepped onto the path. He dragged Cletus's corpse behind him by the ankle. The dead man's neck was twisted at an extreme angle that left no question about the manner of his death.

"No, sir," Sam answered.

"No need for 'sir,' young one. I am not your master. You *have* no masters. But I will be your mentor for a short time. If you are smart, and I know you are, you will listen to me. Call me Manuel."

Sam nodded.

Del Sol looked over at Mackie's dead body and then back at Sam. "Did you drain him dry, Sam?"

"No, Manuel. I didn't."

"Why?"

Sam shrugged. "Ain't hungry no more, not with all the feeding we did before we set that fire."

"If you won't drain him dry," Del Sol advised, "remove his head and his heart, and then take him down to the fire and burn his corpse."

Sam frowned. "Why?"

Del Sol put a cold hand on Sam's shoulder. "The taking of his head and his heart is the only sure way to finish him. If you do not he will rise in three nights. The fire is to hide the evidence of his manner of death."

"Why do we need to do that?"

"Ah, the blissful ignorance of youth," Del Sol sighed. "If he rises in three nights, he'll be *vampiro*, but not like us. To be like us, he would have had to consume the blood of one like us at the moment of his death.

"When he rises he will hunt and kill and hide from the sun, and he would be an obedient thrall to his maker. However, without his maker to command him, he will be little more than a wild animal, without the intelligence to disguise his kills.

"There will be times when he won't bother to drain his prey dry and he will never bother to take their heads and hearts. That will produce more of his kind, all of them savage and oblivious. They would inevitably be discovered."

Sam was still nonplussed. "What difference does that make to us? We'll be long gone by then."

Del Sol smiled patiently. "*Vampiro* have walked the earth as long as mankind. In the past, most of them were like Roscoe will be if he rises again. His kind is a relatively easy kill for knowledgeable humans. They simply followed the trail of carnage to the creature's daytime resting place. Humans almost hunted them into extinction."

"Those like us, intelligent *vampiro*, have existed only since the time of Christ. But since that time, there have been humans dedicated to our extinction."

Sam listened intently, drinking in information as hungrily as he drank blood. Del Sol continued.

"Humans are our favored prey but they outnumber us exponentially. Their superior numbers, in addition to our intolerance of the sun and talismans blessed by the faithful, allow humans to compensate for their physical weakness. We have thrived this long because most humans do not believe we exist. This is why we must burn the plantation, to hide evidence of our passing. The humans will believe raiders set the fires."

"What raiders would do this?" Sam wondered.

"There are many from my country who are still angry about Texas being stolen away from us. And, though the news may not have reached you, war has recently been declared between the northern and southern states. The fire may be blamed on northern raiders.

"A reason will be found for the razing of this plantation. The important thing is that *vampiro* are not suspected. As long as humans believe we are nothing more than myth they will not unite in large enough numbers to endanger us. Something as careless as leaving Roscoe to run wild would threaten the secrecy that protects us. It would also anger *La Secta de la Ascension*."

"Who?" Sam asked.

"It is a cabal of *vampiro* in the old country dedicated to the protection and elevation of our species. They find and destroy wild *vampiros*. They then find and destroy their makers as punishment for their recklessness."

"You can leave Roscoe. His death can be attributed to mundane reasons. As for Mackie, because you are too inexperienced to play master to a *vampiro* in your thrall, you must dispose of his body. Now."

Sam knelt down and took hold of Mackie's ankle. Del Sol nodded in approval, turned on his heel and walked toward the clearing with Cletus in tow. Sam followed. He walked in silence for a time, thinking about all of the things he had learned the night he first met Manuel Del Sol.

There were no real memories of the previous two nights. That time was spent in agonized limbo as his body underwent its dreadful transformation. But he remembered well all of the information Del Sol shared with him before his change.

"The culling," Sam recalled. "You said something about that the other night. What is it?"

A corner of Del Sol's mouth rose in a sly smile. "You are familiar with the word 'culling' yes?"

Sam nodded. "They cull sheep sometimes; goats, too."

"Yes," Del Sol concurred. "There are members of *La Secta de la Ascension* who firmly believe our best chance of survival is to cull humans, to reduce and control their number like so much livestock."

The two vampires reached the clearing and dragged their victims to the top of the slope. They could see the plantation burning beneath them. The raging fires that roared across the expanse of land glowed a beautiful red and gold in the night. Del Sol gave a mighty heave and slung Cletus's body one hundred yards or so into the flames of a burning shed.

Sam stared thoughtfully at the flames for a time and then turned to Del Sol. "The culling... Do you think I can do it?" Sam asked incredulously. "How?"

Del Sol shrugged. "I have no idea. My understanding is that it would be a complicated undertaking. While I've never heard anyone speak of the specific details, I have heard that it could take years, possibly centuries to achieve. Therefore, the *vampiro* who wishes to accomplish this must have supreme determination, cunning, and patience.

"Most importantly, they would need to harbor within them a deep and abiding hatred of humankind. It would take that kind of passion to fuel such a complex endeavor."

Del Sol's words echoed in Sam's mind: *A deep and abiding hatred of humankind. Yes*, Sam thought, reflecting on his natural life. His hatred for humankind was certainly deep and abiding.

"I think you have the traits to bring about the culling. I cannot say that I believe you *will*, but I'm confident that you can. Tell me, Sam, is this something that interests you?"

Sam launched Mackie's corpse into the air, reveling in his newfound power and the carnage he had wrought with it. He watched the body sail end over end in a high, lazy arc. It crashed into the ravenous flames consuming the horse barn that served as a church for the slaves.

Those idiots worshipped a God that cared so little for them that He allows vampires to live in their midst. They *all* deserved to burn.

"Sam is a dead slave. Call me Andre," he said to Del Sol, invoking the name of a French merchant he once observed buying a bull from Boss Sadler. He liked the name and had always intended to take it for his own when he escaped.

"And yes, Manuel, the culling interests me."

CHAPTER ONE
Major's Story

I have a story for you…a doozy of a story. You probably won't believe it, but your belief or lack thereof doesn't change *my* reality. If you don't believe it, maybe you'll at least find it an interesting tale.

And cautionary.

I've already forgotten more about my life than I can remember. As the years pass – and believe me, many more years will pass while I walk this earth – I know I will forget much more. There are three moments in my life, however, that I will never forget. They're memories that not even an eternity can diminish.

The first is what I call my dark baptism. To be more accurate I'll call it the loss of my virginity. I'm not talking about the loss of sexual innocence. That was great. It happened in the mid eighties. It was awkward and terrifying, in a good way, but that's not what I'm talking about. What I'm talking about is the loss of my spiritual innocence. I lost that in the early nineties, in a way no one should.

Richard, Camillia, and Andre; son, mother, and… something else, revealed to me a side of this world that I never thought existed. Richard was one of my two best friends. The other one was Tim. He was right there with me through it all. There were a couple of older guys there, too, named Detective Weller and Father Burns.

I can't remember their first names. Hell, I don't think I ever knew their first names. Before all hell broke loose I didn't know them well enough to care. Afterwards, well, their first names didn't seem to matter much anymore. They were who they were, a cop and priest.

I can't speak for Weller and Burns, but what Richard, Camillia and Andre showed all of us would change Tim and me forever. When we made the idiotic choice to play a part in it, we ended up seeing things that neither of us would ever forget, no matter how bad we might want to.

The worst of it was the end...at least what I *thought* was the end. I can still see Richard and Andre in their death-embrace, both of them impaled on the same wooden stake driven deeply into that tree. Their cold flesh ignited like tinder when the first rays of the morning sun touched their lifeless bodies. Tim, Father Burns, Detective Weller and I watched them burn until there was nothing left of them but ashes at the base of the tree.

The second memory is my wedding day. Six years had passed since Tim and I left Chicago. We couldn't stay home after Richard and Andre. We stuck it out until the end of the fall semester so our grades would transfer from the South Chicago community college to an HBCU (Historically Black College and University) about forty miles northwest of

Houston. I'd never been to Texas. Tim had been in the past when visiting family up in Sealy. It felt right to both of us.

We could have moved to the moon, though, and it wouldn't have made a damn bit of difference. No amount of distance or time was ever going to erase the memories of Chicago during that time. Fighting Andre, Richard's horrific change, and his subsequent honorable suicide were the types of things that gave people lifelong recurring nightmares.

Having already spent one year at a community college, Tim and I finished our bachelor degrees at the Texas university in three years. I chose to stick around and earn a master's degree. Tim went right to work in computer networking and it wasn't long before he was making good money. He lived a single man's dream.

Tim leased a plush loft in Midtown, drove a classic Mustang that he restored and tricked out until it was worth five times as much as a new one, and enjoyed the company of a parade of women that would make a voluptuous video vixen green with envy.

I, on the other hand, met a beautiful woman during my last year of undergraduate work. Her name was Denise but I called her "Kitty." Her sexy phone voice reminded me of Eartha Kitt's Catwoman character from the 1960's era Batman reruns. We fell in love almost instantly and moved in together after only a few months of dating. A few friends and a bunch of family members thought we were moving too fast.

They did not believe we would last. We got married two years later.

The contrast between Tim's life and mine were stark and – if you had known us before the crisis with Richard and Andre – ironic. Tim had always been the one looking for a serious relationship. I was always the insensitive skirt chaser. Tim really hadn't changed very much. He was still looking for a serious relationship but was never able to find the right woman. Until then, he decided he would have as much fun as he could while he searched.

I was the one who had changed. While I watched Richard and Andre burn on that brilliant sunlit morning, something burned away within me. I realized that my flippant attitude and my whole "I don't give a damn" outlook on life had been a shield. It was a barrier I put up to keep from dealing with the seriousness of adulthood. That shield crumbled to ash as surely as Richard and Andre had. From that moment on I took the world and myself much more seriously. And it's a good thing I did. Had I not, I never would have been able to appreciate a woman as special as Denise.

On the morning of my wedding day a tap on my shoulder awakened me. I thought it was Denise but then I remembered she had spent the night at her parents' house. My eyes snapped open and I jumped up. The face that greeted me caused my blood to go cold and my heart to beat like a drum solo from hell.

"Richard!" I yelped.

He sat on the edge of my bed grinning from ear to ear.

"Calm down, Mage," he said in a soothing voice. "I can't hurt you."

"Of course not," I realized. "This is dream."

I knew it was dream, and not just because Richard had been dead for years. For as long as I can remember I've always known when I was dreaming. That knowledge always took a little of the sting out of nightmares no matter how intense they were. I could always force myself to wake up if the nightmare got too bad. This wasn't a nightmare, and even though it was a dream, I was happy to see my old friend.

What made it even better was that it was the Richard I grew up with. His grin contained normal teeth instead of bestial fangs. His skin was medium brown without the ashen undertones of lifeless flesh. His fingers were human fingers with unremarkable fingernails, not long twisted digits tipped with black claws. This was the Rich I knew before Andre entered our lives.

I smiled back. "It's been a while since I've dreamed about you, Rich."

"So are you ready to jump the broom?"

"Hell yeah," I told him.

"Out of the three of us I figured you'd be the *last* one to get married."

I nodded. "Me, too."

"That makes twice you've surprised me, Mage."

"What do you mean?"

"Tim tried to give you a blow-out, 'no ho's barred' bachelor party last night. Emphasis on the ho's. He was gonna rent out a whole strip club for you but all you wanted to do was go bowling."

"I've matured, Rich, but I'm still me. If I'd let Tim have his way I would've got some drink in me, probably a little weed, and had a gang of butt-naked freaks shakin' ass in my face on the last single day of my life. I would've been so deep in trim I'd be too weak to walk down the aisle this morning. Better to start our marriage off on the right foot."

"Glad to see you've grown up a little," Rich said. "Is momma coming down for the wedding?"

"Definitely," I answered. "She said she wouldn't miss this for the world. She can't believe I'm getting married, either. You know what she told me when I brought Denise to the crib one summer and introduced them?"

Richard executed a perfect imitation of his mother. "She said: 'Boy, that girl's too good for you. You better not screw this up!'"

I frowned. "How the hell did you know…? Oh, yeah, this is my dream."

Rich shrugged and smiled. "Something like that. But anyway, congrats, man. I'm really happy for you. Now wake your ass up."

My alarm clock was blaring. I sat up slowly and slapped to top of the clock three times before finally hitting the button to turn it off. Even though I knew I'd been dreaming, it seemed so real that I looked for Richard at the foot of the bed. It depressed me a little when he wasn't there.

The rest of the morning and early afternoon were spent running last-minute errands with Tim, who was my best man, and the other four groomsmen. The day flew by, and before I knew it, I stood at the church altar watching in awe as my beautiful bride and her father made their way down the aisle.

My wife's bright, perfect smile shone like the sun. She looked like a brown angel. Her white dress drifted around her like soft clouds. Her veil was a radiant halo that framed her lovely oval face as she glided to the altar. Before a church full of family and friends we held each other's hands tightly and promised that we would be together for the rest of our lives and, God willing, in the afterlife as well.

My mother-in-law went all-out for the reception. The food was excellent and the decorations were exquisite. Denise led the crowd in a spirited bout of the electric slide, the Harlem Shuffle, and every other line dance she knew (and she knew pretty much all of them). Tim and I, both thoroughly tired of line dancing, decided to watch from the wedding party's table.

Tim raised his glass for an informal toast. "So, how are you enjoying your first few hours of marriage?"

I laughed. "I'm loving it."

"You got a good girl, there, Mage," Tim noted. "The two of you make a great couple. Don't screw it up."

"Don't even sweat that, brother," I assured. "I ain't letting her get away for nothing."

"You know," Tim began, "out of the three of us, I figured you'd be the last one to get married."

"Damn, that's what Rich told me."

Tim looked surprised. "When did he tell you that?"

"This morning."

Tim looked even more surprised. "Say what, now?"

I laughed. "Calm down, man. It was a dream."

"Whew," Tim breathed. "I thought you were losing it." He was silent for a second, no doubt wishing like I was that Rich was sitting there with us. "I still dream about him every now and then, too."

I sighed. "As great as today's been it just doesn't seem right without him."

Tim put his hand on my shoulder. "I'm with you, man. I'm with you. But I think he *is* here." He placed a finger on my chest. "I think he's in your heart and mine, and especially in his mom's heart."

We looked out at Richard's mother and smiled. Except for a few gray hairs she didn't bother to color and a little darkness under her mahogany brown eyes, Camillia Williams looked exactly the same as she did six years earlier.

She was out on the dance floor out-electric sliding most of the people our age. How she had been able to go on after all that happened was beyond my understanding. Andre killed her husband and went on to put her and her son through hell. I was thankful she hadn't been there with us me at the very end. I don't think even she would've been strong enough to endure the sight of her son killing Andre and then himself, to watch them burn in the sunlight.

"So let me ask you something," Tim said.

"Shoot," I replied, glad that he had distracted me from that unwanted memory.

"Does this marriage mean our 'day of memorial' is officially over?"

"Not a chance," I promised, raising my glass. "To Rich!"

"To Li'l Richard," Tim replied. We tapped glasses again.

There's one more memory that will never fade. It's the memory of the circumstances that brought me to this place, to this time, to tell you this story.

CHAPTER TWO

A little over two years after the wedding, Tim and I sped north through Houston, TX, on I-45 in his red Mustang. Hip-hop music from his CD player pulsed from the car's enhanced speaker system. We were both in a solemn mood but we were determined to get our spirits lifted.

My wife would not let me hang out with Tim the way I used to, but there was one day every year that I would not be denied: our "Day of Memorial."

"Does Kitty know you're kicking it with me tonight?" Tim asked.

"She knows what day it is. Even if she didn't, what could she do? She won't be back from that pharmacy tech workshop in DC until tomorrow."

"That ain't what I asked, Mage."

"She knows. I told her last year that we always go out on this day in memory of Richard's death."

"You never told her what really happened, huh?"

"You think she'd believe me? I told her enough: Our lifelong friend was killed by his mom's ex-boyfriend."

"I can't believe she didn't sweat you this time."

"What's the point of sweating me over the phone? Besides, I put my foot down last year when she tried to get me to stay home or bring her with us. She just has to accept the fact that this is a tradition for just you and me."

Tim chuckled. "I bet you didn't tell her *where* we were going this time."

I smiled nervously. "She doesn't need to know all that."

"I've been trying to get you to come out to a strip club with me since the night before you got married. Why'd you decide to finally come?"

"I think 'the curse' is starting to set in."

Tim knew immediately what I was talking about. We'd joked about it more than once. "Oh, shit," he said with a smile, "the married man's curse. So the little woman ain't given' it up on the regular anymore?"

"Not like she used to," I admitted. "I figured at least I could come out here and see some bouncing booties and tig ol' bitties since I don't get to see it that much at home. No touching, though."

"Yeah," Tim grinned. "Just like at home."

"Screw you, man."

"Don't screw me, Nancy. There's gonna be a much better selection where we're going!"

"I'm not even sure I *should* be going," I grumbled.

Tim looked incredulous. "Why the hell not?"

"My resistance is low. A weaker man might slip and end up sticking one of them freaks."

Tim laughed again. "Uh oh. Is the old Major making a comeback?"

I shook my head emphatically. "Hell no. I said a *weaker* man. I know how to stay out of trouble. Like I said a second ago, I ain't touching a thing. No VIP room, no table dances, no lap dances. I won't even stick a dollar in a G-string. I'll just toss money on stage from a few feet away.

Tim kept laughing. "Don't worry, Mage. I don't care how horny you are, you won't be hitting any of these strippers. You don't have enough money for the VIP and you damn sure don't have enough game to get it for free!"

"If this was back in the day though..."

"You weren't exactly a mack back then," Tim teased. "You just targeted the low-self-esteem freaks that gave it up quick. You didn't aim crazy high like Rich did. I still don't know how you pulled your wife."

We pulled into a parking lot on the city's north side. We parked a half a block away because the lot adjacent to the club was full. It was autumn but the weather was uncommonly cool for Houston. We zipped up our jackets and walked down the crowded street in silence for a while. I, like Tim, was deep in thought.

When he broke the silence, he revealed that he was thinking the same thing I was thinking. "Doesn't seem like six years have passed, does it?"

I shook my head. "Nope. As cliché as this sounds, it does seem like just yesterday when all that shit went down."

"It always will," Tim supposed. "Hey, when was the last time you spoke to Miss Williams?"

I thought for a moment. "Since the wedding, I guess."

Tim nodded. "I know. I talked to her night before last and she told me to give you a kick in the ass for not talking to her for so long."

"It's awkward, man. I never know what to say to her."

"Just ask her how she's doing, Mage. She's not expecting you to give her grief counseling. It'd just be nice for her to hear your voice."

"You're right," I agreed. "I'll give her a ring tomorrow."

We came to a stop at the back end of a long line of men and a spattering of women. At the front of the line was a gate of wrought iron bars decorated with fake rust. The gate protected a set of huge, wooden, gothic-style double doors. A man dressed in a medieval jailer costume stood at the gate with a large skeleton key that opened the padlocked gate.

We felt the vibrations from the music pulsing within the two-story establishment. Minutes later, the doors opened inward and the music exploded onto the street. The jailer unlocked the gate and pulled them open to allow a long line of people to exit the club. They were all laughing, cheering and bobbing to the music. It was obvious they had enjoyed themselves thoroughly.

When the last of the group exited, the jailer roared:

"Welcome to THE DUNGEON!"

He motioned for a group of waiting patrons to enter. Tim and I were in that group. The jailer checked the ID's of each person when they reached the entrance. The jailer stopped the people just behind Tim and I and informed them that they would have to wait until the next group exited. I heard the people protest but the sound was cut short when the doors banged shut behind us. There was a small foyer with a booth just inside the club where the entrance fee was collected. After paying, we were ushered into the main area.

Tim had to yell to be heard over the blaring music. "This is it, dog. This is the main floor. They have mini-stages scattered all through the place but there's the main stage."

He pointed to a large circular stage in the middle of the club. Two women danced together with moves that dripped eroticism. "This part of the club is just like most of the strip clubs in Houston," Tim continued. "They only strip down to their G-strings and no physical contact is allowed."

"No, bush? Why the hell would you bring me here? I'm not trying to touch but I *do* want to see some!"

"Calm down, fool, I ain't finished," Tim chided. "That's just on the main floor. If you got enough money you can get one of these dancers to take you to solitary confinement. It's not as expensive as the VIP, but better than the general area."

"I'm liking, continue."

"Once you get into solitary, it's on!" Tim explained. "If you got the money, or if the freak takes a liking to you, almost anything goes. My boy told me he got his link smoked for no extra charge. He was probably lying about the 'no extra charge' part because he ain't that smooth. This other cat said this Latin broad rode his poll for only ten dollars! Him, I believe. I've seen him run game."

"Oh shit!" I swore. "Hold up, though. I told you I ain't trying to screw or anything. Not even touch. I just want to see a little bush."

"You'll have to do that in solitary, then."

"We'll see," I said.

We worked our way to the edge of the main stage. The lesbian show ended and another dancer came out alone and did her thing. I had to admit that the place had some quality dancers. When the second show was finished, a man dressed like Merlin the magician stepped onto the stage. His microphone designed to look like a magic wand. He made a grand gesture and began to speak.

"Now we introduce to you the Oriental treat known all over Louisiana and Southeast Texas: MADAME LOTUS!"

The crowd roared its approval. Tim leaned over to me. "Mage, I heard this freak is tight to damn death!"

A stunning Asian woman strutted out to center stage. Her skin was like porcelain: white, smooth and flawless. Platform heels about six inches high adorned her tiny, perfect feet yet she moved so smoothly it was as if she floated. The crowd roared and continued to roar until the dancer raised her hand for silence. The club went deathly silent as the woman slowly surveyed the attentive crowd. I leaned over to Tim.

"She's sexy and all," I said, "but what's the big deal? The dancer before her had more ass."

"They say she's got some hellacious moves."

"If she has better moves than the sister that danced before her, I *have* to see this."

I briefly wondered what Richard would say if he were here. He used to have a kinky fetish for Asian women. He never actually had one as far as I knew, but he had talked about it more than once.

Right at that moment Madame Lotus's eyes found mine. It was as if she'd heard what Tim and I had just said. It was then that I realized that I recognized her. I turned to Tim.

"I know her, man."

"Yeah, right," Tim scoffed.

"I do, man!" I insisted. "Her name is Su-Yin. I see her at the university library sometimes when I'm doing research. She works in the evenings a couple nights a week."

"You ever talk to her?" Tim asked.

"Just 'hi' and 'thanks' when I check out and return books. I never noticed she was this fine, though. She's a lot less...conspicuous on campus."

"I hope so!" Tim laughed.

She gave a subtle hand signal to start the music and it didn't take long for me to see what all the fuss was about.

Sensuality radiated from her with every fluid movement. Her musculature was perfect: firm but not hard. I guessed her measurements were thirty-four, twenty, thirty-two, with hips and an ass so perfectly round they didn't seem natural. She looked about five feet seven inches tall in those ridiculously high heels. My mind suddenly clouded with sexual images and emotions more intense than any I had ever felt. She moved slowly in our direction as she danced, and it seemed as if she repeatedly looked right at me.

I whispered to Tim, "She's coming this way."

"I can see that."

"Is it my imagination or is she checking me out?"

"Your imagination," Tim said. "She's checking *me* out!"

Tim was wrong. As she eased toward us it was evident that she had focused on me. I expected her to try to ignore or avoid someone she obviously recognized from her other job, her more mundane job. But then again, if she were overly concerned about others' opinion of her she probably wouldn't have been working at a place like The Dungeon to begin with.

She gave a few cursory leers to the rest of the assembly but she was obviously singling me out. The crowd noticed as well. I got a few congratulatory pats on the back and head. Bills of varying denominations carpeted the floor of the stage. She ignored all of it. By the time she reached me she had stripped down to her G-string and platform heels.

Tim sneered. "You lucky motherfucker..."

She turned her back to me and did a few insanely seductive and limber moves that had me fully erect within seconds. More paper money, ranging from one to fifty dollar bills, flew at her from every direction. And then she got down on all fours and turned to face me. The stage was only a few feet high, so with her on her hands and knees and me sitting on a stool, we were nearly at eye level.

"I *know* you..." she whispered seductively.

With those words, my mind was gone. All I could see were her deep, ocean green eyes and her soft crimson lips as they formed the words. I was breathless and speechless and could only nod in agreement. The way I acted probably made me look like a newbie to strip clubs. The people around me laughed at my awed silence and facial expression.

Their laughter seemed to come from miles away. The scene took on a dreamlike quality, which confused the hell out of me. Like I mentioned earlier, I could always tell when I was dreaming and that moment felt *exactly* like a dream. An instant later my mind went completely blank with the exception of one word that echoed in my head.

Su-Yin raised an eyebrow and smiled.

"Solitary," she said aloud.

The patrons within the sound of her voice whooped and barked. I barely heard them. My focus was on a shadowy image in the depths of her beautiful eyes. The image slowly grew, took shape and became recognizable. It was Denise's face. The image shook me into coherence and I slowly shook my head.

"No solitary," I refused.

The people around me apparently thought my refusal was due to a lack funds because money started flying at me instead of her. They tossed tens and fives and ones into my lap. Crumpled bills and coins popped me roughly in the head. Su-Yin reached into my lap and started collecting the money. Her eyes never left mine but her skilled hands had no problem finding both the money and my almost painful erection. She squeezed it gently and leaned closer to put her lips to my ear.

"You're not ready for solitary just yet. Your body is," she gave my attentive member an even firmer squeeze. "But your mind isn't, and I want *all* of you."

She pulled back a few inches, removed her hand – which was good because in another couple of seconds I would've made a mess in my boxers – and her eyes met mine again.

"You will be ready soon, though, Major."

She leaned forward again and this time she kissed me on the lips. I tried to lean away but her hypnotic gaze froze me in place. Our lips touched. My tongue involuntarily darted into her mouth and Su-Yin bit down softly. The move startled me but there was very little pain.

I tasted blood. The taste was initially familiar. I had bitten my tongue countless times over the years. But then the taste changed. There was a quality about it that was indescribable, utterly alien, and it went straight to my head. I had a fleeting suspicion that maybe Su-Yin had kissed me with some kind of drug in her mouth yet I made no attempt to pull away. Her tongue twirled around mine like a snake for what seemed like minutes but was probably only a few seconds. Even if it had been hours it would've still ended way too soon. When she finally pulled back she said:

"See you at work, handsome."

She stood, turned slowly, and glided back to center stage to finish her dance.

Tim leaned over to me. "You frenched her? That's nasty as hell, man. You don't know where her mouth has been."

Su-Yin finished her set but I didn't see it. The rest of the night, at least at The Dungeon, was pretty much a blur. I do remember Tim teasing me and fussing at me for not using the other patrons' charitable contributions to visit solitary with the famous Madame Lotus. He called me a punk. He called me whipped. He described in detail what he would have done if he had been given the same opportunity.

There was an undertone of genuine bitterness in his taunts. He tried to hide it but I could hear it in his voice and I could see it in his face. It was strangely satisfying to me. All I could do was laugh.

Other than Tim's brief tirade, the ride home was quiet. I was lost in thought about Su-Yin. Tim silently fumed about Su-Yin's snub, which was out of character for him. On the other hand, if her dance had the same effect on him that it had on me, I could understand his envy. She gave off a vibe that made me want to possess her. Just the idea of her favoring another man with her attentions made me angry.

"I have to see her again," I said, my head still swimming.

Tim gave me a sidelong glance. "You think Kitty's gonna let you back out of the house any time soon?"

"I'm not talking about seeing her at The Dungeon."

Tim glanced at me. "You're not talking about hitting her up at work, are you?"

"Where else am I gonna see her outside of the club?"

Tim shook his head. "Not smart. Seeing her at the club is one thing. Anything you two do there is work for her."

"What's the difference, Tim? Hell, if we're not in the club I can save some money."

"*That's* the difference, dumbass! In the club it's business. That's what you want it to be: a business transaction that stays in The Dungeon. Anywhere else is personal. Personal leads to people catching feelings. When people start catching feelings people get busted."

Irrational anger surged inside me. "I know you're jealous because she picked me, but you don't have to throw shade."

Tim scoffed in annoyance and frustration. "Do you really think some ho at a strip club noticing you're a mark would make me jealous?"

"So I'm a mark now? Man, fuck you. If you weren't driving I'd bitch slap you."

The tires screeched as Tim stomped on the brake pedal. I wasn't wearing my seatbelt and I would've face-planted in the windshield if I hadn't braced both hands against the dashboard in time.

The Mustang skid to the curb and stopped. Tim shifted into neutral and engaged the emergency brake.

"I'm not driving now, bitch. Go ahead and slap me."

Tim and I glared at each other for a long time. It took everything I had to keep myself from hitting him. Tim was almost a head taller than me and outweighed me by about fifty pounds but that wasn't what stopped me. There was a savage rage inside me that was trying to fight its way to the surface. I knew then that if we started fighting, I wouldn't have stopped until one of us was dead.

"I'm not going to jail behind your jealous ass," I snarled.

I threw the passenger door open and climbed out of the car. Tim didn't give me a chance to close the door even if I had planned to. He peeled out so fast that the momentum slammed the door shut. Fortunately I was only a few blocks away from home.

I was unusually tired when I got home that night. I felt high, too. The high I felt wasn't the dizziness of alcohol. I knew it wasn't the drifting, floating sensation of weed because I never smelled any weed smoke at the club. It wasn't the sensation of coming down from the adrenaline rush of the confrontation with Tim, either.

I was convinced that Su-Yin slipped me a "Mickey." It was a damn good thing Tim had driven that night. I would have been in trouble if I had to drive home. After a shower I went right to bed. Sleep fell upon me like a lead weight the moment my head hit the pillow.

What seemed like a few minutes later, the sound of a heavy door opening and closing in the distance roused me out of sleep. The bedroom was pitch-black. I reached over to turn on the light but my hand struck something metallic. I tried to sit up but my head struck something metallic. It took a moment to realize that I was in some kind of metal box. I cried out but no sound escaped my lips. My throat was so painfully dry that I couldn't speak.

Had someone kidnapped me in my sleep? Had Su-Yin drugged me so someone could come follow me home, kidnap me, and put me in a metal coffin? Frigid panic washed over me. My breathing sped up and my heartbeat did that manic drum solo again. The shivers hit me so hard I could hear the heels of my bare feet thumping against the cold metal beneath me.

Another heavy door opened and closed. This time the sound was much closer. I heard voices. This was it. They were coming to take away to bury me. I fought back the growing panic, held my breath and listened, hoping to hear something, anything, that would give me a clue as to what was happening and how to get the hell out of it.

"You gotta see this broad, man," said a strange voice from outside my box. "She is *hot*."

"Yeah?" said another unfamiliar voice. "She's dead too, so what's the point?"

The voices came closer still.

"I'm not saying we should hump her," said the first one. "She's just...exotic. You have to see her."

"And *you* have to see a shrink."

The voices were just outside of my box now. I tried my best to scream but still I heard no sound. There was a loud click and then I felt the box moving. The top of the box lifted and a pale, bright light momentarily blinded me. When my vision cleared I saw two men leaning over me.

M.J. Stewart

I tried to speak but my lips wouldn't move. My whole body was paralyzed. The two strangers leered at me the way my friends and I leered at sexy women.

"I told ya," said a dark-haired man with horn-rim glasses. "She's so freaking hot."

"What a waste..." said a red-haired guy, "a waste of a perfect pair of tits."

I wondered why the hell they were saying these things while looking at *me*. That's when it came to me. I was dreaming. Nothing else made sense. Once I came to that realization I expected my fear to abate the way it always did when I knew I was in the midst of a nightmare. But the fear didn't abate. This was unlike any nightmare I'd ever had. It didn't feel like a dream at all and, for the first time since I was a grade-schooler, I couldn't wake myself up.

I listened as the dark-haired man continued.

"I told you she was exotic. Look at that muscle tone. She must've been a dancer or something."

The other one nodded. "Her skin obviously paled after three days in the cooler but you can tell she had a nice tan. How does an Asian woman get a tan like that in Chicago?"

"Are you kidding me?" asked the other. "Ever hear of tanning beds? I call 'em sun coffins. Plus they've got that tan-in-a-bottle stuff, too."

"Why are her eyes open?" the other asked. "I see dead, open eyes all the time but hers are creeping me the hell out."

"I closed them," was the brunette's reply. "Post-mortem reflex, I guess. Look at them, though. I've only seen green-eyed Chinese women on TV and in movies."

"Close them," ordered the redhead. "It's like she's looking right at me."

When the dark-haired stranger reached for my eyes my hand darted up and grabbed his wrist. I felt his bones shatter in my grip. I snatched him toward me and used my other hand to snatch his throat out. The redhead's eyes widened with shock. He tried to scream but I was out of the coffin and on top of him before any sound could escape. We crashed to the floor and I was leaning toward his neck when everything went black again.

I felt myself falling. The sensation lasted only an instant before I hit the cold hardwood floor in my bedroom. I was tangled so tightly in my sheets that I couldn't move. It took almost a minute to get free. My mouth and throat were incredibly dry so I went to the kitchen for a glass of water.

I grabbed a full, plastic, one-gallon bottle of water from the refrigerator and a glass from the cupboard. I remembered that Denise was not home to fuss, so the glass went back into the cupboard and I drank straight from the bottle. I didn't realize how thirsty I was until I started drinking. After a few heavy gulps the water was gone.

"Damn..." I belched, tossing the empty bottle into the trash. I replaced it with a fresh bottle that I pulled out of the pantry and then I went back to bed. Once again I was asleep the instant my head hit the pillow.

The next time I was awakened it was by the sound of thunder. It was a long, deafening peal that seemed like it would never end. The room trembled violently from the powerful vibrations the sound caused. I thought I had fallen out of bed again because I was lying on a hard wooden floor. But this floor was covered with dust, soot, and oil. I had no idea where the hell it had come from.

A rhythm became discernible in the clamor. The floor literally shook from side to side and bounced up and down in time to the rhythmic thunder. I heard a bell and the blaring of a horn and knew this was not my bedroom. This was a train.

Another damned dream.

I gathered myself, climbed to my hands knees and looked down at my hands. They were smaller and paler with long manicured fingernails. They were a woman's hands and they were stained with blood. I got to my feet and looked down at myself. I wore a pair of baggy white slacks, a white shirt with sleeves that were way too long, and a white doctor's smock.

Spatters of dried blood covered my clothing. My feet were small, bare, and my toenails were painted. They were a woman's feet.

There was a faint taste of salty copper in the back of my throat and a matching scent hung in the air. My heart was racing again, even faster than before. As my eyes continued to adjust to the darkness of the closed train car, I saw other people. There were three of them. Two men and a woman, all dressed in shabby and dirty clothes, lay sleeping. I wondered how they could sleep so soundly through the racket of the moving train.

My legs started to move involuntarily. They carried me to the closed door of the train car. My woman's right hand reached out and easily threw open the heavy sliding door. The train was passing over a high bridge that spanned a wide river. I walked over to the strange woman sleeping face down on the filthy floor. I turned her over and saw that various parts of her torso were torn open.

I screamed and sat bolt upright, in my own bed again.

"What the hell...?" I complained to the darkness.

My throat was so parched I started coughing. My covers were tangled all about me once again and I was drenched in cold sweat. I untangled myself from the bed sheets, sprinted to, the kitchen, and pulled out the bottle of water I'd earlier put into the refrigerator. It felt like my dream lasted only a couple of minutes but I'd been asleep for some time. The water was room temperature when I put it in the refrigerator but it was cold when I took it out again.

That gallon was gulped down as quickly and easily as the first. Unfortunately, it was the last gallon we had. I filled the empty bottle with tap water and put it back into the refrigerator. Fortunately I was able to make it through the rest of the night without making a third trip for water.

CHAPTER THREE

Work the next day started off uneventful. I was exhausted from the night before and had a splitting headache. It took eight hundred milligrams of ibuprofen to make me barely functional. I hardly acknowledged my coworkers and colleagues as I muddled through the morning.

Su-Yin was the only thing I could concentrate on with any consistency. I'd made up my mind to *not* go see her. I didn't want to start something I wouldn't finish. I was determined to be faithful to my wife.

Sure, I'd been attracted to other women from time to time after I got married but I never acted on that attraction. Women, very attractive women, had approached me on occasion. It didn't happen often, just a few times unexpectedly. A couple of those women were persistent even after I told them I was a happily married man. Never had I come even close to doing anything with them. I always contented myself with just looking.

There was something decidedly different about Su-Yin. I was finished the moment I saw her dance. When she kissed me, well, that was the proverbial nail in the coffin. She had me. There was something about that kiss. The instant our lips touched my mind started to swim and it never stopped.

But Tim was right. A relationship with her outside of The Dungeon would be foolish. Even though I refused to go see her personally, I was not going to go very long without somehow communicating with her. I had to let her know that

I felt something that was much deeper than just lust. Most importantly, I had to find out what it was about that kiss that had messed up my mind so thoroughly.

Talking to her face to face was out of the question, though. I was afraid of what I might do if she put the moves on me. The telephone and email seemed too impersonal, so I decided to do it the old fashioned way.

I sat down at my desk to write a letter. I couldn't believe I was doing it. It felt like I was back in grammar school. It was almost the new millennium, though, so instead of using a pencil and paper I used my computer. As I typed, I changed my mind about giving her the letter. That would be crossing the line. The goal changed to simply typing the letter to get the thoughts out of my head and then deleting the file.

Even while I was telling myself that, something deeper in my consciousness was telling me that was a lie. I would give it to her. I had to... I didn't know why, but I had to. I planned for the letter to start out as a confession of my feelings and to end as an assertion that we could never be together because of my marriage. I took a deep breath, and with my heart fluttering madly, I began to type:

> *Su-Yin, when I saw you at The Dungeon I realized you were the most beautiful woman I had ever seen. I couldn't try to talk to you then. There were too many distractions, too much competition. You probably get*

a hundred offers a night from guys with a lot more to offer than me.

But then I remembered the first place I saw you. It was in the Banks building during entrance testing the night before classes started. You were helping to administer the test to the students taking evening classes. I remember you were wearing green, a green that matched your eyes.

You made a lasting impression on me. I got all excited when I saw you in the library. I said to myself, "Man, I gotta get her number or something!"

I've wanted to get with you from first the day I saw you but there's just one problem. When I saw you I was involved with someone...and we were recently married. I'm ashamed of myself for not telling you last night but I couldn't. I wanted to spend time with you so bad and I knew that if I told you I was married there would be no chance of that happening.

This may sound messed up coming from a married man, but I thought about you all the time after that first time I saw you in the library. Seeing you last night made me realize that I'd still like to spend time with you somehow, although I doubt you'd be down with that after you read this letter (and hell, I wouldn't blame you!).

On the off chance that you do, let me know.

The letter was not supposed to end the way it ended. Nonetheless, when it was finished I folded and pocketed it. I planned to slip it to her at the reference desk and scurry away like a shy, scared little kid.

I'm sorry, Denise, I thought to myself. I felt like shit. The last thing I ever wanted to do was hurt her, and I knew that in time she would find me out. Just the thought of tears in my wife's eyes nearly brought tears to my own. But there was something...something unnatural...pushing me, pulling me, urging me to this insanity.

That evening I found myself creeping up to the second floor of the library. I tried my best to look inconspicuous but I'm sure the attempt had the totally opposite effect. Now I knew how a criminal felt. Even though I hated what I was doing, I felt an adolescent thrill, like I was fourteen years old and sneaking out of the house past curfew.

But that was bullshit. I was a grown-ass man and I was about to risk my young marriage over a stripper that was probably trying to beat me for whatever money I was willing to spend on her. How many other men had she roped in with that dance and that kiss? Maybe she thought I was a good mark because she'd already noticed my attention at work.

Nonetheless, I walked into the periodical section and saw her. She was sitting behind the front desk wearing tinted eyeglasses and reading. She looked up and saw me.

"What took you so long, handsome?" Her smile sent an electric thrill through me.

"I...uh, it was just..."

"Your wife?"

My eyes must have gotten as wide as tennis balls. "How did you know?"

"I know things. And don't worry about that letter you want to give me. The answer is yes."

"What did you do to me last night?" I demanded. I tried my best to come off as stern as opposed to how curious and nervous I really felt.

"I kissed you," she answered. "You kissed me back."

"But I didn't want to kiss you," I said.

Su-Yin tilted her head and gave me an incredulous smirk. The slight movement and the face she made were sexy enough to make my knees almost buckle.

"You know what I mean," I accused. "I wasn't *trying* to."

"Well, I was. And yes, I do want to hook up with you. Tonight."

"No," I refused. The fact that she knew what was in the letter didn't surprise me until I thought back on it later. Right then I was trying desperately to get back in control of the conversation. Things were moving faster than I was prepared for. "I can't just leave the house and stay gone. Hell, I don't even know if I want to do this."

Su-Yin chuckled. "We both know you *want* to do this."

She glanced down at my semi erection. I couldn't understand what was happening to my self-control.

"You just don't know if you *should*," she continued. "Take some time and build up your courage. When you finally get the nerve, you know where to find me."

She was challenging me, taunting me. It was obvious she was playing on my ego to get me to do what she wanted. It almost worked, too. I was ready to go off with her right then and show her how much of a man I was. I caught myself, though, and refused to take the bait.

"Yeah, right," I said sarcastically.

I turned and walked away. Quickly. My initial intention was to demand that she tell me what she had in her mouth when she kissed me but I didn't trust myself to go back and confront her. All I could think of was the kiss itself, and how much I wanted another one...and much more.

I was still tired when I got home that evening, though not as tired as I'd been earlier that day. The only time I'd felt any real energy was when I talked to Su-Yin. Once I got home all I wanted to do was take a nap. I walked in and saw my wife sitting on the couch drinking a soda and bobbing her head while listening to some Jeffery Osborne with LTD from the seventies. I kissed her on the cheek and we hugged.

"Hey baby," she greeted.

"Hey, sugar," I answered. I went to the bedroom and stripped down to my boxers. "How was your trip?" I called into the living room.

"All right, I guess," she replied. "I missed you, though."

"You know I missed you."

"Major," my wife called.

"Yeah?"

"I rented a movie. You wanna watch it?"

"Kinda tired, babe. Let me take a nap for an hour or so then I'll watch it with you."

"All right," she said. "An hour."

I fell across the bed and went immediately to sleep. When I opened my eyes I noticed that the sun was down. I looked at the clock and saw that it was ten thirty in the evening. Denise walked into the bedroom wearing nothing but a bath towel. She looked annoyed.

"You're up now?" she asked.

"Damn," I said. I didn't know I was that tired."

"I never watched the movie," she said matter-of-factly as she dropped the towel and proceeded to don a pair of pajamas. "And just so you know, it was a flick."

"Porn?" I asked, surprised. "Since when do you watch flicks?"

"I was hoping we could spice things up a little."

"Damn," I swore again. "You should've said something before I went to sleep."

"You said it would be a short a nap. I wanted you to be well rested for what I had planned for you. Besides, I wanted to surprise you with it."

"Why didn't you wake me up earlier?" I asked.

"I tried. You wouldn't budge so I let you sleep. Move over. I'm about to crash." She lay down next to me and closed her eyes.

"I'm awake now," I volunteered. "Let's watch it."

"Too late. I'm sleepy now. We'll watch it tomorrow."

We talked a little while before Denise started drifting off to sleep in the middle of her sentences. I tried my best to talk her into engaging in a little erotic show of our own but she was having none of it. Fifteen minutes later she was sound asleep. I watched her. She had the prettiest mouth. The corners of her lips curved upward just a bit when she slept. It made her look like she was smiling. She said it was because she loved sleeping so much. It was beautiful.

Hours went by. I looked at the clock and it was one in the morning. To my surprise I was wide-awake. At first I assumed that I threw off my sleep pattern by taking that long, late nap. As the moon shone into my window I realized that not only was I awake, I was incredibly alert. There was no hint of the exhaustion I felt during the day.

The chirping of crickets was like music. Night birds cried out in the darkness and it felt like they were singing to me. It was enchanting. I got up and looked out the window. The moon was as bright as the sun to me and I suddenly had an incredible urge to go walking or jogging, anything to get out into the clear night air.

And then I had a stronger feeling. I had to take a leak.

I went to bathroom and did my business. As I walked out of the bathroom I passed the mirror and something about my reflection struck me as odd. In the mirror I looked somewhat pale. It was barely noticeable but I saw it. I stepped closer to the mirror for a closer inspection. I was taken aback when I noticed my teeth. My canines were longer than before, a lot longer, and pointier. I couldn't stop staring at them and I could swear they grew a bit more even as I watched.

I gasped and took a step back. Countless images flashed through my mind. A few of them were of Eric, a tall, pale, gaunt white man with a shaved head. Some of them were about Andre – the *real* Andre, the bloodthirsty creature with wicked claws and two-inch long fangs. Most of the images were of Richard. I saw him the way he looked when we were kids, and then as teenagers. And then I saw him as a thing not very different than Andre.

The realization struck that the same thing was happening to me. My heartbeat began to race, my breath quickened, and my entire body shuddered. I staggered out the bathroom on legs stiffened by shock, bracing myself with a hand on the wall to keep from falling over.

I stumbled into the bedroom to get dressed. I had to get out of there, to put some space between my wife and me so I could think things through, and for her safety.

Denise could was a sound sleeper at times and this was one of those times. She lay still as I dressed silently and crept out of the house got into my car drove to South Main. That was a strip that came alive at night with clubs and restaurants. There were lots of people there and I needed to be surrounded, to lose myself in a crowd while I tried to wrap my mind around what was happening to me.

I parked, got out of the car and then I just walked. The moment I stepped onto the street I sensed that something was different. The sounds on South Main were always loud but they seemed much louder than usual. There was a strange hum in my ear. It was just barely audible but it was constant. The strange thing was, even though I heard it, I was not distracted by it. I could clearly hear every word that was spoken in my vicinity.

After walking several blocks I wandered into a tavern and claimed an empty stool at the bar. While sitting there, I followed every conversation going on around me. All the while that hum buzzed on in the background. I began concentrate on that continuous drone in my ears. That was when I realized that the background buzz wasn't in my ears. It was in my *head.*

I tuned out the external conversations and concentrated only on the sounds in my mind. The hum began to break up here and there and I thought I heard a few words. A little more concentration confirmed that they were words, partially formed sentences, in fact. I visually focused on a small group of people and noticed that the words I heard in my mind were not the words their lips were forming. In some cases, what I heard would totally contradict what they mouthed.

A man's mouth would be saying "I love you" but in my mind I heard: "Damn, I bet she tastes good." I was hearing his thoughts. The experience reminded me of watching one movie while listening to the dialogue of a different movie. The thoughts of everyone around me were as clear in my mind as their words were in my ears. I could follow conversations just as easily as individual people.

I slipped off the stool and left the bar, my stomach roiling with fear. Something was seriously wrong with me. I already knew that. At the same time, though, that fear was dampened by a tinge of curious excitement as I stalked the streets listening to words and thoughts. And then, all at once, the sounds in my head and in my ears grew muddled. I felt a presence, a strong urging for me to look to my left. So I did.

Su-Yin was leaning against a wall across the street. My eyes met hers and she mouthed the words:

"Come."

After navigating through a maze of people and cars I was within arm's reach of her. She turned and walked away. I followed her into a dark alley, where she took a dozen steps into the shadows, turned and waited for me catch up.

"What did you do to me?" I demanded.

She smiled. "You know what I did."

I grabbed her by the collar of her blouse and lifted her off of the ground. "Why, dammit? Why me?" I snarled.

Su-Yin knocked my hands away easily, but she didn't drop back to the ground. I looked down in disbelief to see her still hovering at least six inches above the dirty alley floor. The next thing I felt was a crushing blow to my midsection, and then I felt myself sailing through the air.

My back slammed into the wall on the other side of the alley and I sank to the pavement. I coughed for a second and looked up to see her standing right in front of me. This time her feet were firmly on the ground.

"I'll explain it to you," she offered. "But only if you come fly with me."

"I'm not going anywhere with you."

"Tell me, Major, why did you come out tonight? Won't Denise be upset?"

"I'm just taking a drive, and a walk." I struggled to my feet. "And don't worry about Denise."

"You're hunting, Major. You just don't know it yet. Come with me if you want to learn some things."

Kiss her. I said to myself. *She wants you to kiss her*. I wanted to kiss her. I stepped toward her and then hesitated.

"That's you," I accused. "You're trying to make me kiss you. I'm not that easy."

She appraised me thoughtfully. "Impressive."

She stepped toward me, reached out with both hands and held my face. My heart pounded against my sternum like a jackhammer at her touch. She pulled me close and kissed me. This kiss was like the one she gave me when we first met, only much longer. Painful lust raged through me and every other thought in my mind blew away like a leaf in a hurricane. I reached down and grabbed two handfuls of her soft buttocks. I was going to take her right there in that alley.

A random thought pushed its way up from the deepest corners of my mind. It was a simple observation, really.

Su-Yin was about an inch shorter than Denise.

I pushed Su-Yin away.

"I'm going home." I turned and bolted.

"You'll be hungry soon," she taunted as I ran away. "You'll be hungry for a *couple* of things. You know where to find me. Don't make me wait too long."

When I got home I stripped silently and took a shower. I tried to convince myself that what was happening to me wasn't really happening. I failed miserably.

The shower curtain flew open. Denise stood there.

"Where did you go?" she asked.

"I took a ride. There's a lot on my mind right now."

"Let's talk about it," she said.

"Not now..." I told her.

Denise looked away for a second then looked back.

"If it's bad enough for a midnight drive it should be important enough for you to talk to your wife about it."

"Not yet," I whispered.

"Well..." she began. I heard the words in her mind before she spoke them. "Let me know when you're ready to share your life with me again." She closed the shower curtain and left the bathroom.

How could I tell her what was happening to me when I didn't want to believe it myself?

Let me tell you about temptation.

I worked with two attractive women. One was in graduate school and the other was a junior. The grad student was laid back as well as soft-spoken. Her soft-spoken quality, however, was not a result of timidity or an introverted nature. It was the calm, introspective nature of a confident woman whose mind was constantly at work. She was mysterious in a subtle way that made men curious as to what was going on behind her thoughtful eyes.

The other young lady was more outspoken. She seldom hesitated to say what was on her mind and could be brutally honest. When she smiled it was sincere and pretty and it made the people around her smile. When she didn't smile it was best to tread lightly around her. I could tell she had a soft heart but she guarded it closely. She had mentioned to me that it had been broken recently.

As attractive and interesting as they were, there had never been any kind of sexual tension between us. The grad student was cordial but she was all business. When things got slow at work she busied herself with research or writing her thesis. If she was even the slightest bit attracted to me she did a great job of hiding it.

The undergrad gave subtle and likely unintentional hints that she might have thought I was cute. I'd occasionally catch her checking me out on the sly but she never did anything flirtatious. She would confide in me from time to time or ask for advice about men, and in one such discussion she'd made it clear she did not "mess with married men." She said it while complaining about a married instructor of hers who had been hitting on her. I got the impression she was giving me a not-so-subtle hint for future reference, you know, in case I ever got any ideas.

After Su-Yin's kiss, temptation started getting the better of me. My desire for other women grew stronger every time I saw one. No matter what I was doing, my mind constantly strayed to things, perverted things, especially about Su-Yin. I've always had a dirty mind but my thoughts had never reached the level of strangeness and depravity that had been plaguing me the last two days.

When my coworkers were near me, and if I took a deep breath, I could taste their scents on the air. Their perfumes and scented lotions were acrid on my tongue. Beneath that, though, I could taste their natural essence, which was more intense and alluring than any artificial scent. Whenever they touched me, whether it was an accidental bump in passing or a playful punch on the shoulder, the contact sent tingling through every nerve in my body. It was crazy.

I'd always been playful with them and they never took me seriously. Anything I said that might be construed as flirtatious was ambiguous enough that they would take it as a joke or an awkward compliment. Those two days after the kiss, however, I grew flirty.

My playfulness became less like joking and more like obvious come-ons. I skirted dangerously close to crossing the line and propositioning them. I saw it happening and so did they, but I could barely stop myself.

There was no question about why my inhibitions were slipping away. I couldn't deny what was happening to me but I foolishly thought I could resist it. I knew how it worked, though. Su-Yin had only nipped my tongue and I hadn't drunk any of her blood. There was still a chance I could beat this. The first thing I had to do was master my base emotions. The thought of my wife had been enough to bring me back under control before so I was confident it would again.

That second day, though, it became more and more difficult to pull myself back from that precipice. I felt like a different person, like I was on the outside looking in at another guy's life, and I didn't like that guy. He didn't just want these women. He wanted them *badly*. He wanted to feel their warm skin on his fingertips, to taste the salt of their sweat and tears. He wanted to bite down into their flesh and –

Eventually, inevitably, I crossed the line.

Amara, the undergrad and outspoken one, came in to work early on Monday morning. Mr. Barr, the coordinator of the lab, was on a business trip. Michelle, the soft-spoken one, was not scheduled to come in until two hours later. I was working on my computer when Amara came into the lab.

I watched her through the large glass windows set in the wall of my office. She walked through the teachers' work area, waved hello to me, and then took a seat at her workstation. I continued punching keys on my computer keyboard but I could not take my eyes off of her. Her fluid movements were mesmerizing and I found my mind wandering yet again.

Amara did some work on the computer for a few minutes and then came into my office. She would often sit and talk with me when there was nothing to do in the lab. No teachers or teacher assistants were in the lab so it was pretty quiet. Amara pulled up a seat behind me and started talking.

"You know what happened this weekend?" she asked.

"You got a ticket."

"How did you know?" she demanded.

"Just a lucky guess," I lied. "You've been talking about getting an inspection sticker for days. I knew if you didn't hurry up and get one the law would catch you."

"Well, I'm not paying it," Amara said defiantly.

"C'mon Amm, how are you going to get around paying it? You were caught straight up with an expired sticker."

"I've already thought of something," she answered.

She went on to explain her scheme for beating the ticket. Her words and thoughts faded to a faint background buzz as I found myself lost in her appearance and her scent. The aroma of her peach-scented lotion permeated the air. My wandering eyes traced the shape of her breasts beneath her close fitting blouse. My breathing fell into rhythm with the rise and fall of her chest as she talked and took breaths of her own.

Instead of listening to what she was saying I watched her pouty lips form the words. Her breath smelled of mint toothpaste and mouthwash and the chocolate latte she drank on her way to work. The deep red lipstick she wore made me think about the hot, pulsing blood running through her veins. My eyes found her neck...her soft, flawless neck. I could almost taste her –

"Major!" she barked. Her sudden exclamation startled me out of my reverie. I almost jumped out of my chair.

"What?" I asked, acting puzzled.

"Why are you looking at me like that?"

"How was I looking at you?"

"I don't know, but I didn't like it."

"Sorry, Amm. I was thinking about something else."

"Yeah, I *bet* you were. Keep it up and I'll tell Denise you're in here looking at people freaky."

Denise.

"It wasn't even like that," I lied again. "Whatever you're wearing smells like peaches. It made me think about lunch."

"You *are* a freak," Amm said. "Anyway, I'm going in the back to make a cup of hot chocolate."

"Didn't you have a chocolate latte already?"

"How did you know?"

"That's your routine, right? You've mentioned it before." I had no memory of her ever mentioning that to me.

"Have I?" she asked.

Amm gave me another curious look before she stood and went into the back room. My eyes followed her until she rounded the corner and was out of view. Before I knew it, I was out of my chair and moving right behind her. When I walked into the room Amm was reaching up into the cabinet.

"I want you," I said.

The box of hot chocolate fell to the floor. Amm turned.

"What?" she asked in disbelief.

"I don't want hot chocolate. I want you…all of you."

"You are really tripping now, Major," Amm said with an uncomfortable laugh. "And you need to *stop*."

That's when I saw it in her thoughts. Amm was uncomfortable for two reasons. The first reason was the fact that I was married. The second reason was that she was a virgin. The revelation surprised me, and excited me even more. She tried to look away from me but I wouldn't let her.

"I'm not tripping, Amm. Come here."

Su-Yin had been able to project her desire and make me think it was mine. I instinctively knew I had the same ability.

"No," she whispered.

She took a step in my direction anyway. I raised an open right hand to her. She took it with her left. The warmth of her touch flowed through me.

My sense of smell grew so acute that I could detect the heady, natural scent of her body through the peach fragrance she wore. My mind went cloudy and all I could think about was the taste of her flesh. The taste of her blood.

I pulled her to me and softly lowered her eyelids with my thumb and forefinger. She sighed deeply. I felt her relax as all resistance faded. I pressed her soft lips against mine. She kissed me back but the rest of her body fell limp as if she was unconscious. She didn't fall, though. I kept her upright by the sheer force of my will.

As we kissed, I felt her heart beat. The blood coursing through her veins was a rushing river to my ears. I kissed her chin, her neck, and her throat, drinking in the salty taste of her skin. My lips went to her throbbing jugular vein. I traced it with my tongue from just behind her ear to her collarbone.

She was so vulnerable at that moment that I knew I could do anything to her I wanted. All I wanted was her blood. The sound of her heartbeat pounded in my ears like a bass drum. The room...the world...began to whirl and dance around me.

The only thing in my universe was her smooth, perfect neck. I opened my mouth and bared my teeth...

The sound of the front door of the lab opening brought me out of my blood trance. By the time Amm opened her eyes I was back at my computer typing away as if nothing happened.

Shelley, too, was coming in to work early. She waved hello and went straight for the telephone. Before she reached it, however, Amm peeked out from the back and called Shelley to come talk to her for a moment. The two ladies went into the back room together. Even though Amm was whispering as softly as she could, my recently enhanced hearing easily picked up what she saying.

"Girl, I just had the craziest daydream..."

While my outward appearance seemed calm, my heart raced, my palms were sweating, and my knees shook. I tried to tell myself again that this couldn't be happening to me. But why was it so hard to believe? I saw Andre and my best friend with my own two eyes. It was obvious I had the same affliction yet my mind simply wouldn't accept it.

I had to talk to someone that would understand what I was going through. There was only one person in Texas I knew of that could.

CHAPTER FOUR

I went to Tim's house as soon as I got off work at five that evening. He was still pissed with me and I was sure he would slam the door in my face. That didn't matter, to me. He was my best friend. I had to try. I drove up to his apartment building. His Mustang was out front so I knew he was home. I knocked on his door until he snatched it open.

"What the hell is wrong with you?" Tim demanded.

"We gotta talk, man."

"I ain't got shit to say. Go home and talk to your wife."

"I can't go home. I'm afraid of what I might do."

Tim was slightly curious. "What are you talking about?"

"Let me in, man...please."

Tim reluctantly opened the door wider and stepped aside. "Make it quick."

"I'm sorry I blew up at you the other night, man," I began. "I've been acting real flaky lately, I know. Some weird shit has been happening to me."

"Are you talking about Su-Yin?" Tim was growing annoyed and he didn't try to hide it. "I don't wanna hear about her anymore. If you wanna screw up what you and Kitty have for a stripper, keep it to yourself."

I looked into Tim's eyes and tried to sound as serious as I could. "She's changing me, Tim."

Tim just stared. "No shit."

"No, man. She's *changing* me...like Richard changed."

I'd never seen Tim move as fast as he moved right then. He reached out with both hands, grabbed me by my collar and shoved me against the wall. The look he gave me left no doubt in my mind that he wanted to punch me.

"You've always been a triflin' asshole, Mage, but I didn't think you could stoop this low. How can you compare your bullshit to what Richard went through?"

I wanted to be angry. I wanted to be mad enough to toss him across the room, but I couldn't. He wasn't really angry. He was in pain. The thought of Richard's fate hurt me, too.

"It's true," I said calmly. "God knows I wish it wasn't, but it is."

"Prove it," Tim challenged. He let me go and took two steps back. "Show me something to make me believe you."

"It's not that easy, Tim. I can't control it. Sometimes I think things, sometimes I feel things..."

"But what can you *do*? If you can't prove this is happening why should I believe you?"

"Because we're best friends," I countered. "We grew up together –"

"And you've been a bull shitter all that time."

I started to get pissed. "That's what you think of me, huh? After all we went through with Richard and Andre... You think I would lie about this?"

Tim just stared at me. The look in his eyes was answer enough. At that point I was too hurt to be angry.

"I don't give a damn what you think of me, Tim. Not anymore." I felt my voice quivering. "We don't ever have to talk again. Just remember, no matter what happens from here, I came to you first. You'll always be my brother."

"Whatever," Tim mumbled as I left his apartment.

The house was empty when I got home. I pulled off my shirt and tossed it in the dirty clothes hamper and saw that it was empty. I concluded Denise went to the Laundromat, or "washateria" as they called it in that part of Texas. I lay down on the couch and thought about the last few days, yesterday in particular. I thought about the letter that I had planned to give Su-Yin...

My heart dropped. My mind was so scattered I forgot about the letter I'd left in my pants pocket. My pants were in the hamper that morning. Denise was washing clothes. I almost shit myself.

I tried to take a nap but the thought of my wife finding that letter was too distressing to let me rest. I found myself watching the clock, counting the seconds until she came home. An hour or so passed before I heard a key being inserted into the lock at the front door. Denise pushed the door open with her shoulder because she held a basket of clothes in both hands. I rose from the couch and took the basket out of her hands.

"How you doing' baby?" I asked.

"Tired." There was no sign of anger or sadness in her face or posture. I was tempted to read her mind. That temptation was thwarted by the fear of what I might find there. "There are more clothes in the car."

With a sigh of relief, I went to retrieve the rest of the clothes. I wasted no time finding the pants that contained the letter. After a quick check of the pockets I found it. The letter was still damp and the ink had been all but washed away to the point where it was impossible to read. I wadded it up and tossed it in the trash when I brought in the second load.

The dinner I cooked that night was delicious, if I do say so myself. Guilt and incredible relief forced me to cook the best meal I had in years. Even if my wife didn't know about the things I'd done or wanted to do, I still felt like I had to make it up to her.

"Dinner is great," she said. "What'd I do to deserve this?"

"I just felt like hooking you up, sweetheart."

"Oh," she said. Then anger shrouded her face. "I thought you felt bad about this..." she tossed an envelope across the table. It landed next to my plate and I picked up, confused.

"What's this?" I asked, but I had a pretty good idea.

"Open it," she commanded.

Again my heart started pounding. I opened the envelope and low and behold –

"What you threw away was an old grocery list that you left in *another* pair of pants," she answered. "*That* is the letter you wrote."

"Look," I started.

"No," she cut me off. "I don't wanna hear any weak-ass explanations. Who is she?"

"That's not important, Denise. What's important is that I didn't give her the –"

"Who is she?" Denise repeated. "No, never mind. You're right. It's not important who she is. The fact that you didn't give her the letter doesn't mean shit to me. You might have given it to her tomorrow."

"I wasn't gonna give it to her at all."

"Why don't you go give it to her now?" she suggested. Her calm voice unnerved me. It was the soft hiss of a burning fuse before the fireworks start. "And pack some suitcases so you can take all of your shit with you."

"Let me explain, please."

"I don't wanna hear it."

And then she exploded.

Her arms flashed from left to right. Dishes, food and silverware went flying. "How could you do this to me?" she screamed. She got up so fast that her chair clattered to the floor. She strode into the bedroom and slammed the door.

The emotions I felt are hard to explain. I was angry with myself and sad for Denise. She didn't deserve this.

I went to the door and knocked softly. "Denise?"

She didn't answer. I tried to open the door but it was locked. I knocked a little harder. "Denise?"

Still no answer. I went to the living room and sank down onto the couch. Tears welled up in my eyes but they wouldn't fall. Time passed and I just stared at the blank wall in front of me. I'm not sure exactly how much time went by, but when Denise came out of the bedroom she was composed once more... She was almost too composed.

"Your bag is packed," she said. My eyebrows went up. "You can send for the rest of your stuff."

"Hold up..." I started as I rose to my feet. "What do you mean my bag is packed?"

"What do you think I mean?" she countered with an irritated sting in her voice.

"We gotta talk about this first, Kitty. Let me explain what's going on."

"There's nothing to explain. You want another woman? Go get her, and *stay gone.*"

"Listen to me, Kitty – "

"You don't get to call me that any –"

"LISTEN TO ME!" I exploded. Rage erupted from a dark place in my soul. The moment the words escaped my lips I knew all hell was about to break loose.

"Now you wanna scream at me?" she challenged. "Get out of here before I call the police!"

My anger left as quickly as it came. It turned into guilt and crushing sorrow.

"Do you love me, Denise?"

"How can you ask me that?" The anger in her voice was tinged with grief.

"If you love me now, if you ever loved me, you have to listen to me." My grave tone got her attention. She was quiet, for a little while, at least, as I continued.

"It's going to be hard to believe what I'm about to say. When I'm finished, you can call Tim to confirm at least part of it. Remember us talking about Richard and Andre?"

"Yeah," she said impatiently. "You're friend that was killed by his mom's ex."

"Exactly. Only he didn't really kill Rich. Rich killed him and then killed himself."

Mild surprise flashed in her expression and then the angry frown came back. "What the hell does that have to do you and this other bitch?"

"Richard and Andre were vampires. Richard turned Su-Yin and she chose me because I knew Richard. She bit me and put me under a trance. She's trying to turn me."

Denise's laugh was incredulous and bitter. "You've lost it! Are you really joking with me at a time like this?"

I didn't expect her to believe me. Still, her dismissal of my confession, no matter how hard it was to believe, soured my sadness and desperation into anger again.

Searing heat built up in my chest. My head began to throb and I could literally feel my eyes turning red. I was spilling my heart to her and she laughed at me. Her thoughts were worse. They were mocking and biting, things she was too kind to say aloud even in a fit of anger. They provided more fuel for my anger.

"You don't believe me?"

Denise saw the look in my eyes and fear crept into her own. The fear was swiftly pushed back by her anger.

"Get out," she snapped. "Let me get the door."

She turned her back to me to go to the front door. I wish I could describe the shock and fear in her face when she saw me already standing there. She looked behind her to see if I was still there, but of course, I wasn't. Slowly, she turned back to face me. "How did you...?" she was breathless.

"I just told you how."

"No," Denise said to no one in particular.

She shook her head in disbelief and hurried into the bedroom. After closing and locking the door, she turned to face the bed only to see me sitting on it. She barely stifled a scream and began to fumble at the lock. When she finally unlocked it, I got up from the bed. As she opened the door, I stepped up behind her and closed it.

Denise turned frantically, trapped between the closed door and me. Her breath came in ragged gulps of air and the speed of her heartbeat increased threefold.

"I won't hurt you," I promised. Her fear appeased my anger. The heat in my chest cooled. My guilt and sadness returned. "I'll never hurt you. I love you. You're right, though. I do have to leave."

I waited for a reply. For the first time since the argument began, Denise was speechless.

"Call Tim," I suggested. "Tell him what you saw tonight. He didn't believe me earlier. He'll believe now."

Denise watched as I picked up the bag she packed for me. Angry, afraid, and confused, her eyes never left me as I stalked out of the bedroom and through the front door.

The club where Su-Yin danced was crowded that night. Perverted, corrupted thoughts saturated the air as thickly as the cigarette, cigar and weed smoke. Some of the men were thinking about their wives and what they would say if they knew their husbands were here.

"You weren't thinking about Denise when we met, were you?" came Su-Yin's voice from behind.

She was reading my mind as sure as I was reading the people around me. I turned to her.

"I'd appreciate it if you stopped eavesdropping."

"Major, there is a lot I want to show. You must have questions. Let's go somewhere so we can talk in private."

"You're early," I observed. "Don't you have to work at the library?"

"I quit yesterday."

I was surprised for some reason. "Why?"

"Because I was tired of it. I only work normal jobs from time to time to maintain the Su-Yin identity, not because I need the money. I make more than enough here."

"I'm surprised you even live on the grid. Seems like you'd want to lay low."

She scoffed. "Do you know how hard it is to get a decent place to live without a job and credit? I'm not going to live in some off-the-books dump, or on the street, or in the woods. I'm a vampire, not an animal."

"Makes sense," I conceded. "I don't mind going somewhere to talk, but aren't you dancing tonight?"

She smiled. "I do what I want. Pedro owns the club. I own Pedro. Come."

A short cab ride later I found myself in a two-story house. Houston, TX has the fourth largest population among US cities and is in the top ten in geographical area. It also has a lot of forested areas within the city limits. This house sat right in the middle of one of them. It was built in the middle of an acre of cleared land in a larger wooded area about a quarter mile away from an affluent Houston neighborhood.

We sat in her living room under a dim light. I was never real big on interior decoration, so I couldn't say if there was a particular style or theme. All I could tell was that the house was expensively decorated. There was soft carpeting, leather furniture, and a big screen television adorned the far wall.

The house appeared empty but I had a feeling something else was there besides the two of us. There was no foreign scents, sounds, or thoughts, and the feeling quickly went away. I chalked it up to simple paranoia.

"This place is posh," I noted.

"Pedro pays me well. I also have friends who buy me nice things. You'd be surprised at what men and women will give for just the possibility of sexual satisfaction, let alone the actual act."

"Why work at all, then?" I asked. "Couldn't you just *persuade* people to provide you with everything you want and then some?"

"We have to use our abilities discreetly," she explained. "In many ways it's better for us to blend in to some degree."

"You keep saying 'we' and 'us,'" I observed. "You're not just talking about you and me, are you? How many vampires have you made?"

"Pedro is the only one, until you."

Su-Yin fell silent for a while and just stared at me. She was trying to read my mind again. This time I concentrated on stopping her.

"You're blocking me," she said with more than mild surprise. "You're change isn't even complete. I've had Pedro for over two years and he still can't do it."

"Why?" I asked.

"I don't know," she answered matter-of-factly. "He can't hear thoughts either. Maybe he's just slow."

"No," I said. "I meant why did you do this to me?"

She performed a slow, seductive spin. "Before I dance, I scan the minds of my patrons; a quick sweep of the crowd to find the easiest or most challenging target. It depends on how I feel on a particular night."

"Which category did I fall into?"

"Neither. When I read you I saw a familiar face. You were reminiscing about how you, Tim and Richard used fake ID's to get into strip clubs. Richard was my maker."

I was distracted by the memory of the last moments of my best friend's life. Su-Yin used that distraction to slip into my mind again.

"That's right," she said. "Before he killed himself, he admitted to you and the others that he made a kill that night. *I* was that kill. He didn't quite finish the job."

"But why me?" I asked again.

"There are several reasons. Pedro is starting to bore me, for one. I needed a new playmate."

"But why *me*?" I repeated angrily.

"I am very particular about who I turn," she said as if it was a compliment. "I only share this gift with people I know I can trust to do what I want them to do."

"You mean people weak enough for you to control," I snarled. "There's no shortage of people like that. Why did you pick me?"

"You knew my maker. I thought you could tell me about him." She poured herself a drink and took a long swallow. "The other reason was that you wanted it."

"That's a lie," I argued.

"You envied Richard," Su-Yin said. "Do you deny that you wondered what it would be like to have any woman you wanted? What it would feel like to have all of that power?"

"I was curious," I admitted. "I never wanted it."

"In any case," she said dismissively, "it's too late now."

"Is it?"

Su-Yin laughed. She tried to enter my mind again but I blocked her again. She laughed again. "I don't have to read your mind to know what you're thinking. You think you'll become human again if you can somehow destroy me before you give in to the hunger."

She was right.

"Let me put that thought to rest, Major. You're not in a transitional period. You won't revert to your human form, not even if I die before your first taste of blood. You see, you've already had that first taste."

Pain seized my gut and doubled me over. The room tilted. The floor flew up and crashed into the side of my face. I lay there shivering in agony as Su-Yin sat down cross-legged in front of me.

"Yes. That drug you thought I gave you when we first kissed was my blood. The blood of your maker turns you faster than human blood ever could."

"You licked your teeth," I gasped. "You cut your tongue on your teeth before you kissed me."

"Your mind was so clouded with lust you paid it no attention. You can forget about becoming human again. The only question is how it will take for your change to be complete. You have two choices: Feed or die."

The pain passed almost as quickly as it overtook me. I took a deep breath to be sure I still could before climbing unsteadily to the couch. The front door opened and two men walked in with four women.

The man leading the way was a tall Latino that couldn't be anyone other than Pedro. I recognized three of the women immediately as dancers at Su-Yin's club. The fourth woman was a dark haired beauty unfamiliar to me. A look into her mind revealed the name Debra. She was a nineteen-year-old college student spending the weekend at home. Her only thoughts were soft moans and erotic visions of Pedro.

Pedro didn't have to entrance the man. I pulled the name Trevor from his mind. The promise of an orgy with beautiful people he'd never see again was enough for him to come to this house with these strangers.

Idiot.

Pedro was the only vampire among them. The rest were the meal for the night.

Su-Yin stood and announced: "Company's here." She gestured to the Latino. "You've probably guessed this tall strapping man here is Pedro." She turned to him. "Pedro, this is our new playmate, Major."

Pedro walked over to me and held out his hand. I stood up to shake it and winced as he squeezed unnecessarily and unnaturally hard. From the pain and the look of my hand, I expected to hear the sound of my bones breaking. I could even feel them scraping against one another. Surprisingly, the bones bent but didn't break. It hurt like hell but wouldn't give him the satisfaction of anything more than the wince.

"You're gonna let this *maricón* join our club?" he asked in a thick Cuban accent.

"Yes," Su-Yin said. "Do you have a problem with that?"

"Guess not," Pedro said before he let my hand go.

My hand remained contorted the way Pedro crushed it. I growled and flexed it. The pain of my bones popping back into their regular places was, for lack of a better word, exquisite. Tears welled up again and again they did not fall.

"Let's begin, then," Su-Yin commanded. She picked up a remote control and pressed one of its buttons.

The lights dimmed. A new song began to play. A slow, sexy track with thumping, mesmeric bass pulsed from the speakers. I sat back down on the couch and watched. Debra and Trevor went over to Su-Yin. Two of the dancers stayed with Pedro. The other dancer came to me and commenced a seductive dance.

I listened for their thoughts. Pedro and Su-Yin shielded themselves. Debra's sordid thoughts were the same except Su-Yin had taken Pedro's place. The three dancers were absent of discernible thought. They were being overwhelmed by the carnal emotion projecting from the vampires. And there was something else.

Beneath the unnaturally lewd desire was the smallest hint of dread. The dancers and Debra both felt it. Deep in their subconscious a whisper warned that something was terribly wrong. The vampires' projections of lust, however, kept those whispers pushed back into the shadows of their thoughts. Only one person's mind was crystal clear.

Trevor. His thoughts were of the eight of us sprawled across the floor in a tangle of naked, sweaty flesh. There were three men and five women. Trevor had already been scheming on how to get two of them to himself. The second woman didn't matter as long as Su-Yin was the first.

The dancer swaying in front of me was even better than Su-Yin. She was sexier, too. That was when I realized that neither Pedro nor Su-Yin was controlling her. She was under *my* trance. The vampire in me instinctively took over and drew the prey to the predator.

What's your name? I breathed softly into her mind.

"Christina," she answered aloud. That was her real name. Her performing name was Flayme. She thought spelling it with a "Y" made it sexier. I wanted her real name.

Her smooth, artificially tan skin was flawless with the exception of a dusting of freckles on her bare shoulders. Flaming red hair swayed to the left and right as she gyrated in time with the slow driving beat of the music.

She hitched up her mini skirt, straddled my thighs and lowered herself onto my lap. Her skirt was pulled up just cnough to reveal to me that she was indeed a natural red head. Her heartbeat boomed in my ears. The blood whooshing through her veins roared in my ears.

"Christina," I began, "how does it feel?"

She rubbed against my growing erection and said, "It feels good."

"Not that, Christina. How does it feel to know you're about to die?"

"Mmmmmm," she purred. "Sexy."

The scent of her passion and underlying fear made my head swim and stomach growl. I pulled her to me, took a handful of her red hair and snatched her head to the side to get a good look at her neck. Her jugular pulsed, beckoning me until I couldn't hear the music anymore. My mouth opened wide. My gums tingled as my canines unsheathed.

A glance over Christina's shoulder showed me Su-Yin. Her blouse was open. The doomed man sucked on her left nipple while she drank blood from Debra's ruined neck. Debra's eyes rolled up in her head and her eyelashes fluttered like the hummingbird wings.

I looked into her mind during her last moments. She screamed for God to save her. She asked why this was happening to her, a young woman who had never hurt anyone. And then there was nothing.

Her thoughts were snuffed out like a candle in a gale. The moment she died my mind snapped back to lucidity.

"No," I growled.

"What do you mean?" Christina demanded.

She sat back to give me an incredulous look. She saw my glowing red eyes and scythe-like canines and screamed. Her cry brought the others out of their trances.

The women with Pedro panicked and tried to run. He had a vice-like grip on the neck of one of the women that choked off any sound she wanted to make. He had the other woman by the hair and snatched her to him. Her scream turned into a blood-choked gurgle as Pedro tore into her throat.

Christina leapt from my lap and ran to the front door. Trevor tried to follow. Su-Yin didn't let him. She grabbed his head with both hands and snapped his neck with frightening ease. He crumpled to the floor.

My maker literally flew after Christina. The poor woman was struggling with the locks on the front door when Su-Yin fell upon her. Meanwhile, Pedro tossed the lifeless body of the first dancer to the floor and ravaged the other one.

I froze. The grizzly scene played out in less than a couple of minutes that felt like hours. When it was over, Su-Yin turned and walked toward me. Blood dripped from her chin and hands. Dark red gore stained her white blouse. She leveled a blazing red glare at me and bared her fangs.

"What is wrong with you?" she snapped. "Are you trying to get us caught?"

Pedro dropped the dancer's corpse and wiped the blood from his mouth with the back of his hand.

"Let me kill him," he snarled.

"Not yet," Su-Yin commanded, still staring at me. "We were all a little frightened when we were first made." She took another step toward me. I was too stunned to move.

"Get out, Major. Now." She snatched me to my feet. "Pedro and I are going to finish the gentleman over there."

"But Su," Pedro interrupted. "He's already dead. You said we aren't supposed to –"

Su-Yin turned on Pedro. "He's not dead yet you stupid fuck," she said, clearly irritated. "Can't you can smell? Can't you hear his heart beating? You are so fucking slow."

She faced me again. "Like I was saying...we're going to finish him. You can join us if you want. If you choose not to, don't be here when we finish or you're next."

They turned and went to Trevor. Su-Yin ripped open his neck with her fangs. Pedro bit into his wrist. The monster in me urged me to take the other wrist. The human part of me was still stronger. I found the strength to stand and walk away. In my confusion, with my trembling hands, it took me a while to figure out the locks on the door. When I finally got it open I sprinted into the night.

I lost track of time as I ran. When I couldn't run anymore, I walked. With no idea where I was or where I was going, I just kept moving. I tuned out the thoughts of the people around me and concentrated on my predicament. A deep craving lurked in my gut and my mind. The vampire growing within constantly reminded me how hungry I was.

The pain came back with a vengeance. It took all of my strength to stay upright. My breath grew labored from sharp pains repeatedly striking my stomach. The throbbing ache made me dizzy, made me stagger like a drunkard. I was in such a daze I barely noticed a man walking deliberately toward me.

The stranger punched me hard in the face one time, grabbed me by my shoulders and pulled me roughly behind a building. He drove his forearm into my throat and forced me against the wall. I looked into his eyes and saw madness. His mind was a drug-induced kaleidoscope of hatred, paranoia, rage and addiction.

He moved fast, and in my weakened condition I couldn't stop him. No words were spoken. There were no threats, no taunts, no nothing. There was only violence. He pulled a hunting knife from his pocket and stabbed me again and again in the stomach and chest. I slid slowly to the ground and he stooped down with me, stabbing all the while.

I looked down at the knife in stunned disbelief. My blood was all over him, spattered across his face and torso. He got a kind of sexual satisfaction from the massacre. After twenty-seven piercings of my midsection, he finally stopped. My eyes bulged and my mouth hung agape. Blood oozed over my bottom lip and down my chin.

The would-be killer took a few breaths to compose himself before searching my pockets. He took my wallet, keys and loose change. Only then did his frenzied thoughts settle into exhausted satisfaction.

I was his eighth victim in as many nights. All of his previous victims had been women. He chose me for his first male victim because I was smaller than him. My drunken appearance made me look like an easy kill. Pride filled him and the bastard had the nerve to crack a smile. He planned to cut my picture out of my driver's license and tape it to the underside of the lid on a chest he kept in his apartment. Thinking I was dead or surely dying, he turned his back to me and headed for the street.

He took one step onto the street just before my bloody hand reached around and clutched his face. I covered his mouth with one hand, my extended claws digging into his cheek, and dragged him back to the scene of the stabbing. I pinned him against the wall the way he had just pinned me. He pulled his knife, but this time I grabbed his hand and squeezed. His bones shattered like brittle glass.

My upper and lower fangs extended. His pain and terror-stricken face was awash with the crimson glow of my eyes. I smiled with all the dark mirth of Satan himself. His eyes bulged until I thought they would pop out of his head. I remember thinking how cool that would've been. The fear exuding from his mind and his scent made me stronger and hungrier still.

"Now it's my turn," I growled.

I licked my lips with an elongated tongue and sank my fangs into his pulsing jugular. Warm blood spurted against the roof my mouth and down my throat.

The stranger's mind shrieked. His thoughts were wild and incomprehensible, not entirely unlike they were when he attacked me. Only this time there was no rage, hatred, or addiction. Instead, there was loathing, confusion, and terror. Those emotions added enough flavor to his blood to lessen the bitterness of the drugs and alcohol polluting his system. When his heartbeat began to slow and his blood pulsed weaker, I sucked as hard as I could. I instinctively knew to stop drinking the instant before his heart stopped beating.

My vampire came to the fore of my consciousness and cried out in triumph. His warm blood invigorated me. It extinguished the sweltering heat of the hunger and made me feel superhuman. I hoisted the dead body easily and tossed it into a nearby dumpster. My mind raced. My hunger was finally appeased.

Now what?

I my ripped shirt open to inspect the stab wounds. They were gone. The only evidence that I'd been attacked was the drying blood. My change was done. I could feel it. The power that burned through me was unlike anything I'd ever known. I felt like I could fly...

So I did. I leapt into the air and kept rising. The ground rushed away beneath my feet and an instant later I was standing atop the roof of a sixteen-story office building. I stood on the ledge and stared with satisfaction down at the ground. A subtle change in the sky snapped my gaze back up and to the east.

The eastern sky was no longer black. It had lightened to purple with a tinge of orange. My wave of newfound strength began to ebb with the coming of the morning sun. Fading power was replaced by a rising surge of dread.

I'd become a vampire. I had to find shelter.

CHAPTER FIVE

A drop of cold water on my forehead woke me up. The first thing I noticed was a disgusting smell that made sent me into a coughing fit. The smell was a reminder that I had slept through the day in the shadows of the sewer. I heard the footsteps and thoughts of dozens of people on the street. That wasn't a good place to emerge.

A thirty-minute walk through the dark putrid tunnels brought me to a place where there were very few people above. The sewer grate overhead was far beyond the reach of my outstretched hand, but then I remembered what I could do. I didn't even have to jump. I simply willed myself to rise six feet in the air. The heavy iron cover was easily brushed aside and I floated to the sidewalk above. The few people on the block turned at the noise, but by the time they noticed me I was already walking briskly down the street.

The sun had just surrendered to the night. The western sky still shone with a purple and orange hue. Nightfall was as beautiful to me as the sunrise had been when I was human.

The hunger returned while I marveled at the darkening sky. It wasn't as painful a craving as it was the night before but it grew with every step. I rushed to reach Su-Yin before she left for the evening. A hunter's moon crept across the darkness. I didn't want to hunt alone.

Su-Yin had no idea that I was in her mind long before she picked up my scent from a block away. She was thinking about me.

For reasons she didn't understand she couldn't let me exist unless I was under her control. She thought pursuing me was a waste of time the night before and she would've rather left me to my own devices, but an irresistible compulsion urged her to come after me. She planned to track me, to find me so she could enthrall me. Option two was to kill me if she couldn't make me her slave.

Her thoughts immediately clouded over when she caught my scent but it was way too late. I'd reached gently into her mind a mile before I reached her block. She opened her front door to find me sitting on the stoop.

"I knew you'd be back," she lied.

I humored her. "Of course you did. I need you."

"I'm glad you realize that."

She grabbed me by the collar and pulled me through the doorway. Again I felt the presence of something else in the house with us. My mind probed carefully but found no thoughts. Other than the hairs tingling on the back of my neck, I could not sense anything. The paranoia was quickly forgotten when Su-Yin started projecting sexual desire. The scent of her lust was strong enough to taste on the back of my tongue. The flavor reminded me of over proof rum and was exponentially more toxic.

"We followed your scent a few hours after you left last night," Su-Yin revealed. "I was curious to see if you'd do something stupid. You did. You left the remains of your meal in a dumpster for anyone to find with no attempt to disguise his manner of death."

I shrugged. "I wasn't thinking straight."

"Damn right you weren't. If Pedro hadn't moved the body we could be in a real shit-storm right now."

"What are you so afraid of?" I asked. "I only put myself in danger."

"You're almost as clueless as Pedro," she snarled. "*Try* to understand this: If your stupid actions bring hunters sniffing around, or worse, if it attracts the attention of *La Secta de la Ascension*, all of us are in danger."

I knew what she meant by hunters. Hell, I'd been one, at least on an amateur level. From the way she said it, though, there must have been a more organized group. I had no clue about the other thing she mentioned.

"What the hell is *La Secta de la Ascension?*"

"You don't want to know," she assured me. "Do a better job of covering your tracks so you never have to find out."

The mental haze she used to cloud her thoughts grew even denser. She really didn't want me to know about *La Secta de la Ascension*. I decided not to press the issue.

"So what's on the menu for tonight?" I asked.

"I've had a taste for Greek," she purred. She pulled off her tight midriff shirt. A light sheen of sweat already glistened on her bare breasts. "But I'd like my desert before the main course."

"This is just an appetizer for me," I said as I ripped off my shirt.

The rest of our clothes followed and moments later we were writhing on the stairs of her foyer like feral beasts. Her nails extended into claws that raked my flesh relentlessly. The bloody lacerations knitted closed mere moments after they were opened.

The pain excited me. My canines extended to fangs that lightly punctured her skin. Her black vampire blood burned my tongue and quickly evaporated. It didn't sate my hunger the way human blood did. Instead, it sent bursts of euphoria straight to my brain. The rush was stronger than any alcohol or drug I had ever experienced.

When we were done, we lay together on the floor.

"How is it that we both ended up in Houston?" I asked.

"I don't know how about you," Su-Yin answered. "I came because Houston is a good hunting ground."

"Why not New York or LA? Hell, you were already in Chicago."

"It would've been stupid to stay in Chicago," Su-Yin explained. "I'm sure they noticed a missing corpse and two dead morticians."

I thought about the dream I had. Those were Su-Yin's memories. Did she project them to me? Did I pull them out of her mind without her knowledge? Is that what happened when a vampire's blood was ingested?

She continued. "I spent time in New York, Vegas and LA. Many of our kind like the glamour of those cities. They're saturated. The competition is fierce."

"Chicago isn't saturated?" I asked.

Su-Yin shrugged her smooth, bare shoulders. "Don't know. I didn't stick around long enough to find out. I didn't know what was happening to me at first, but after what I did to the morticians I knew I had to get out of town before the police started looking for me."

"So you came to Houston," I said. "Huge population, lots of room to move around...and since it doesn't get as much attention as those other cities, it doesn't attract as many vampires."

"Exactly," Su-Yin confirmed. "Besides, there are just as many flavors here as in those other places. It's just not quite as loud or congested."

There was more to her reasoning than what she said aloud. Even without reading her thoughts I could tell she was holding something back, though I didn't know why. Maybe even she wasn't certain what it was.

She scooped up her clothes and stood. "Get dressed," she commanded. "It's time to leave."

When we finally emerged from her home the moon was at its apex. So was our hunger. Su-Yin's vehicle for the evening was a convertible Porsche. The brisk night wind caressed my face as she drove along the Houston highways with absolutely no regard for life or law.

Countless curses were yelled and thought at us by drivers that had to abruptly brake or even swerve out of their lanes in an attempt to avoid the speeding sports car. We were pulled over several times by HPD and constables and sheriff's deputies and state troopers, but in each instance the ticketing officer was convinced to let the enthralling Su-Yin go with only a verbal warning. After about thirty minutes of driving we reached a Greek restaurant and found Pedro sitting at a bar waiting for us. He inhaled through his nostrils and wrinkled his nose.

"Su, you should take longer showers after being with this puke. You still have his stink on you."

Su-Yin grabbed the back of his head and gave him a long, passionate kiss.

"Don't be jealous," she cajoled. "It doesn't become you. Remember, I don't belong to you. You belong to me."

"Got anything lined up for us?" I asked, surprised at how quickly I was settling into my new existence.

"I ain't got shit for you, rookie," Pedro spat. "But for you and me, Su, I got a couple of young couples. If you want to share with the little one over there, that's your business."

Su-Yin turned to me. "You game?" she challenged.

I smiled. "I'm hungry."

"What's their story?" Su-Yin asked.

Pedro's mind was so easy to read it was scarcely necessary for him to speak. He was more intelligent than Su-Yin gave him credit for but he was too arrogant and smug to care if we read him or not. The only people he cared about deceiving were the humans he fed upon, and only then because it was part of the hunt.

Pedro chuckled. "One is a married couple. The other couple is married, too, but not to each other. They all swing. Their plan is to hit a few more clubs tonight then end it with a nice little party with just the seven of us."

"Greek?" Su-Yin asked.

"That was your order, right?"

"Lovely."

"They've already been drinking and smoking weed," Pedro explained. "We'll hit this spot I know to top them off with a little 'x' and meth."

"Then what?" Su-Yin pressed.

Pedro smiled. "They're into that nature shit. We'll find a secluded area in a park somewhere and feed by the light of the moon. Their night ends with a tragic car accident. The bodies will be burned nearly beyond recognition."

"Hiding any evidence they were preyed upon," Su-Yin added. "You're getting better, lover."

The night went on according to plan. We were all in the shadows of Herman Park by three in the morning. Our prey was full of liquor, food and drugs, so aroused that we didn't even need to beguile them. They indulged in one last hit of meth before the carnal festivities began.

By then my hunger was so strong that I had the shakes. My vampire urged me to stop pussyfooting around and feed. Su-Yin and Pedro, however, were old hands at this. I knew that if I wanted to survive undetected I would have to take every opportunity to learn from those with more experience.

Pedro was uncomfortable with the outdoor setting but he would not attack until Su-Yin gave the command. His trepidation was even evident to the couples. They teased him between tokes of the pipe they passed around and called him an "obvious virgin" to this kind of thing. Pedro chuckled nervously but I could smell his anger.

Su-Yin was as uneasy as Pedro but she did a much better job of hiding it. I couldn't read her so I didn't know exactly how long she intended to play this game. She breathed deeply from the pipe and swooned for a moment.

"Good shit," she giggled as she passed the pipe to me.

What was I supposed to do? I was the only one who hadn't hit it so I took a long pull.

Nothing.

I didn't feel the slightest twinge of intoxication. I'd gotten more of a rush from a drag on a cigarette when I was human than I got from that pipe. I sat there with a blank expression waiting to feel something. One of the young Greek women took the pipe from me.

"You didn't feel anything?" she asked. "You must be a vet, eh? A meth vet!" She laughed at her own wit.

Just play the game. Su-Yin advised, easing her thoughts into mine. *It's fun.*

I shrugged and forced myself to chuckle. "Not a meth vet, baby, I just hide it well."

Su-Yin decided to get the party started as the pipe went on its second rotation. I felt her and Pedro projecting erotic thoughts and emotions into the minds of our prey. They didn't really have to but it did hasten things along. We all shed our clothes. The young Greeks disrobed faster than us. The married couple slithered over to Pedro and helped him undo his trousers. The other man went to Su-Yin and she allowed the remaining woman to slide over to me.

You owe me... she whispered into my mind.

I took the woman in my arms and inhaled deeply, drinking in her scent. Everyone's scent is unique. Each person I came into contact with had slight variations to the rhythm of his or her pulsing blood. Each heart beats at a slightly different pace. The tastes are unique, too.

The woman shuddered when I licked her neck. Her lusty scent provided the head-rush I expected from the drug I'd just inhaled.

And then I heard it again. Her subconscious cried out in terror. Somewhere at the core of her being she knew she was about to die. I heard her beg for her life in a psychic scream that sounded like a faint echo from a deep, dark tunnel.

My vampire implored me to ignore the pleas and sate its hunger. I closed my eyes in anticipation of the coming euphoria and immediately thought of Denise. She was at home, crying. I heard her tortured thoughts from across town as if she were right next to me.

Why was this so difficult for me? It wasn't like I'd never killed before. The psycho I fed on should have obliterated my inhibitions, yet there I was, too reluctant to feed.

The Greek beauty was suddenly snatched from my arms. Pedro stood before me holding the woman up by her shoulders. Her eyes were wide with horror but they closed when Su-Yin came over and whispered a mental command for her to sleep. Pedro dropped her to the grass. Su-Yin turned, reached down and wrapped a strong hand around my neck. She snatched me to my feet and then even higher. My maker's eyes shone red with fury.

"I'm tired of you," she sneered. "I thought you were different, special. You're a coward, too afraid to kill unless you're attacked. I need *hunters*."

Pedro chimed in. "He was a waste of your blood, Su."

"And now that you're a vampire," Su-Yin observed, "your blood can't even satisfy my hunger."

"Fucking useless," Pedro added.

Su-Yin roared and flicked the clawed hand that clutched my throat. Blood...my blood...sprayed across her face and I could no longer breathe. My eyes trailed her bloody fist as it lowered to her side. She opened her hand and a portion of my windpipe fell to the floor. I wheezed and panicked, clutched my neck and fell to my knees. The remains of my throat burned like fire. Su-Yin licked her fingers and spat.

"Disgusting. Pedro, finish him."

Even through my pain and hysteria I could feel Pedro's mirth. I looked into his mind and saw that he intended to pull off my head, snatch out my heart, and burn my body somewhere on the outskirts of the city. He wasn't quite sure where he would dump the body but he'd worry about that when the killing was finished.

Pedro considered putting me in the car with the slaughtered couples. He thought better of that because a red flag would be raised with medical examiners if they found a headless, heartless, charred corpse in a car wreck.

My vampire took control as Pedro reached for me. I dissolved into mist and all Pedro got was a hand full of air.

"Fuck!" he swore. "Where the hell did he get that?"

"Some of us can do little tricks like that and some can't," Su-Yin admitted. "It doesn't matter. He's weak and confused. He can't hold that form for long and can't go far. Find him while I do the girl."

Su-Yin was right. I materialized about one hundred yards away and reached out for Pedro's mind again. He caught my scent the moment I re-formed and bolted in my direction.

Something crazy happened. He morphed into a big gray wolf as he came at me. Those eyes, however, were as bright red and feral as they were in his human form. I took a few sluggish steps then went airborne. Somehow I'd found the strength to fly.

My throat stung as my vampire tried to heal it. My terror and Pedro's murderous rage prodded me on. As I gained altitude the earth below became a dark blur. Pedro howled in indignant disbelief when he realized he would not catch me. His thoughts eventually faded as I glided away.

I don't know how far or how fast I flew. I just kept going until my strength gave out. The fire in my belly had grown greater than the agony in my ruined throat. With no more anger or fear to feed upon, and weakened by neglected hunger, I couldn't go any further.

The earth rose quickly up to meet me. I knew the landing would hurt but I was still shocked by the pain of the impact. My vision blurred as oblivion crept upon me. For a fleeting but terrifying instant I thought it was death, and then I chuckled weakly at my own stupidity. I was willingly surrendering to unconsciousness when I remembered that I was lying in the middle of an open field, where I would be completely exposed to the sun at dawn.

My ordeals that night left me too weak to walk, let alone go airborne again. By then I was so dazed and disoriented that even if could walk, I wouldn't have known which way to go. My augmented sense of smell was overcome by exhaustion so I couldn't use that to guide me to shelter.

Instead of going up, I chose to go down. I started digging. The night was cool but typically humid for southeast Texas so the earth was damp. I focused all of my being into my hands and arms and used the last of my fading strength to burrow into the ground like a mole.

Even through my mental pall I could sense the dawn approaching. It was a growing feeling of dread blooming from the pit of my stomach that burned on the inside but chilled on the outside. The fear didn't prod me to dig faster, though, I wasn't physically capable, but it did stop me from giving up.

The last thing I remembered from that night was worming my way into that hole and pulling as much of the dirt in behind me as I could before everything went black.

"This is so far beneath you," someone said.

I opened my eyes and turned to the sound. I was lying in the middle of a cow pasture. The sun had not yet risen but I could clearly see a dead bull sprawled on the grass a few feet away. My newly enhanced vision pierced the darkness and I saw a monster that I prayed I'd never see again.

"Andre." Surprisingly, I wasn't afraid. I was curious. "It can't be. I watched you burn."

"You watched my body burn. My essence endures. I exist beyond the detection of man and all but the most gifted of our kind."

"This is a dream," I insisted.

One of Andre's eyebrows twitched. He looked a little irritated by my assumption. "Call it what you want."

"Why are you here?" I asked.

"You're not a thief in the night," Andre said. "You should be sitting on a throne of granite and human bone."

I frowned at the image but stayed silent.

Andre continued. "Your potential dictates that you feed discriminately, yet you feed on derelicts and animals like common vermin. You refer to your power as 'your vampire,' as if it were a different entity. There is no vampire inhabiting your body. You *are* the vampire. Don't run from it."

I shook my head tiredly. "I don't know what you're talking about and I don't care. Get out of my head so I can get some sleep."

"As you wish," Andre said. "But you'll never sleep peacefully again. Such is the fate of our kind." He took a step back and stopped. "Noah's flood was nothing compared to your fire. In time, I can help you ignite it."

"Whatever," I sighed.

Andre's form faded into the darkness. I stretched out in the grass and closed my eyes. I wasn't concerned about being above ground because I knew I was dreaming. My body was still a few feet underground. I just hoped I was deep enough to be protected from the sun.

Sometime later I felt something wet on my face. Something was licking my cheek. I opened my eyes and was immediately blinded.

Intense heat seared my retinas. A sensation like millions of white-hot needles piercing my flesh brought me to searing tears. It took a while for my eyesight to return. It took just as much time for those superheated needles in my flesh to cool to a bearable level. When my vision finally cleared I saw the source of my pain.

It was the sun.

I was lying in a small crater in the middle of a cow pasture in broad freaking daylight. My burrow had been dug open. Dirt was scattered to either side of me. Fear paralyzed me. Would I melt? Explode into flames? I rose to a sitting position and waited fearfully for whatever was going to happen to me.

There was a throbbing ache at the base of my neck and just behind my eyes. My exposed flesh was acutely sensitive and continued to sting slightly in the sunlight. The softest breeze brought pain to my irritated skin. It even hurt to breathe. The air I inhaled burned from the inside of my nostrils to my lungs.

But I was still there. I reached for my throat. The flesh there was very tender and my breathing was uncomfortable.

But I was still there. I was still whatever the hell "alive" is for a vampire.

A dog sat a few feet away, watching me with his head cocked to the side. It was a big, muscular Cane Corso. When I say big, I mean *big*, even for a Cane Corso. Standing on all fours he had to be about 40 inches tall from paw to withers. As imposing as it was, I wasn't afraid of it. It had no desire to attack me. That was obvious by its relaxed posture and scent.

I looked into his mind just to see if I could. His thoughts were more like vague impressions. They were a patchwork and fleeting mix of urges, random intentions, and pictures that he somehow filtered down into the choices he made.

"Where am I?" I asked the dog as if he could answer. The dog twitched and it looked a lot like a shrug.

The sound of flies buzzing behind me aggravated my already throbbing headache. The smell of blood filled my nostrils. I looked over my shoulder and saw the fallen bull. Its neck was ripped open but there was a lot less blood around the body than there should have been.

"Did I do that?" I asked the dog.

The dog gave a sharp bark that I translated loosely as *of course* and then trotted over to the bull's carcass. He found a spot on the bull's thigh where the hide of the animal had been torn away. He buried his snout in the exposed wound and began to eat.

Blood covered my hands and shirt and I could feel it drying around my mouth and on my nose. I could only imagine how my face looked.

"Say, dog," I called, just for the hell of it. To my surprise the dog stopped eating and turned to me. As startled as I was, I kept talking. "Where can I get cleaned up?"

The dog gave another shrug and went back to his meal. I stood and stretched, hoping my improved senses would allow me to smell a pond or a stream in the distance. All I smelled was blood and cow shit. Wait, I could fly. Maybe higher ground would be the key. I levitated about ten feet high.

My headache began to throb with a vengeance. The heat of those needles of sunlight flared and my stomach lurched. I dropped back to ground ass-first. It wasn't hard to figure out that I was a lot weaker in the daytime. I picked a direction at random and started walking. After a few hundred feet of stepping over and around cow chips, the dog began to bark at me. I turned and the dog barked more. He turned and ran a few feet away before stopping, turning toward me, and barking again. He wanted me to follow him.

We'd walked for about half an hour when I heard the sounds of cars somewhere far off. Another half hour and I was looking at a highway rest area. It was one of the larger ones. It was a building that housed vending machines, park tables and benches, and generally well-kept restrooms.

Stepping into the station immediately made me feel better. The sun's rays didn't affect me when they did not touch me directly. Residual sunlight weakened me and caused my head to ache a little, but the burning pain on my skin receded to a mild irritation.

The facility was empty. I found the men's room and washed the blood from my skin. My clothes were hopeless. I needed to change. The dog did not like the smell of the rest area so he went and waited outside. He barked just as I heard two approaching cars. I reached out with my mind to see if I could "listen" to the thoughts of the occupants.

A young couple sped down the highway in separate cars. The male drove a black Mazda RX-7. The girl drove an electric blue Camaro Z28. Both cars had Oklahoma license plates. He and his girlfriend were the same age. The girl had just purchased the RX-7 from a dealership in northeast Houston and they were taking them home by way of Dallas.

The male had to take a dump. The female was concentrating on the joint she was smoking. They pulled into the rest area and came to screeching halts. The young man came rushing to the men's room. I ducked into a stall.

I scented his blood even before he entered the restroom. My stomach lurched and the hunger had me again. The bull's blood I'd ingested kept me alive but it made me nauseous and slowed my healing.

I needed human blood.

Crouched in the fourth stall, balanced easily with both feet on the rim of the toilet seat, I looked into his mind. He wanted to go to the first stall.

Su-Yin could project desires and impressions to other people. Why not see if I could, too? The teen reached for the door of the first stall.

Fourth stall.

He hesitated. The pressure in his stomach overcame my will and he reached for the door again.

Fourth stall is cleanest. I was more insistent.

He pulled back and walked down three doors. His surge of fear and surprise exhilarated me when he opened the stall door and saw me. My eyes blazed. My fangs were bared. I was on him before he could cry out.

The thought occurred to me that I didn't have to kill him. I could have taken just enough blood from him and his companion to get my strength back. That would leave them infected, and my vampire whispered to me that they could make useful thralls. I might be able to use them to my advantage when I saw Su-Yin and Pedro again, and I was determined to see them again. But how could I control two new vampires when I could barely control myself?

It would've been dangerous to turn them and then leave them on their own. Somehow, I knew that on an instinctive level. I also knew that I was nowhere near ready to start creating thralls.

This kid was food, nothing more. His girlfriend was, too.

I didn't close my eyes that time because I didn't want to see Denise. I didn't want to see anything that would have stopped me. All I allowed myself to see was survival. Later, the bloodless bodies of the young couple shared an embrace in the Z28, which was consumed in roiling flames in a dry creek bed about two miles away from the rest area.

I didn't expect to feel bad about what I'd done. I was a vampire, even though I was walking around in the daylight. This is how my kind survives. The wolf doesn't feel remorse for the sheep.

The thing was, I *did* feel remorse. I felt terrible for the victims and was appalled at myself. There must have been some vestige of humanity clinging to me. A faint voice screamed at me that I was a monster. A part of me was desperate to do what Richard was brave enough to do years earlier, when he cured himself the only way he could.

That consideration was dismissed as quickly as it had risen to the surface of my thoughts. Maybe Richard was more stupid than brave. Yes, the price was appalling, but the power was worth it. The sooner I could get past the guilt the better. The alternative was out of the question. Su-Yin didn't give me a choice when she turned me, but I chose then, to survive.

Their blood returned most of my strength. My senses, while dulled by the blazing sun, were sharp enough for me to pick up the sounds and smells of Houston about 50 miles southeast of where I stood. I focused my aching eyes on a sign about two miles down the road and saw a Highway 290 sign. I decided to conserve my strength and use the R-X7.

The Cane Corso jumped through the car window and settled himself into the passenger seat. I stared at him.

"You're riding with me?"

The dog just panted and stared at me. I climbed in on the driver side and used the boy's key to start the car.

"I'm not ready to head back to Houston just yet," I explained to the dog. "We've got full stomachs, a car full of gas, a pocket full of someone else's credit cards and cash, and all the time in the world. Let's see a little more of Texas before I go see Su-Yin and Pedro again."

CHAPTER SIX

The dog turned out to be invaluable. He became my constant companion. I never named him. He was feral and free, not mine to name. Besides, I didn't need to call him aloud. I projected thoughts to him as easily and as clearly as I could to humans. He guarded me while I slept and I repaid him by letting him join in on my kills.

We spent the next few weeks wandering the Texas highways. We stayed clear of the cities and survived mostly on livestock and deer. After I drained them dry the dog ate the meat. It kept me functional even if it wasn't as good as human blood. I was still reluctant to feed on humans, and it wasn't just because of the guilt. The reluctance also came from practicality.

Controlling my preternatural appetite became an endless battle. At times I could feel the human part of me recede as the vampire took over. The urge to gorge on human blood often threatened to overwhelm me. I found myself following people involuntarily. It happened while driving a stolen car or on foot in a rest area or a gas station convenience store. The whole time I'd be looking for the best opportunity to attack. I was usually able to stop myself.

Though the human part of me receded, it always left behind enough of a residue for logic to temper the hunger. I'd already seen news reports about the couple from the rest area. If more people went missing in the same part of Texas a manhunt would be inevitable. A large enough manhunt would make it that much tougher for me to travel and feed.

The other reason I rarely targeted humans was, for lack of a better description, plain old stubbornness. I refused to let the hunger control me on general principle. Nothing would control me if I could help it. I would force myself to go for days without human blood just to see how long I could do it.

Eventually the hunger for human blood would get to be too much to bear. During those times the hunger ignited a feral madness within me. It promised to devolve me into a mindless animal that would not be the least bit concerned about logic or discretion or self-preservation of any kind beyond its next feeding.

Even in those extreme situations I was careful about how and when I chose human prey. I would only take the occasional driver or hitchhiker, and only then if a mind-peek revealed they had no family or friends that would miss them. After I fed I took great pains to hide the bodies thoroughly. The corpses would be left damaged enough to mask the bite wounds, weighted down in deep lakes or rivers, or burned whenever a convenient opportunity presented itself.

My abilities made it easy for me to break into closed convenience and department stores along the highway. There weren't as many back then as there are now but there were enough for a change of clothes every few days and to keep dog food on hand.

The dog didn't like store-bought, but disappearing livestock would attract unwanted attention and there were times when wildlife large enough to satisfy him was too far away for a convenient hunt. Truck stops provided my showers. Sleep was had when and wherever possible. Sometimes I rested during the day and sometimes at night, sometimes in a car and sometimes on the ground. The dog always stood guard when I slept.

The road was lonelier than I could have imagined. Before my change there was always someone to talk to' my wife, and friends, my coworkers. I missed TV and movies. The dog was the only thing that kept me from going completely stir crazy. It wasn't a pleasant existence but it was better than not existing at all.

More than a month passed. I changed vehicles randomly so as not to establish a pattern. I visited city and university libraries from San Antonio to Austin to Dallas and did as much research on vampire lore and vampirism as their resources allowed. The Internet as it's known now was still fairly new to me in the mid nineties. There was little useful information to find online regarding vampires.

My heightened senses made me a faster reader. I no longer needed water or normal food so I could spend hours on end reading without any breaks. As long as the hunger was sated I could take in and retain more information than I ever could as a human.

Later I went down to Galveston and found even more interesting reading. Some of the descriptions and experiences were similar to mine. There were passages about distinctive types of vampires and how abilities and vulnerabilities differed from one individual to another.

Some, like me, could fly or morph into mist. According to some of the texts many could project and manipulate simple emotions. The more powerful ones could read minds and project ideas into the minds of their prey. There were descriptions of shape-shifters that could change into different kinds of carnivores and scavengers. I even read about a breed of vampire that fed on energy and emotions as well as blood.

One book spoke of vampires that, like me, could tolerate sunlight. According to the text, and as I could attest, their strength was diminished and flesh irritated to varying degrees by direct sunlight. On the other end of the spectrum, there were others so severely affected by the sun's rays that their flesh would ignite upon contact. That was what happened to Richard and Andre.

What made me different from them?

I was curious about what literature there was regarding the danger of religious artifacts. Some of the texts spoke about religious paraphernalia as transmitters. They contained no power by themselves. When consecrated, however, they were powerful conduits that converted a true believer's faith into a form of telekinetic energy.

The holder's religion didn't seem to matter. If their faith was real, that energy could repel or even harm some vampires – the stronger the faith, the more harmful the energy. The text explained that only the more powerful vampires were more sensitive to the power of faith. The weaker ones with limited abilities were not as vulnerable. They were, however, easier to kill using mundane methods.

There was also information about vampires' inability to enter someone else's home uninvited. I was certain that was movie bullshit but there was a surprising amount of writing on the topic. Though they all agreed it was dangerous to enter a home without at least one of the residents' permission, the authors didn't always agree on the severity of the harm.

Several texts suggested vampires would only be slightly weakened. Others asserted that we'd lose our power and become little more than human. Some authors insisted it could be fatal. Based on all I'd read to that point, I agreed with those few that believed the extent of the damage was similar to a vampire's susceptibility to blessed talismans: the more powerful the vampire and the more devout the people living in the home, the more dangerous it was to intrude.

I found passages discussing vampire mortality. All vampires have the ability to regenerate damaged flesh and bone. Wounds made by a weapon of pure silver or wood healed slower. Apparently the heads and hearts are the only things that don't grow back.

I learned a lot during my travels but there was so much more to learn. Mortals compiled most of the literature. Some of them claimed to have had dealings with vampires. A few of the authors claimed to *be* vampires. Who knows if any of those claims were true? There's really no way of knowing and it didn't matter right then. Time would tell.

After discovering as much as I could within the I-35, I-10, I-45 triangle, I decided to go east. The Louisiana Gulf Coast seemed to be as good a place to feed as any, and probably better. I didn't think I'd have to be as selective with my prey and I was right. That region was alligator country. They were convenient waste disposal systems for the remains of our feedings. I was surprised at how many people lived in such close proximity to those prehistoric throwbacks.

There was a small community living in the swamp that had little if any contact with the outside world. I observed them for a short time from the shadows, eavesdropping on thoughts and voices. Their dialect was a mix of French and English so uniquely accented that no one outside of the community would recognize it as either. It was like a foreign country on the geographical edge of the United States.

They had no use for organized law enforcement. They handled conflicts internally. If one or two people went missing now and then, the news stayed within their isolated society. Disappearances were dismissed as feuding neighbors or carelessness around hungry gators.

It seemed a convenient place to live and feed for a short time. I tested that theory my third night in the Louisiana swamplands. Beneath a hunter's moon, I traveled among the high limbs of cypress trees. I used the darkness, elevation, and heightened senses to spy both human and wildlife.

The things I thought would make the swamplands of the Louisiana Gulf Coast a good place to hunt were the same things that made them troublesome. The people lived virtually side by side with man-eating reptiles so they were on constant alert. They were more in tune with nature than the average American and hyper-aware of their surroundings.

They were deeply superstitious and profoundly religious. Their deep belief in the supernatural included vampires, werewolves, and revenants among other monsters, and they protected themselves accordingly. Every home had at least two things in common: multiple firearms and multiple pieces of religious paraphernalia.

Most of the paraphernalia consisted of talismans rooted in Christianity, and it wasn't there just for decoration. All of it must have been consecrated. Energy radiated fiercely with the power of the owners' faith. It was difficult for me to stand near most of the homes let alone enter them. Many of them had consecrated silver ammunition crafted from silver.

Crucifixes and shrines to the Holy Mother were decorated with rosaries. Some of the talismans included elements of voodoo. Strings of garlic bulbs hung behind many a window. Some people owned crossbows with consecrated wooden and even silver crossbow bolts. These people or their recent ancestors must have had vampire trouble in the past. They wanted to be prepared in case it happened again.

None of that was going to stop me.

I caught the scent of two hunters from this isolated community doing some illegal late-night white tail deer hunting. They were set up in a camouflaged deer stand in the middle of a clearing and outfitted with night vision goggles and scopes. To my pleasant surprise neither of them wore any faith-based protection. Almost fifty yards separated us but I would have felt that kind of energy from fifty yards further than that. They were young and fearless, dismissive of the old superstitions.

One of the hunters had a healthy buck in his sights at the edge of the clearing. He dropped the buck where it stood with one well-placed shot to the head. The moment the two hunters emerged from the stand, I leapt from the tree and the dog burst from the bushes where it hid downwind from the buck. His black coat made him difficult to see even in the moonlight. My dark jeans and t-shirt did the same for me.

The dog ran so fast and smooth and silently that he looked more like a ghost streaking above the ground than a massive dog charging in to take down live prey. The cool autumn air buffeted me as I soared down toward the hunters.

The dog couldn't run as fast as I could fly but his hiding place was closer to the men than mine. I timed my approach so that we struck at the same time. The men heard the dog, or maybe some primal instinct warned them. They turned, lifting their rifles, but it was far too late.

I crashed into the shooter. With my right hand I slapped the rifle out of his hands. I used my left to grab his face and twist his head until his neck snapped. He was paralyzed and my teeth were locked into his neck before we tumbled to the damp earth.

The other hunter got off a shot. He hadn't even brought his rifle completely to bear on the dog so the shot went wide. The dog barreled into him and bore him to the ground. The dog's incredible weight kept the rifle and the hunter's arm pinned to his ribs as the dog savaged the man's throat. I could hear the cartilage snapping and the choking sounds the man made as he died. His mind was filled with a long, agonized scream that never made it past his crushed larynx.

My kill died quietly on the outside but his mental scream was worse than the dog's victim. The dog's kill was still confused. Pure shock would not allow him to grasp what was happening. Mine knew exactly what was happening. He recognized me for what I was when he felt my fangs slide into his carotid. That knowledge filled him with far more terror. Just before is mind's eye closed forever, he wondered with morbid curiosity if he would come back as a vampire.

He wouldn't.

I drained him of every drop of blood. Guilt and self-loathing washed over me with each swallow. A wail of despair over my lost humanity echoed in my head. The hunger quickly consumed it, as it did all of my negative emotions, as voraciously as my physical being consumed the doomed man's life force. The combination of my victim's misery and mine enhanced the flavor and spurred me to feed even more ferociously.

Satisfied, I sat back and watched the dog worry at his meal's belly with glee. It had been weeks since I allowed him to feed on a human so he enjoyed his repast immensely. The scent of blood in the air stirred my gluttonous hunger but I was sated for the night.

The dead man was at least two hundred and eighty pounds and I hoisted the corpse over my shoulder as if he weighed next to nothing. I contemplated what to do next as I rose to my feet. My plan was to take him to a congregation of alligators I'd spotted closer to the coastline earlier that day.

Just before I went airborne I detected something watching us from the brush.

The dog sensed it, too. His head snapped up. His hackles rose, his ears went erect and his tail curled down between his legs. Not only was he alert, he was afraid. I'd never seen the dog afraid.

I searched the darkness, my eyesight cutting easily through the shadows, my nose catching every scent. My ears picked up every sound, no matter how miniscule. One of the sounds was a booming heartbeat.

It was a wolf. For a moment I thought Pedro had tracked us down, but that was not Pedro. Pedro turned into a gray wolf of slightly larger than average size. The wolf watching us was black as pitch and taller than an Irish wolfhound. And the scent told me it was female. Her back, chest, and shoulders were unnaturally broad. Her black coat was shaggier than any breed of wolf I'd ever seen. Everything about her seemed supernatural.

Her eyes gleamed with golden light as her baleful glare went back and forth between the dog and me. She bared scythe-like fangs and blue-black gums. Her forepaws looked more like large human hands with canine claws instead of fingernails. She was not a shape-shifting vampire taking a canine form. She was a werewolf.

I thought back to a question I'd asked Eric, Andre's servant, years earlier when he told Tim and me vampires actually existed.

"So you're tryin' to say that werewolves, fairies and all that other shit is real?"

He said he didn't know. Now, I knew.

She sized us up while we did the same to her. I reached out to her mind to see if I could find any human thoughts or emotions. Most of what I found was an incoherent haze of malevolence and hunger. Just beneath that, though, was the barest trace of human intelligence.

And then she morphed. She stood up on her hind legs, rising over seven feet tall, and began to shrink. Her torso contracted in both length and width, as did her wolf's snout. She snarled in pain during the transformation and I could see her teeth grow smaller and slightly blunter.

The long human hands shrank into dainty ones as her claws retracted into long human fingernails. Her arms shrank while her legs remained the same length. All four appendages changed in shape and, for lack of a better word, shagginess. The heavy pelt covering her entire body retreated into her skin everywhere with the exceptions of her head, eyebrows, eyelashes, and crotch.

When the transformation was complete, the only things that remained unchanged were her shimmering golden eyes.

A woman faced me, pale and naked and unashamed. In her human form she was downright tiny, standing an inch or two shy of five feet tall. Her arms and legs were lean but not skinny. She had a flat, smooth stomach and frizzy black hair that fell riotously past her shoulders.

If not for her generously proportioned breasts and hips, as well as the faint lines in her unremarkable face, she could easily be mistaken for a child.

We stared at each other for a long time, each waiting for the other to break the silence. Her nakedness began to stir my hunger and my lust. She could sense the former and smell the latter so she broke the silence with a low growl that warned me against acting on either.

I knew all of this because her thoughts were clearer to me while she was in human form. I soon realized that reading her mind was unnecessary. Her bearing spoke volumes and it was in perfect accord with her thoughts, which she finally spoke aloud.

"I could tell you knew what I was even before I changed." She spoke in broken English with a thick New Orleans accent. Her "I's" sounded like "ah's." She pronounced "even" as "eem." Her "before" was chopped down to the single syllable "fo." Yet even with all that her speech was far more comprehensible than the residents of the swampland. She definitely wasn't a local.

She sniffed. "And I damn sure know what you are. So, we gonna have a problem?"

I kept her gaze, wary to be the first to break eye contact. "Only if you want one."

"All I want is live deer meat," she assured. "But I'll take human, dog, or vampire if I have to."

The buck was brain dead but his heart had not stopped. The werewolf wanted badly to sup on him while he still had living blood in his veins. Had either the dog or I been alone with the deer and the humans she would have attacked without hesitation. Together, despite her bluster, she wasn't certain she could take us. I wasn't certain she couldn't.

"What's your name?" I asked.

She chuckled as if that was the silliest question she'd ever heard. That was fine with me. I didn't expect her to tell me, at least not out loud. Though she didn't say her name aloud, it immediately rose to the surface of her thoughts.

Corinne.

I took a deep breath through my nose, scenting and tasting the air in an attempt to catch anything else out of the ordinary. The werewolf smiled. She wasn't a mind reader but she was observant and smart.

"Sniffing for more like me?" she asked needlessly.

"How many werewolves are around here?" I asked.

"We ain't like regular wolves, you know. We don't travel in packs. We don't have to."

"You didn't answer my question," I noted.

"Why you wanna know? Thinking about settling down around here?"

I scoffed. "Not hardly, I just –"

"I'm asking one more time," she interrupted. "We gonna have a problem? If not, you best be moving on."

With that, she dropped back to all fours. In the time it would take a person to cough once or sneeze, she morphed back into the massive wolf. The abrupt change startled the dog. He barked once, shuffled backward a few feet, and then dropped into a wary crouch.

The three of us stood there as still as statues, waiting to see who would attack first. With every second that passed, the buck came closer to death and the werewolf grew more anxious to have him before he died. She inched forward, her growl rumbling across the forest. The dog inched forward in response, causing the werewolf to rear up on her hind legs again. This time, though, instead of transforming she brandished her claws in challenge.

I remained still. As interested as I was in knowing who would win this confrontation, an instinctive sense of self-preservation dictated my next move.

"Let's go, dog," I suggested. "She can have the buck. That's not what we came for, anyway."

The dog huffed and turned back to his kill. He clamped his powerful jaws around the dead man's torn throat and dragged him awkwardly but quickly out of the opposite side of the clearing. With my kill still hanging limply over my shoulder, I took to the sky. It was time to feed the gators.

When I looked back I saw the werewolf lope cautiously across the clearing. She looked into the darkness of the surrounding wood and to the sky to make sure the dog and I were still moving away from her. When she was satisfied we were not coming back, she went for the buck.

The dog and I went east to New Orleans after that night. I found an all-night library with better information than the other places I'd visited. They didn't, however, go into as much detail as I would have liked. I asked the woman at the front desk if they had any books other than the ones on the shelf. The little old librarian looked at me with more than a little curiosity.

"Detailed works on vampirism and vampire legends?" she asked. "No one's asked about those old books for quite some time."

She went into a back room and returned with three dusty volumes. When I say dusty, I mean *dusty*. There had to be at least ten years' worth of dust layered on the top edges of all three books. I picked one at random. At least I assumed it was random. Looking back on it, though, I think a part of me knew exactly which volume to select. It had never occurred to me to ask about archived books at any of the other libraries I visited, and the one time I did I was rewarded with several.

Dust plumed when I cracked the leather cover. A stale odor accompanied the dust. Something about it set off an alert in my subconscious. It didn't quite alarm me but they definitely got my attention, so I began to read. I had no frame of reference to determine if what I read was accurate or not. I looked for details that weren't part of the popular lore often depicted in Hollywood and mainstream literature.

I weighed the tale against my limited personal experience. This particular tome spoke of the origin of vampires. The words seemed to ring true to me for some reason. I was compelled to read it and as I did, images and sounds formed in my mind's eye. The sensory information was clearer than the images and sounds at a movie theater.

Denise and I loved to go to the movies, but for the life of me I couldn't remember the last time we did. The loss of that recollection stung. The vampire within me had started to whittle away pleasant memories. It preferred to linger on painful thoughts. It fortified itself with the anger and hopelessness I felt at being stripped of my humanity.

I shook those thoughts away, pushing positive and negative alike to the back of my mind. Knowledge had to be my sole focus. Concentrating on learning as much as I could about my kind distracted me from potentially dangerous emotions. I had to hold on to logic and reason. That was the only way I could suppress my feral and predatory nature in the presence of the few humans milling about the library.

So I read. I never bothered to take note of the number of pages and lost myself in the prose. Once I was immersed in the text, the words became visions and sounds and smells and emotions. The huge book went into great detail about events spanning two millennia. I know it now like vivid memory of lucid dream. It's way too much to recite here so I'll paraphrase it for you with the most relevant parts.

A child was born more than two thousand years ago. This was not a child born in a manger. Not the child whose birth was signaled by the divine beacon of the North Star. There was no celebration for this birth, at least none in the earthly or heavenly planes. This child was born far to the north in the cold and barren wilds of that land that is now known as northeastern Europe.

There was no ceremony. There were no wise men. No one was there to bear witness or present gifts to this grim child of the darkness. The sky was so overcast that not even the stars cast their light on the birth of this child.

Blood of the Third

On that night, in that place, there was only the mother, the son, and the agent of the fallen one sent to oversee the arrival of his abomination.

The mother cared for her son over the years, but not in the loving way most mothers care for their children. She cared in a strictly utilitarian sense. There was no love, only effort. She served the child the way a slave woman tended to the master's child. She fed and clothed him. That was the extent of her interaction with the child.

The clothing part was easy. The child was relatively unaffected by the cold air and harsh winds. When the child was an infant, a cloth or a fur was sufficient. As he grew older, simple breeches and shirts were fashioned from animal hides. While the mother cowered in their flimsy wooden shack, wrapped in layers of furs and huddled by a weak fire, the child frolicked and played with the beasts of the wilderness in the dead of night.

She never even named the boy. There was no need. There was only the two of them. As he grew older, the woman dutifully taught him to speak her native language. Other than that they had very little interaction. The boy instinctively knew how to do many things on his own.

The mother fed her child but never did she suckle him. Suckling was never necessary. The child was born with a full set of teeth. The mother would hunt small game and cook it for herself and her son. The boy, however, did not seem to get the proper nutrition from cooked food. His mother cooked his food less and less as time passed.

Eventually, she would cook half of her catch for herself and give the other half to her son raw. The bloodier and the fresher the carcass, the more the child enjoyed it. At the age of four the boy was as strong as a man. He was agile and intelligent enough to catch his own food.

His mother would look on in horrified amazement as the boy pursued, captured and devoured small game. Eventually the child barely consumed the meat. The blood was enough. In this way, the boy indirectly helped his mother. When he was finished with his meal his mother collected the blood-drained carcass for the meat.

In his ninth year, the child asked his mother why they were so different from one another. He wondered if they were the only people in the world. All the boy had ever known was his loveless mother and the cold and the mountains and the crawling and flying beasts of the wilds.

Were there others like them, like him, in some other part of the world?

The mother laughed nervously at the question. The child was irritated by her hesitance. Until then she had always tended to his every whim without question. She answered his every question without so much as a moment's pause. How dare she hesitate to answer his question?

He slapped her. When he did, his long jagged fingernails tore bloody tracks into the flesh of her cheek. His acute eyesight picked up a faint hint of pink vapor as his mother's warm blood met the chill air. The scent of her blood hit his nostrils.

And then he was on her. Before he realized it, his canines were piercing her left jugular vein and her blood was pulsing onto his tongue in frenzied bursts. Her blood was sweeter than that of the beasts of the mountains. Her blood fortified him more. The taste of her blood sent heat through his flesh, blood, nerves and bones. His awareness and strength grew exponentially.

The boy pulled away from his mother. He knew instinctively how close she was to death and knew he could not kill her yet. He still needed her. The boy released his dazed mother and walked away as she collapsed onto the cold, windswept earth.

Days passed. The boy noticed a change coming over his mother. In many ways she became like him. Her appetite for blood mirrored his. She started to move like he moved, hunt the way he hunted.

But unlike him, she could not tolerate the daylight. He himself did not care for it but it did not harm him. His mother however, cried in pain when the sun touched her skin. Its rays seared her flesh and blinded her.

Weeks passed. They fed the way they always had, but the boy had tasted his mother's blood and he wanted more. One night he decided to take it. She foolishly attempted to deny him.

He discovered that she indeed had some of his strength when she had the gall to defend herself. He was stronger, though, in both mind and body, and eventually tasted her blood again. It wasn't the same. Her blood had none of the sweetness it had that first time. It had a dizzying effect instead of its original invigorating quality.

The boy realized that it was he who had polluted her. As her soiled blood washed down his mouth and throat, her memories flooded his mind.

There were other beings like his mother had been before his infectious bite. They roamed the lands to the south, where the gentler weather was kinder to their weak flesh.

He learned how his mother was stolen from one of those southern clans by what she called a demon. She thought of it as more animal than man. It could continuously change its form so that it could be mistaken for a man for short periods of time as long as it stayed in the shadows. It could hold this near-human form just long enough to stalk its prey from a relatively close proximity.

That was how it singled out his mother to bare its seed. It looked for specific traits: someone with enough vitality to survive the horrid existence she would have to suffer; a strong enough will that – once bent to its master's purpose – would dutifully adhere to her charge.

His mother was a girl of fourteen when she was stolen from her family. Hers were a robust and nomadic people that scarcely settled down for long periods of time. The demon followed them, occasionally feeding on those unwary enough to stray too far from their itinerant campsites.

She was one of those. One night, while wondering at the stars, it fell upon her with the intent of feeding. When it looked at her, and looked into *her the way only its kind could, it saw the traits of the human female that its master, the sovereign of the underworld, had been seeking since the birth of man.*

While she was biologically able to bear a child, her body had to mature to make it physically possible for her to do what was needed. The beast could impregnate her but her womb did not yet have the strength to nourish its ravenous seed. Instead of feeding on her, the beast took her away.

It took her farther north, where humans scarcely wandered, where the winters lasted all year and the days and nights could drag on for weeks. It knew more humans were coming. Those pale, nomadic creatures constantly migrated in every direction. It was only a matter of time before they encroached upon its domain. The beast's time on this plane was short. It would take steps to ensure that at least one of its bloodline would protect its dreadful legacy.

The girl was held captive for years. The hold the beast had on her was physical and psychological. Sometimes it would chain her within a cave or to a tree outside. Sometimes it would allow her to roam free but with subconscious instructions that kept her from wandering too far. There were times when it physically tortured her for its own amusement.

It also protected her fiercely from creatures that would harm her, including itself. The most difficult part of the undertaking was denying itself the sweet taste of her flesh. It was important that she remained pure and healthy while carrying its seed. She was well fed and forced to labor in ways that would strengthen her body and increase her stamina.

After four years of imprisonment, torture, and mental conditioning, she was finally ready. She knew what awaited her. The beast told her when it first abducted her. She knew exactly what it planned for her yet she was powerless to stop it. Her immature, fourteen year old mind had not been strong enough to resist his control. By the time she turned eighteen she had been thoroughly conditioned to accept her fate.

Her captor told her that it had lived for thousands upon thousands of years. Its kind roamed the earth long before man, spawned by the fallen one himself, and reigned supreme over the creatures that dwelled here. But then the humans came.

The beast and its kind fed on humans as well as all of the other animals, but humans proved to be different. Over time, they multiplied exponentially and evolved into intelligent enough creatures to pose a threat. Humans, including monotheists, polytheists, and atheists, hunted and killed its kind until it was the only one left.

The girl would be the bridge between the beast's world and the human world. Their progeny would be able to walk among mankind undetected. Humans would never know what this new species was until they chose to reveal themselves. One day, its bloodline would reign over all of humankind.

She had nightmares of what would eventually become of her, but when the night finally came her ordeal easily surpassed the worst of her nightmares. The beast came to her shortly after sunset in its true, bestial form, with a wolf's brow, ears and eyes but the upturned nostrils and stunted snout of a bat. Countless teeth protruded from its cavernous maw like dozens upon dozens of brownish mini scythes.

Its body was hunchbacked and only vaguely humanoid. It had long, spindly arms that that ended in simian hands with curved claws. Leathery wings – webbed through with black and purplish veins and covered with patches of soil-brown, bristly fur – connected the underside of its arms to the bottom of its freakishly long torso.

The beast walked on thick, short legs and canine paws with claws as fierce as those on his hands. Short, coarse, foul-smelling hair covered most of his body with the exception of his chest, stomach, and intimidating crotch.

Red wolf's eyes radiated like fire from the hell described to her by her family and clan holy men before she was abducted.

Beneath the stubby fur its skin seemed to crawl over his body as if it were an independent entity. The epidermal surface jerked across his body in fits and starts, causing patches of dark fur to twitch almost nervously. Other times, sinewy muscles and bones were accentuated as its skin crept over his body.

The worst part of the beast, by far, was its mating organ. The young woman had seen the male organ and the sexual act a few times as a child while sneaking through the night to spy on adults, so she had a faint idea of what would happen to her.

When she saw his member she was sure their coupling would kill her. It was half the length of her arm. It pulsed and swayed like something akin to a serpent. Like the rest of the beast's body, it was covered with patches of bristly fur and changed shape slightly from moment to moment.

Her heart seized with fear and panic until she thought it would burst. The monster's hellish lantern eyes bore through her as it approached. When it took her, she felt as if she was being torn apart. Its organ seemed to swell within her, to fill her completely and agonizingly. Its bristly fur hooked into her flesh and bled her both inside and out. Her entire being was blinding fire and all-consuming pain.

She screamed until the sound became a harsh rasp in her raw, inflamed throat, and then she screamed soundlessly. She asked God why He would allow her to suffer so. In reply, the demon ravaged her even more savagely. Her mind snapped. She could almost hear the psychotic break through the beast's deafening growls and roars.

It took care not to kill her and took even greater care not to taste her blood. Though her womb was befouled with its seed, her blood had to remain uninfected. The beast continued to abuse her as the night wore on and on, never slowing in his frenzied assault until moments before sunrise when the demon had to melt back into the shadows to find shelter.

She lay in pool of her own blood, completely naked, her skin raw and torn, barely-conscious half of the time and completely unconscious the other half.

Her pain was constant. There was pain in her dreams and pain during the brief periods she was awake. It washed over her in waves that ebbed only long enough for her to remember where she was, and then she wished she had not.

She did not move for over two days, but at some point she noticed that she had been moved into a cave. She thought she would die of thirst in the dry, harsh winds that whistled through the cave and pierced through her like frozen knives. In hazy dreams her captor would come to her in the darkness and sprinkle droplets of water on her tongue or spread some sort of coppery, salty paste on her lips for her to consume.

Wolves guarded her unconscious form night and day. Several times she opened her eyes to see at least one of the beasts staring at her hungrily. They licked the blood soaking the earth around her but did not so much as even nip at her flesh.

After another two days she could walk, but just barely. She began to find little bits of food left in different places around the cave in which she was imprisoned. It took another week before she could get around well enough to acquire her own food. She fed herself on berries, nuts and fish from a cold stream.

In another two weeks she could see the bulge in her stomach. She remembered the pregnant women from her clan and how it took a few months shy of a year for them to carry and birth a baby. With her, however, the child was in her womb for only four months before it matured enough for her to give birth in the dead of winter.

More than once she thought to kill the boy while he was an infant but a stern warning from her tormentor stayed her hand. The beast assured her that if any harm ever came to the child, no matter the cause, the night of his conception would be pleasurable in comparison to the punishment to which it would subject her.

Instead of killing her son, she cared for him. She never saw the boy's sire again. She knew the demon was watching, though. Whether it hid in the darkness or watched them through the eyes of its nocturnal creatures, she could feel its attention upon her.

After seeing his mother's experiences, the boy knew what he was and what he was meant to do.

He attacked his mother one last time. Fueled by his new purpose, he overcame her easily. He drank her blood yet again and reveled in the way it made the world spin about him. He drank and drank until she was dry, finally granting her the solace she prayed for so fervently before his conception.

He let her still body crumple to the ground. Once again the carnivores and scavenger let her lie undisturbed. This time, though, it wasn't because she was guarded. They could all scent her unnatural taint and wanted no part of it. By the time the sun came up and burned her body to ash, the boy was traveling south to meet his destiny.

And then it ended. There was no mention of what the boy did after he went south, but if the story was true, I had a pretty good idea. Most of the vampire lore I'd read placed their origin in Northern Europe.

I looked down at the book. I'd just read it from cover to cover and it was at least three inches thick. Still curious as to what it was about the book that resonated with me, in lifted it and held it just under my nose. One long deliberate inhalation through the nose told me what I needed to know. I didn't recognize it initially because of its age and the way it had been chemically treated.

Only a vampire's nose or complex machinery would have been able to discern that there were two different scents. The ink had been infused with the barest hint of human blood. The inner surface of treated leather cover was lined with human skin. I closed the book, returned it to the front desk, and walked out into the irritating mid-day sun. I got curious looks from the morning staff. The graveyard staff told them during the shift change how long I'd been there.

One evening, while doing research on the Internet, I came across something that captured my attention. I found a link to an organization called the Third Millennia Sect. This was not the first such site I came upon during my studies but it was the first to peak my interest.

I'd read about organizations that were clearly groups of weirdoes who liked to dress Goth and cut one another. TV news shows had infiltrated their fabricated world to film them. They got high on a variety of drugs, cut one another with little blades and tasted tiny specs of each other's blood. The cameras would then cut away as the freaks settled in for full-fledged orgies. It was all bullshit.

The Third Millennia Sect, on the other hand, seemed different. If the group really was as bogus as the others, at least the founders took the time to do a little research. The author included details that were similar to things I'd read and even some things I'd experienced. The group was founded in New Orleans, which didn't surprise me.

The Texas chapter was in Galveston and they were meeting at midnight that very night for a meet and greet for potential new members. They called the meeting the

"Gathering" and it was for serious participants only. I wondered if the sect was a group of genuine vampires attempting to lure unsuspecting victims or a bunch of sadomasochistic psychos. I decided to drive back to Galveston and find out.

CHAPTER SEVEN

It took me a little over six hours to drive I-10 West and then 45 South to get from New Orleans to Galveston. Before my change I would've made that same drive in five hours. After my change I started driving at a slower pace, often as much as five miles per hour below the speed limit. That makes other motorists crazy, especially in Houston, where most drivers treat posted speed limits like polite suggestions.

Thankfully, whoever owned the car I'd stolen that night was a Hiphop lover. Music had been the furthest thing from my mind lately, so it had been weeks since I listened to it. I was happy to see a CD booklet resting on the passenger seat. The collection was regional, "Dirty South" Hiphop. I preferred East Coast and Midwest rappers like Common, EPMD, Wu Tang, De La Soul and Tribe Called Quest, but I was more than content listening to OutKast, Goodie Mob and Ghetto Boys as I rode down the highway.

Flying would have been faster. It would have also been more physically and psychologically draining. It took a fair amount of concentration to stay airborne for extended periods of time and flying leached strength from my body. I had no need to rush anymore. All I had was time…and hunger.

That stubborn, voracious fire within my belly flared about a quarter of the way to Galveston. It had been several days since I tasted human blood, and that night I knew animal blood would not satisfy me. I stretched my awareness into the night, evaluating the drivers around me in search of ideal prey.

There were many drivers on the highway that night but only once did I identify a person that fit my criteria of minimal risk. The problem was that she was driving on the eastbound side of I-10 and I was driving on the westbound side. We were on Atchafalaya Basin Bridge, also known as the "Twenty Mile Bridge".

It was a problem because the Atchafalaya Bridge is composed of *two* bridges, parallel but spaced dozens of yards apart. One of the bridges was for eastbound traffic and the other was for westbound traffic. There was no discreet way to ditch my car, cross the distance between the two bridges by air or water on a fairly busy highway, and get into her car.

It ended up being a long and hungry drive back to Texas.

The meeting in Galveston was actually a party. It took place in an abandoned airplane hangar on an acre of private land near the beach. The landing strip near the hangar obviously hadn't been used in very long time. The entire length of it was cracked and broken, almost completely reclaimed by grass and weeds. It was used as an impromptu parking lot for the partiers inside the hangar.

I ditched the stolen car two miles away. The dog went off to do whatever it was he did when we weren't together. He'd find his way back to me later the way he always did. I flew the rest of the way. I was weak because I hadn't fed in a while but the same hunger that weakened me spurred me to hurry. It took me less than a minute to reach the party. Judging by the number of cars, the place was packed. Hundreds of minds permeated the inside of the hangar, hundreds of potential victims.

The riot of thoughts and the frenetic techno music created a dizzying cacophony. There was something unsettling within that grouping of minds that I couldn't quite pinpoint. My inability to identify it almost repelled me. The scent of blood was the only thing that kept me from turning around and searching for other prey.

The person watching me through the peek-hole wasn't sure if he would let me in. I was dressed in a leather jacket, t-shirt, blue jeans and a pair of Air Jordans. My attire was way too plain for their dress code. A strange feeling came over me as I eavesdropped on his thoughts. It took a few seconds to realize it was trepidation. So much time had passed since I last felt that emotion that I almost didn't recognize it.

But why did I feel it?

I stopped about ten yards from the door. The man behind the door watched me as I looked up at the stars and faked an air of uncertainty. The trepidation didn't make me hesitant. If anything, it fed my curiosity, but I wanted my spy to think I was nervous. He was sizing me up and I wanted him to underestimate me.

I also wanted to use that time to keep trying to identify what made me so uneasy. It took another few seconds for me to figure it out. His thoughts were, for lack of a better word, just *wrong*. Humans thought much faster than they spoke. Their thoughts are often images and impressions, words and phrases strung together almost randomly that had to be filtered and reordered before the person speaks out loud.

The bouncer watching me was different. His thoughts were slower, more deliberate. He thought the way the average person spoke aloud. I expanded my awareness again to the jumble of thoughts, emotions and music radiating from within the hangar. Instead of taking in the mental noise as one big sound, I focused on individual thoughts. That was when I realized what was so unsettling.

A large percentage of the people in the party had the same weird thought cadence as the bouncer. At the same time, there was a significant amount of people whose thought patterns were normal. And then there were a few instances where I could sense a person's presence but he or she did not generate coherent thoughts. Their minds were hazy like Su-Yin's when she blocked me.

There were real vampires in there.

The bouncer was still undecided about me so I projected a profound sense of fear into him. I didn't make him fear me specifically. I made him fear what might happen if he didn't let me in. It was a subtle, significant projection, a suggestion, like the instinctive fear of a prey animal in the proximity of an unseen but vaguely sensed predator.

The man opened the door before I took another step. He stood in a dark vestibule with an inner set of double doors behind him. He beckoned and called out to me:

"You here for the Gathering?"

I looked quickly at him as if he had surprised me.

"Yeah!" I called back. "If you're still accepting more members, I'd like a shot."

"Come on, then," he invited. "You're the last guest for the night."

I made sure my feral canines were retracted – my growing hunger had caused them to ease out involuntarily –

and gave him a friendly, appreciative smile that took him slightly by surprise.

"Thanks," I called to him as I jogged to the entrance.

I sized him up visually the way he had appraised me. The man was huge. He had a blonde buzz-cut and stood six feet seven inches tall and was three hundred pounds of artificially enhanced muscle. I'd never smelled steroids before but there was definitely an unnatural chemical scent about him, and by the look of him, steroid use was the obvious guess. He was a dangerous man. I could see it in his eyes. But he was just that: a man, not a vampire. The vampires were on the other side of the inner vestibule double doors.

Another man of identical size and build stood in front of the inner vestibule doors. He was a black man coiffed with a low-top box fade similar to the other man's buzz-cut. He ran a metal detector up and down my body and patted me down. Once he was satisfied I wasn't "packing" he took a step back and faced me.

"How did you hear about the Gathering?" It seemed more like a challenge than a question.

I had no idea if there was a certain answer they expected. A look into both of their minds didn't help. They weren't thinking about the answer. It seemed almost intentional. Without any hint of a passphrase, I decided to tell the truth.

"I was doing some research on vampires and came across an ad. It looked authentic and I wanted to see for myself."

The answer seemed to satisfy him. He nodded and opened the inner doors. Sensory overload almost knocked me to my knees. The vestibule had been soundproofed very well, because the music leapt through the open door and struck me so hard it knocked me back a step. The multitude of smells hit my sensitive nose just as forcefully.

Neon lights and spotlights of all colors flashed and beamed chaotically. The walls were lined with floor-to-ceiling mirror panels that reflected the chaotic lighting and made it even more discombobulating. The mirrors had the added effect of making the hangar look exponentially bigger. The party seemed to be designed to overpower the senses.

The bouncers watched me as I stepped unsteadily across the threshold and then they closed the door behind me. I stood there for a full minute forcing my senses to adjust to the violent onslaught of sights, sounds, smells and thoughts. While the lights disoriented me and the music painfully assaulted my ears, intensely varying emotions along with wildly random thoughts and strange thought patterns disconcerted me so much that I had to lean against the mirror-wall to keep myself upright.

The smell was the worst, at once cloying and acrid, so thick its touch was palpable, like warm slime on my skin. The stale air of the ventilation system and the displacement of air by the patrons as they danced and milled around pushed the wraithlike stench around the room. The scents of alcohol, tobacco, marijuana, and crack cocaine saturated the air. Those smells combined with human and the sharper vampire musk, all of which was poorly concealed by numerous perfumes, colognes, and deodorants. The body odors were accented with fear, excitement, lust, and barely concealed rage.

Beneath it all was the tantalizing scent of blood.

It wasn't just the sensory overload that made me so unsteady. The hunger did its fair share of damage. I had to feed before the hunger took over and I lost control. I still wasn't sure what was going on in the party, though, so I continued to observe from the perimeter.

None of the other vampires were attacking the humans, which made me wonder if there was some kind of protocol in a Gathering. If there was, I didn't want to be the one to break it, so I concentrated on holding my hunger at bay. I pushed myself off the wall and walked slowly around the crowd, reconnoitering as I went.

The majority of the vampires were open books to me. They made no effort to hide or muddle their thoughts or emotions. They thoroughly enjoyed playing with their food before the feeding frenzy began. I zeroed in on vampires who hid their thoughts. Even if they couldn't read minds the way I could, they were at least aware of the possibility. If Su-Yin were an accurate indication, those would be the more powerful vampires. They would be the more dangerous ones.

Of the ones I couldn't read, I noticed that, with the exception of a few, they didn't cast reflections. The ones I could read easily did cast reflections. Some were vaguely translucent while others were almost as opaque as the human reflections. That suggested to me that the more powerful the vampire, the more transparent the reflection. The problem with that theory was that there were some I couldn't read but I could see them clearly in the mirrors. I thought back to Su-Yin dancing at the club and remembered that she cast a reflection, too.

I looked for my reflection and couldn't find it, so I tried something on a hunch. I focused on the mirror, where my reflection should have been, and concentrated. It took some energy and tweaked my growing hunger, but my reflection eventually flickered in the mirror for a couple of seconds.

After my image disappeared, I knew I didn't have the strength to try it again. My hunger started to feel like a knife in my gut. I made it a point to step away from the mirrored walls and deeper into the crowd. The humans didn't seem to notice the semi-transparent or missing reflections but I wasn't taking any chances.

Every human I focused on had the same strange thought pattern the bouncers had. It was too deliberate, too weird. I wondered if there were any other vampires there who could look into minds. If so, did they also notice the irregularity?

"Are you as hungry as I am?" asked a woman who had walked up behind me.

Even if she had not spoken I would've known in an instant that she was a vampire. Her scent gave her away immediately. She was probably an inch or two taller than me barefoot, so she had to look down on me from her six-inch stiletto-heeled thigh-high boots.

If Su-Yin was hot, this woman was nuclear. She was a light-complexioned black woman with flawless skin the color of eggnog with a touch of bourbon. Not quite buxom, she was nowhere near thin, with soft curves that were pronounced and exquisite beneath her black fitted mini-dress.

Her silky black hair was pulled back into a loose ponytail, putting her deep widow's peak in full display. She made no attempt to hide the red gleam in her big brown eyes. The devious slant in her perfectly arched eyebrows looked even more devious when she parted her full red lips to smile. Like the red light in her eyes, she made no attempt to hide her fangs.

"I'm Renee. What's your name?"

I tried to look into her mind to see if she was telling me the truth and found that she was one of the vampires who could hide her thoughts. I didn't feel her attempting to read me. I didn't know if she couldn't or if she had that ability but simply wasn't bothering to use it on me.

"Major. My name is Major. It's very nice to meet you. And yes, I am freaking starving."

She laughed softly. Her voice was throaty but absolutely feminine. Like Su-Yin, everything about Renee was so sexy that she had no need to project erotic emotions and she knew it. She tilted her head to study me with a raised eyebrow.

"Cool name, Mr. Major. I usually wait for males to approach me, but you make me curious. You're different."

"Oh yeah?" I asked. "Different how?"

"I don't know, but I'd like to do a thorough inspection to find out."

I grinned, showing her *my* fangs. "Sounds good to me. Maybe after we feed."

"Speaking of feeding," Renee said, "there are more of us here than there are humans. Any idea when the *real* party is supposed to start? We need to get close to our meals so we don't get left out."

I shrugged. "I was gonna ask you the same question. I've never been to one of these things before. If you're worried about the numbers, you and I can share if you like."

She gave me an uncertain look. "That's generous of you, but I'm rather stingy with my –"

There was a sudden rise in the intensity and cadence of the humans' deliberate thought patterns. Before Renee could ask why I was distracted, the wild lighting went dark. Everything else happened almost at once.

Even if the vampires couldn't read the humans' thoughts, there was no way they missed the other cues. We could hear all of the humans' heart rates accelerate at the same time. The scent of their anxiety saturated the room. The vampires I could read thought the humans were merely surprised and frightened by the sudden darkness. I knew they were wrong.

In the next instant, brilliant white light flooded the cavernous interior of the repurposed hangar. When I felt an uncomfortable tingle on my skin and heard the pained bestial roars of all the vampires around me, I realized it was ultraviolet light. It might have been artificial but it burned vampire flesh almost as severely as sunlight.

Renee screamed. Her perfect face bubbled and blackened before my eyes. The wall she'd constructed to veil her mind collapsed as well. One thought came racing out. It was a mental scream as desperate and shocked and agonized as her vocal scream. Her hair and body ignited with pale orange flames as she collapsed to the floor.

Almost identical psychic screams from the other vampires who had been concealing their thoughts blasted into my mind. It felt like a superheated hurricane behind my eyes. It hurt my head as severely as my hunger hurt my stomach. I can't remember when I fell. All at once I was on my knees vaguely taking notice of people moving cautiously but purposely toward me. My body dissolved into mist just as their weapons came out and cut harmlessly through me.

I willed myself to rise to the ceiling, focusing through the pain of the UV lights, which had grown more uncomfortable in my vaporous form. My disembodied consciousness took in the mayhem on the floor.

The humans produced all kinds of weapons. I saw machetes, hatchets, katana swords, scimitars, even a freaking broadsword, as well as metal and wooden stakes. All of the metal was silver that gleamed painfully in the intense light.

All of the vampires were dying, but not all of them died as fast as Renee. They burned at varying intensities, dying at different speeds, but none fast enough for the humans. They tore into the dying vampires with a savagery as feral as ours. The vampires, in their pained and weakened states, were relatively easy pickings. I say relatively because many of them still fought back violently enough to kill one or two humans before they were brought down.

That was when the fire sprinklers came on.

I was dispersed loosely near the ceiling by then but a few tendrils were low enough to catch some of the streaming water. The pain burned infinitely worse than the hunger. The pain was so distracting that I almost reverted to my solid form. It took a raw and primal survival instinct to keep my focus and my vaporous form. Instead of turning solid, I flattened myself against the ceiling and out of the range of the dangerous water.

The sprinklers spewed holy water. They'd somehow consecrated the hangar's water supply. It took almost a minute for the pain of that fraction-of-a-second contact to subside enough for me to move again. I started drifting toward an air vent in the ceiling near the front corner.

I took note of what was happening below. The people that had been closing in on me looked up and around in frustration. They brandished their weapons as if they expected me to reappear in their midst. That was not about to happen. The ultraviolet light might have been uncomfortable but the holy water was deadly.

My attackers waited for several heartbeats before giving up and going after different targets. They didn't have much to choose from by then. The ultraviolet light combined with the holy water settled things for good.

A few vampires ignited even brighter, as if the holy water was gasoline. They had violent spasms and contorted into unnatural shapes before they collapsed into charred husks. Some of them sizzled like cold water on a hot skillet and crumbled into wet ash. Some melted into boiling slime, first the skin, then the blood and meat, and then even the bones. In every case they all generated a thick, foul, grayish steam that choked and temporarily blinded the humans.

That was probably why they saved the holy water for last. Their decreased visibility allowed a handful of vampires that hadn't yet fallen to put up a spirited but brief fight. They lasted a little longer but were still chopped to smoldering pieces. The massacre was over in less than two minutes. None of the humans were bitten. Less than a fourth of them were killed. We outnumbered them almost two to one yet I was the only surviving vampire in the room.

I listened to the humans talk as I wafted slowly through the air vent. The sprinklers were still running but their hiss didn't hamper my ability to hear the conversations. They were congratulating one another on a successful ambush and comparing notes. One of them mentioned me.

"We missed one," he said. It was the bouncer with the buzz cut.

"Yeah," added the bouncer with the low-top fade. "It was the last one we let in. That bloodsucker turned into smoke. I've never seen one do that before."

"Me either," buzz cut agreed. "I didn't think they could really do that. I thought that was bullshit from movies and books. Danny, did you know they could turn into smoke?"

A middle-aged, fit, tall, dark-haired man of Italian ancestry stepped forward. His bearing and the attention the others gave him easily marked him as the leader.

"It wasn't smoke, Mike. It was vapor. That's a very rare ability. I'd never seen it before but I've heard of it."

"The UV lights didn't bother him," low-top fade noted.

"I saw, that too, Wes," Danny acknowledged. "I've never seen that before tonight, either. I've read about it, though."

"What was it, then?" Mike asked.

Danny shrugged. "I wish I knew. I'll have to call some of our researchers. They may be able to give us some intel."

"How far do you think he's gotten?" asked Wes. "We have to kill him. There's no telling how dangerous he is."

"You're right," Danny said. "If we're lucky he'll be too exhausted to hold that form for a long time. We might find him somewhere close when he gets solid again."

The conversation faded out of earshot. I was well away from the hangar by then. The Italian was right. I couldn't hold that form for long. I went about a quarter of a mile before I reverted and dropped from the sky like a rock.

Severe exhaustion and dangerous hunger kept me from flying, so I trudged through the darkness. The dog found me before the hunters from the party could. We stalked to the beach and found a happy young couple walking hand in hand along the shoreline.

Ten minutes later we were replenished and riding down the highway in their cobalt blue late model IROC-Z.

CHAPTER EIGHT

A couple of relatively uneventful weeks passed as I traveled back and forth between east Texas and west Louisiana. After losing count of the libraries I'd haunted to study vampire – and now werewolf – literature, I was satisfied that I was ready to return home. By home, I mean Chicago, not the house Denise and I occupied in Texas.

The trick was figuring out how to get there. The thought of travelling by air under my own power was tempting. The only thing faster would've been an airplane, but that was not even a consideration. I couldn't remember the last time I had my wallet. It was a few years before the 9/11 tragedies so identification wasn't a big concern. My biggest concern was money. I had neither cash nor credit cards, and going to the house to try and retrieve either was out of the question.

I wasn't ready to go that house, whether Denise was there or not. That part of my life was behind me and I felt it was best to keep it there.

My other option for air travel came with its own set of problems. The effort needed for flight was exhausting, which would mean several stops to feed. I wasn't sure how many stops would be required but I knew it would be a lot. Animals would not adequately replenish the kind of drain that would be caused by flying that distance. The hunger would compel me to drink human blood and I knew I wouldn't be able to fight it if my fatigue got bad enough.

Maddening guilt was already gnawing at me from taking that couple on the beach. They were good people. They were truly in love and intended to spend a long and happy life together. I saw it in their minds and I felt it in their hearts as I was taking their future away from them. Killing them made me feel like shit and I didn't want to make it worse.

Flying was a big risk from a practical standpoint, too. A lot of time would be wasted finding ways to hide bodies and disguise the causes of death. I didn't want to leave a trail that could be used to follow me home. Effective concealment would be necessary to delay the detection of a pattern by attentive law enforcement and, more importantly, hunters. After Galveston I had a healthy respect for hunters.

Travelling by car would be less taxing, therefore allowing me to feed on wildlife and the occasional livestock along the way. That would keep me below the radar of hunters and the FBI for a time. However, driving a stolen car or a string of stolen cars over a distance of more than a thousand miles was asking for trouble.

I settled on the same mode of transportation to return to Chicago that Su-Yin chose to flee Chicago. It was a choice that required the dog and me to part ways. He was feral, so I didn't think he'd respond well to being cooped up in a train car for hours on end. Additionally, he was fond of human flesh. I didn't know how many people we'd encounter along the way and I only had so much control over him.

Besides, he was way too conspicuous for me to walk around with in any city. That would have been true even if he had been domesticated and well trained. People would remember a Cane Corso damn near the size of a donkey. They'd also remember the guy walking around with it.

One night I projected the suggestion to the dog that we go our separate ways. He gave a brief but questioning whine. I showed him my memories of Houston traffic on I-45 and Highway 59 at rush hour and the crowded sidewalks of the Galleria and Midtown. Those memories were followed by images of bumper-to-bumper traffic on Chicago's Dan Ryan and Eisenhower Expressways. I showed him the congested thoroughfares in downtown Chicago, particularly Michigan Avenue and State Street.

The dog wrinkled his nose in distaste at the images. He was familiar with the big city and wanted no part of the pollution and multitudes of densely packed people. He bumped me roughly with a broad wither as he turned to leave. I watched him lope away from the roadside and disappear into the woods just outside of Beaumont, TX. He let loose a single, thunderous bark but he never looked back.

It was a ridiculously long trip by freight train. The frequent stops and protracted delays made me lose track of time. I was fine with that. It didn't matter how long the trip took. I wasn't on a schedule. My perception of time, and my concern for it, had already started to change.

The stops allowed me to go on short expeditions to feed. Scenting out deer and wild boar, or horses, cattle and goats helped me resist the temptation to victimize the handful of hobos and train-hoppers that came and went along the way. Sometimes I had to ride on the top of train cars to put a safe distance between them and me. Even with a full belly from gorging on animal blood, my hunger still responded to scent of human blood.

The train chugged along through clear days and overcast days. Brilliant sunshine and starry, moonlit nights alternated with gloomy skies, heavy downpours and spectacular thunderstorms. The temperature dropped steadily as we crept northward and I learned something new. The cold didn't bother me. I felt it but I didn't suffer from it. The rains and winds didn't affect me, either. Only sunlight bothered me. It continued to irritate my skin and weaken me. I rode inside one of the cars on sunny days.

Most of the train hoppers could tell something wasn't right about me. The majority of them had ridden the rails for a few years or more. Their relative seclusion and self-reliance put them more in touch with their primal instincts than the newer riders. The veteran riders learned to listen to that little voice of warning, that sixth sense that alerted them to danger that their other senses couldn't detect. All humans have it yet they often ignore it, especially in developed countries.

Contentment and comfort tended to dull that sense. The monotonous grind of everyday life distracted people from it, often to their detriment. Veteran riders didn't have that problem. They gave me a wide berth and convinced the less experienced riders to do the same. I helped the situation by projecting fear to anyone I sensed near me, and for that reason, when I rode inside a car I usually had it all to myself. That was exactly how I preferred it. The closer the humans were to me, the harder it was to control the hunger.

I was content to watch the landscape slide by in solitude. Days and nights eventually blended together and stretched into one long, gray blur. And then I was home.

The freight train approached the outskirts of Chicago before dawn. I saw the glow of the city on the horizon from one hundred miles away. The smells and sounds of predawn Chicago hit my nose and ears a few miles closer. I climbed to top of the rail car to watch our approach. The glow of the big city grew closer and dimmer with the coming of the day.

I wanted to get where I was going under cover of darkness so I could be settled in by sunrise. A look into the minds of the other riders assured me that none of them were watching me. They were thinking about me, though, wondering who and what I was, but they were far too afraid to ask me or to spy on me. No one was around to see me when I took to the air.

The cow blood I drank the night before gave me the strength to gain the height and speed I needed. I moved through the still-dark skies undetected by human eyes. Familiar streets rushed beneath me but I felt not one bit of nostalgia. In the past there had always been longing and homesickness because I was only visiting for a brief time before returning to Houston. This time was different.

I passed over parks and schoolyards where Richard, Tim, and I played blacktop basketball, stickball with makeshift bases, and football. We saved tackle football for the wintertime when we could use the snow to cushion our falls. We still got busted up pretty bad, of course, but boys will be boys. Bare concrete would've been much worse.

In the distance I saw dance clubs where we partied all night to House Music and Hiphop; movie theaters where I stole kisses. It was strange…I knew I did all those things but I no longer remembered doing them. It was like someone told me about it and I believed them, but the images were gone.

From the air, in my new, damned existence, none of it even mattered anymore.

Blood of the Third

A few minutes later I stood atop the roof of a hospital building located within a south side, lower middle class, residential area. The entire medical complex was relatively small, taking up only about half of two adjacent avenues, with a parking lot taking up the other half of the easternmost avenue. Even though the complex was small, the main building I stood upon was six stories high. That was easily higher than the two-story houses and three story brownstones that made up the rest of the neighborhood. It was my old neighborhood. The hospital complex was almost at the exact center of an imaginary triangle drawn from my childhood home to Tim's childhood home to the home where Richard lived with his mom before he died.

I could see all three houses from where I stood. I could also see three men dressed in dark jeans, black windbreakers, and black sweater caps. They crept through the shadowy back yard of a home situated three houses away from the end of my block.

That house belonged to the Ellis family. I knew them well. They had three children, all of them younger than me. The oldest, a daughter, had just graduated from college and lived in an apartment in Naperville, IL. The other daughter and their youngest, a son, were away at college. The parents had already left for work so the house was empty. The men slinking toward the back of the house knew all of this, which was precisely why they were there.

They were from the neighborhood, too. They were the son's friends and classmates from high school. They'd been in the home many times and knew exactly what they planned to take and where to find it.

Their felonious objective pissed me off. The Ellis's were a hardworking couple and good neighbors. They didn't deserve to be robbed, and the fact that the thieves were betraying someone who thought they were friends pissed me off even more. My anger tweaked my hunger. I had to fight back the urge to pay the would-be robbers a visit. I had other things to do. If I was lucky, the trio would get comfortable in the familiar house and take their time.

There was movement at my house, as I knew there would be. Mom and Dad were getting ready for work. Mom had recently been promoted to management at the main Post Office downtown. It paid more and allowed her to work days instead of nights. She carpooled with Camillia Williams, Richard's mother, an office manager for a company with offices in the Sears Tower. The two buildings were close enough for them to take turns driving to conserve gas. Dad worked as a ramp-service shift manager at O'Hare Airport, overseeing baggage handlers.

I caught them at the perfect time: early enough to catch them before they left for work but late enough to avoid the long conversation they would certainly want to have with me.

I had second thoughts about seeing them. What would I say? Did I really want to answer their questions? The answer to the first question was that I had no idea what I would say. The answer to the second question was: Hell no. I didn't want to answer any of their questions.

I didn't feel like I had a choice, though. That made me wonder, as I had many times, about what kind of vampire I was. Monsters aren't supposed to give a damn about what humans thought. But they were my parents. I loved them when I was human and I obviously still felt something for them, something that wouldn't allow me to disappear without giving them a reason. I owed them that much and more.

It took less than two seconds to go from the hospital roof to the alley that ran behind my parents' home. I landed in the shadows just outside the pool of light cast by a streetlight at the mouth of the alley. Satisfied that no one saw me, I walked to the sidewalk perpendicular to the alley and followed it around the corner and down the block. I reached out with my mind, ignoring the random thoughts and dreams of the surrounding neighbors, and focused on my parents.

They were both preoccupied with their morning routines. Mom made coffee while dad splashed after-shave lotion on his face. By the time I got to the front door they were just about to sit down at the kitchen table to have a cup of coffee and slice of toast together. It was their ritual; it reminded me of the similar ritual Denise and I once had.

Ten years earlier I would've been right there with my parents, drinking a glass of orange juice and eating a bowl of cereal, waiting for them to leave for work so I could smoke a little weed if I happened to be holding. After that I would use the eye drops to clear the redness, wash up, brush my teeth, get dressed and then head off to high school.

The memory gave me a strange feeling. It took a moment to realize the feeling was a sort of sad nostalgia, the emotion that eluded me as I flew over the city. The emotion had to fight its way past my lingering anger and the bloodlust it stirred, but somehow it pushed through. It didn't last, though. My vampire quickly consumed the melancholy and replaced it with annoyance.

"Lets get this shit over with," I growled reprovingly to myself as I rang the doorbell.

"Who the hell is ringing the doorbell this time of morning?" my dad asked both himself and my mom. He spoke softly but I heard him easily through my sensitive ears and through my mind. Through my dad's eyes I could see mom shrug.

Dad set down his coffee cup and trudged through the long hallway of the bungalow-style home. The foyer stairs creaked and then he looked through the peephole. I heard his heartbeat quicken when he saw me. I felt a surge of happiness and relief, which were soon overcome by anger and disappointment.

Then came the jingling, clicking, and turning of the three locks on the front door: the chain, the deadbolt, and the lock on the doorknob. He pulled open the door and just stared at me, frowning, through the iron-gated glass door that replaced the screen door we had before the neighborhood started going bad. He masterfully kept the look of anger plastered to his face, but inside, his disappointment and anger turned into grave concern. I looked through his eyes and immediately knew why he was worried.

I hadn't seen my reflection since Galveston so I had no idea how bad I looked. My appearance was exactly what you would expect from someone who had just ridden over a thousand miles inside and on top of a freight train: dirty, ragged, and tired. The torn t-shirt I wore was woefully insufficient for Chicago in late autumn, at least for a human, and I was as thin as a rail. I was always a skinny kid but I'd just started to fill out as I approached my thirties. I was twenty pounds lighter than when Dad last saw me, and the weight didn't appear to have been lost in a healthy way.

"What the hell happened to you?" he implored.

It was obvious he was asking about a lot more than my appearance. The first thing he thought about after looking me over was that I was strung out on crack or maybe heroin and I couldn't blame him. At that moment I wished I'd found somewhere to wash up and change clothes.

"I've been having a rough time, dad. I had to ride up here on the train. It's good to see you."

He wasn't sure if it was good to see me or not, and he chose not to lie about it. "On the train?" he asked. "Like a hobo? I know you didn't ride Amtrak looking like that."

"I don't feel as bad as I look," I said, and it was true, just barely. "But yeah, money is tight. I did the hobo thing."

Dad looked me over again and decided, reluctantly, to unlock and unlatch the outer gate. He didn't push it open. Instead, he simply let the inner door hang open and went back up the foyer stairs. I pulled open the gate and stepped across the threshold…

And almost collapsed to my knees. The foyer spun madly as an unfamiliar energy repelled and repulsed me. I could have gone into the house but I would have been almost too weak to stand and sick to my stomach. I used the doorframe to steady myself and I backed out to the porch.

Dad stopped at the top of the stairs and turned to look back. I was able to straighten up just before he saw me.

"You coming?" he asked.

I just stood there. The sickening energy still wafted from within the house. It wasn't the painful waves of power that radiated from those consecrated homes down in Louisiana, but it was enough to effectively keep me out.

"I know I look like crap," I began. "And I know you and mom are mad as hell at me for not calling for so long. I didn't want to assume you would let me –"

"Get your ass in this house, boy!" Dad snapped. "You're momma is worried sick about you." He was, too, but he wasn't about to say it. "And lock the damn door behind you."

In the past I would've chuckled at my dad's familiar gruffness. At that moment, in my condition, all it did was irritate me and stoke my anger. My hunger responded, reminding me how easy it would be to break his back and drink the living blood from his paralyzed body.

I fought back that urge and realized that he had just given me permission. The repulsive energy faded away from the threshold and I was able to walk into the house in relative comfort. I turned to close and lock both doors. When I turned back my mother was standing at the top of the stairs.

Mom didn't even recognize me when my back to her. She was just turning a questioning glare to my father to ask why he had just a derelict in the house. When I turned and she realized it was her son, she gasped and took a step back. Her quickened heartbeat thundered in my ears. So much shock and worry emanated from her that it filled my nostrils and I could feel it on my skin.

"Oh, my God," she cried, and in a flash she was down the stairs and in my arms.

She hugged me as hard as she could for two seconds. It was just long enough for me to get a good, deep inhalation of the blood rushing through her jugular and carotid. I tensed up at the slight elongation of my canine teeth just before she ended the hug. I was so thin she was afraid she'd hurt me. That made me chuckle, but I was careful to keep my mouth closed because my canines had not finished retracting.

My smile eased the fear that she'd hurt me but her other concerns remained. Mom was frightened by how cold I felt in her arms. Even though it was a cool autumn day, she knew the chill coming off me was too cold for the weather. The fear that I was on crack or heroin or some other dangerous narcotic dominated her thoughts. She pulled back to arm's length, wiping the tears from her face with one hand and keeping a tight grip on my shoulder with the other; afraid her baby boy would disappear again if she let him go.

And then she got mad.

"Where the hell have you been? We were worried sick about you! Denise told us you left her! You *left* her? Have you lost your mind? And why couldn't you call us after you left her? It's been weeks since I talked to you. Weeks! I'm gonna have to call in sick today. William! Call Camillia and tell her I can't come get her this morning! Are you ok, Major? Come in here and get something to eat. When *was* the last time you ate? You look like you're starving."

The moment she started talking she started walking. She pulled me up the foyer stairs behind her and walked me, well, it was more like towing me, to the kitchen. By the time she ended her rant I was sitting at the kitchen table and she was ducking into the refrigerator.

I held up a hand to stop her. "Believe it or not, mom, I fed not too long before I got here."

Mom frowned at the strange choice of words. Who the hell says *I fed* instead of *I ate*? But as the human mind tends to do, her mind translated my words the way she wanted to understand them.

"Really? I sure can't tell." She turned and called out: "William! Have you called Camillia?"

"Call her yourself!" he yelled from the bedroom. "I'm getting ready for work! The boy ain't going nowhere!"

"Momma, go on in to work," I insisted. "I'll be alright. I just need a shower and a nap. If I get hungry I'll find something in the fridge."

"Ok, but *please* shower. You smell like a dead goat. Put those funky clothes in a trash bag. Better yet, double-bag it, and then put the bag in the trashcan in the alley. Your daddy's got some old shirts and pants that might not hang off you too bad."

Dad stepped into the kitchen. "You better wash your ass *real* good before you put my clothes on."

Mom scoffed. "What do you care? I said *old* clothes. You got pants from ten years ago that you'll never fit in again."

"You don't know that, Mae," dad huffed. "I could lose some weight and get back into them."

Mom smiled for the first time that morning. Dad did, too. And then he looked at me and the smile shriveled.

"I'm glad you're home, son, but we need to talk."

"I know, pops." And then I told the truth. "I promise I'm not on drugs. I've just been having a really tough time since Denise and I... It's been harder than I thought it would be."

Neither of them believed me about the drugs but they didn't feel like arguing about it. Dad folded his arms, shook his head slowly, and sighed.

"I can't believe you left that nice girl for a piece of ass."

"Pops, I didn't leave her. I did mess around on her, though, and she put me out. Look, it's a long story. Let's talk about it when you and mom get home from work."

"You'll still be here?" Mom asked. "You promise?"

I forced a smile and saw it through mom's eyes. It looked convincing enough. It convinced my mother, and she had always been able to see right through my fake smiles. My vampire was making me a better deceiver.

M.J. Stewart

"Yes," I lied.

Dad climbed into his Four Runner, mom ducked into her LeSabre, and they were off to the daily grind. Both of them thought about me with equal parts anger, relief, and worry. Mom lived only a couple of blocks from Camillia Williams's house but I was back on the hospital roof and watching well before she got there.

I gave Ms. Williams's home my full attention. My intent was to listen in on her or see through her eyes. When I reached out, the painful energy of holy consecration pushed back. It was even more intense than the power that radiated from the homes in Louisiana.

I pulled back, and then I noticed a strange car parking in front of the house. Two men got out and strode up the walkway. One of the men was a Latino. He had dark hair, was medium height, and appeared to be in his late twenties or early thirties. The other man was a little older with distinct Anglo features, with dark brown hair just starting to go gray on the sides. He was a couple of inches taller than his companion. Both men were fit and had similar haircuts.

My first thought was that they were cops but I suspected they were more than that. I filtered out the background noise of the city, including the conversations and thoughts of the hospital staff and patients just beneath my feet, and focused on Ms. Williams' visitors.

The Anglo was as easy to read as most other humans. He was annoyed by what he thought was a waste of time. His young partner's enthusiasm annoyed him even more. He was thinking that the downside of being an agent in the God branch of the organization was all the wild geese they had to chase. He believed there were no such things as vampires.

My eyebrows lifted when the word "vampires" rose to the fore of his conscious thoughts.

The younger man thought about the questions they planned to ask Ms. Williams. And that was it. I couldn't tell from his thoughts whether he was bored, annoyed, or excited. His thought pattern was similar to the hunters in Galveston. It was too deliberate, like a person reciting a memorized and well-rehearsed speech. I realized that I could only see or hear what he allowed to hover on the surface of his thoughts.

Was he a hunter? His partner certainly wasn't.

Ms. Williams was stepping out onto the porch just before the men reached it. As she pulled the door open, my sensitive hearing picked up a muffled click and catch. It was the sound of a handgun cocking. I could tell she was curious about the strangers' identities and was prepared to defend herself, but that was all I could get.

Her thought patterns were just like the Latino agent's. That was no surprise. Neither was the gun. It was probably loaded with silver rounds. Living on the south side of Chicago was enough to make anyone cautious. Her unfortunate experiences with Andre and her son made her that much more vigilant.

One hand remained hidden in her purse while she pulled the front door closed with the other. She turned just as the men approached her small porch.

"Can I help you gentlemen?" It seemed more like a challenge than a question.

They both produced wallets that contained FBI picture identification and badges. Brown-hair's thoughts gave them away, at least to me. He smiled inwardly at the craftsmanship of their fake credentials. The other's thoughts continued to be repetitive and generic acknowledgement of his surroundings. Brown-hair felt that, as the ranking operative, he should do all the talking, so he did.

"I'm agent Benjamin Mitchell, my partner here is agent Jorgé Barboza. We're with the FBI. We'd like to ask you some questions about some murders that took place here a few years ago."

As he spoke, he appraised the woman standing before him. I looked through his eyes and saw Camillia standing there, relaxed but wary, as attractive as she was when I last saw her at my wedding. Her hips were a little curvier beneath her smart business skirt. A few more swaths of gray swept through her hair. Neither did anything to diminish her appeal.

Tim and I never told Richard, but both of us had a little crush on her when we were in high school. I understood why

Andre coveted her. Her beauty, passion, and strength were captivating. The sight of her stirred my vampire's lust.

The only thing that marred her allure was the crucifix at her bosom, hanging from a thin gold chain around her neck. It reminded me of the one I used to wear. I stopped wearing it after Andre and Richard died, thinking I no longer needed it. If I'd worn it that fateful night at the Dungeon, Su-Yin likely would have never targeted me.

I wasn't so lost in my memories that I missed the rest of their conversation. Through my ears and Mitchell's, I heard Ms. Williams' reply.

"The serial killings," she was saying. "Yes, he was my ex-lover. But he died that night…him and my son. I don't see how I can help you."

"People *thought* he died twenty years before that," Mitchell pointed out rather curtly.

Camillia gave him a cold stare. "We *know* he died that night. There were witnesses who saw him burn."

"We're sorry for making you recall such a horrible ordeal," Barboza said with sincerity. "That case is closed, I can assure you. But there've been some abductions and murders down in Texas and Louisiana that people have found uncomfortably similar to what happened here.

"We think it's a copycat. If it is, and if he's sticking to Andre's script, we thought you would be able to give us some insight on how the killer might operate."

Ms. Williams shook her head. "I was able to help back then because it really *was* Andre. I have no earthly idea who might be copying him down south."

My mom pulled up beside the agents' parked car, buzzed down her window, and waved to Ms. Williams.

"Everything ok, Camillia?" Mom called suspiciously. She instantly mistrusted the strangers.

"Yes, Mae," Ms. Williams called back. "I'll be done here in a second." She turned to the agents. "I'm sorry, gentlemen, but I have to go to work. I'm just a few years away from retirement so they're looking for a reason to fire me and keep that pension money."

Mitchell raised an eyebrow. "Retirement? I don't believe it. You're way too young for that."

Ms. Williams gave him a sideways glance. "You know exactly how old I am, agent Mitchell. I'm sure the FBI knows everything about me. Flattery won't get you anywhere with me."

"What about dinner, then?"

"Good day, agents," she said, both polite and firm, as she locked her door.

The three of them walked to the street. The agents got into their sedan while Ms. Williams walked over to the passenger side of mom's SUV, one hand still tucked in her purse. I tried to peak into her mind one more time as she swung the car door open.

She released the door handle and wrapped her free hand around her crucifix, and then she did something that freaked me out a little. She glanced around furtively but not at street level. Her eyes swept the surrounding trees and roofs.

My perch was over a block away, barely peeking over the rooftops and treetops. The sun was behind me and had risen high enough to hide me in its glare, yet it still seemed as if her eyes found me as she scanned the area. I was certain she didn't see me, though. Her gaze never hesitated and there was no reaction when her eyes moved past me. What she demonstrated was the natural alertness that came with having peeked into my new world, the world of vampires, and surviving the experience.

When she and mom pulled away, I refocused on the fake FBI agents. Barboza had started the car but he had not yet driven away. The two agents held a brief discussion as the car idled. The car was insulated so well even I couldn't hear what they were saying, so I had to watch through Mitchell's eyes and listen through his ears.

"Ben," Agent Barboza was saying. "I can't believe you asked her out. I didn't know you were into the sisters."

Agent Mitchell looked at the younger agent. "I don't discriminate. Sexy is sexy. You saw her."

"Yeah, I saw her. I heard her too, and she didn't sound very interested."

Mitchell shrugged. "I had to try to salvage something from this wild goose chase. Vampires, George? Really?"

"You have twice the experience in the GOD branch as me. I know I've seen some crazy things so I can only imagine what you've seen. How can you *not* believe in the existence of vampires?"

"Because I've never *seen* one, George, and neither has anyone I know. I've seen crazy bastards who filed their teeth into points or wore fake fangs. None of them turned into bats, though. Nor were they allergic to garlic, silver, or sunlight."

"That's why you don't do the mental shielding exercises," Barboza accused. "You should, you know. And it's not just about vampires who may or may not be able to read thoughts. What about telepaths?"

"I've never crossed paths with one of them either."

Barboza gave his older partner a questioning look. "Why are you even in the GOD branch, man? You don't believe in anything we're supposed to investigate."

"Let me tell you what I *do* believe, youngster. I believe in monsters, but most of the ones I've come across were human. I believe they should be put down like the sick animals they are. The GOD branch does the best job of finding and eliminating them, so this is where I want to be."

Barboza grinned. "Nice speech. So how do we go about finding the sick animal down in the Gulf Coast region?"

Mitchell gazed thoughtfully through the windshield for a moment. "This is a waste of time for the organization. Do we still have our SHROUD contacts?"

"We do," Barboza confirmed. "Our Midwest contact said a couple of their Chicago operatives are going down there."

"Really? SHROUD has enough manpower to send people down south without Chicago being short-staffed?"

"In Chicago, yes. They moved a lot of assets here after what happened a few years ago. Besides, the two they're sending are investigators, not muscle. Anything they can contribute here can be done from there via telephone phone."

Mitchell turned to Barboza and frowned. "Don't tell me they're sending those two old guys."

"Yes, them. No one in their Gulf Coast region has their amount of experience. They're to serve as consultants and leave the wet works, if it comes to that, to the younger guys."

"That's good," Mitchell said with satisfactory nod. "Let's farm this out to SHROUD for now. That's their wheelhouse, anyway. We'll stay in touch with our contact in case they need any help."

Blood of the Third

I thought about Barboza's and Mitchell's conversation as I leapt from the hospital roof. They posed as FBI agents for Ms. Williams but were actually part of something they simply called the organization, in the GOD branch, no less. Mitchell's thoughts indicated that G-O-D was an acronym for their branch of the organization, but what the letters actually stood for never came to the surface of his thoughts. It didn't matter. Their organization was obviously some high-level clandestine agency with a fair amount of clout.

Their conversation was pushed to the back of my mind when I landed softly on the roof of the Ellis home. Those three idiots were still there. Their familiarity with the home and the Ellis's schedules made them comfortable enough to take their time and bold enough to even grab a few snacks out of the refrigerator.

Just like I was hoping.

They couldn't discount the possibility that someone might come home early so they assigned a lookout. Travis got the job, which meant he sat on the radiator by the living room picture window eating a fried hot dog sandwich and watching television. He wasn't happy about the sandwich. Fried bologna was his first choice but they didn't have *any* kind of lunchmeat. He wondered what the hell kind of people didn't keep lunchmeat in the fridge.

He had the TV turned up loud to hear the daytime game shows over the sounds of Chad and Trey stomping around upstairs. He cast an occasional glance through a crack in the closed curtains, just to be vigilant. His infrequent peeks never revealed anyone so he was startled by the sound of the front doorknob turning.

Travis dropped his sandwich and pulled his loaded Desert Eagle. Weed, malt liquor, and crack logic convinced him to turn down the TV volume, as if the person at the front door hadn't already heard it. He crept to the front door and peeked through the peephole while pressing the nose of his Desert Eagle against the door. Travis was ready to blast right through it if he didn't like what he saw.

He didn't see anything. The downed forty-ounce put pressure on his bladder and the noise scared him a little bit, so he had to take a piss. He unlocked the door and opened it just wide enough to scan the porch without leaning across the threshold, aiming the Desert Eagle from his hip. There was already one in the chamber so he was all set. When he was satisfied no one was there, he closed the door and turned.

The Ghetto Boys' Hiphop classic, *Mind Playin' Tricks On Me,* started playing in his mind. He chuckled and bobbed his head as he made for the bathroom. After only two short footsteps the doorknob started jiggling again, more urgently than before. Travis froze in his tracks and listened. The doorknob kept moving, the urgency growing until the entire door shook.

Travis lifted the Desert Eagle and turned back to the door. He held it shoulder high, aiming right where the chest would be for someone about his own height. The knob continued to shimmy and the door continued to shake as Travis reached for it. At first he was hesitant, but the feel of the gun in his hand and the substances clouding his mind bolstered his confidence. And he *really* had to piss.

"Hell with this," Travis grunted.

He unlocked the door as quickly as he could and snatched it open. There was no one there. He stepped out onto the porch, scanning left and right, ready to blast. A verbal challenge was at the tip of his tongue just as his back foot cleared the threshold. Whatever he was about to say was cut painfully short by a rush of wind, a vice-like grip on his throat, and the sensation of flight. He never made a sound.

By the time Chad and Trey came downstairs with their arms full of the Ellis's property, I was on the roof of the hospital draining the blood from Travis's carotid artery. By the time the two would-be robbers noticed that Travis was missing and the front door was hanging open, Travis was already dead.

CHAPTER NINE

There was a twinge of guilt from feeding on a human again. The fact that those guys were assholes took some of the sting away but not nearly enough. In an attempt to preserve energy after dropping the bloodless corpse about a mile out from a deserted stretch of Lake Michigan shore, I used Travis's money for public transportation.

I rode the CTA bus to Midway airport, ragged clothes, dead-goat-smell and all. There would be no more train hopping for me. It was easy to ignore the disgusted stares of the other commuters. I had so much on my mind I barely noticed. And they were food. I didn't care what they thought.

Mitchell and Barboza were on my mind. They kept referring to something called "Shroud". Barboza guarded his thoughts too carefully for me to get a clear description of what it was. Mitchell was in such denial about the existence of creatures like me that he didn't bother to think about Shroud beyond the name of the group. I inferred what Shroud was from the context of their conversation. The hunters in Galveston were likely a part of that group.

The agents' discussion made one thing clear to me. I couldn't stay in Chicago. Andre was six years dead but the damage he did put the entire region on high alert. Chicago wasn't saturated with vampires the way Su Yin said New York and LA were. Chicago was saturated with hunters.

I seriously considered making Houston my permanent home. It didn't feel like home the way Chicago did but I felt a connection, like I was supposed to be there. It wasn't the city itself as much as the area, the *land* on which Houston and the surrounding area were built. Is that what drew Su Yin there? She was right about the relative lack of competition, but was that just a secondary reason for her to stay?

There were two problems with Houston, though. The first was that the Gulf Coast region of Texas was now on hunters' radars. The Galveston incident was proof of that. The other problem was Denise. As long as we were in the same city I'd never be able to stay away from her. My vampire constantly fought to change my love for her into obsession. The only thing that would keep me from turning her against her will was distance. I scoffed at the irony. There was a time when she was the only reason for me to live in Houston. She had become the only reason I couldn't.

While settling down in the "Bayou City" was out of the question, I had some loose ends to tie up there. I wanted more information from those with more experience with this life than I had. It was time to get in touch with Su-Yin again. I doubted she would welcome me back and I didn't care. I was intent on learning as much as I could. Su-Yin would enlighten me whether she wanted to or not.

The wary eyes of airport security scrutinized me as I strode through Midway Airport. I never attempted to enter the ticket line. Instead, I took a few seconds to scan the departing flights and then ducked into the first men's room I saw. It was fairly crowded so I had to wait in line until a stall was free. I sat on the toilet, not bothering to latch the door, and then melted into mist.

That form allowed me to move through the airport without being noticed. I stayed loosely dispersed and close to the ceiling to minimize the chance of an observant person catching sight of a small cloud moving purposely through an enclosed area. It was a quick trip through the terminal, across the waiting area, and out through the ramp that connected the terminal to the airplane's passenger entrance. From there I drifted through the narrow space between the enclosed, tubular loading ramp and the plane to get to open air. In another few seconds I was drifting into the luggage compartment of a plane heading to Texas.

In Houston, I used the rest of the day to find a change of clothes and a truck-shop shower. By then I was sick of my own filth. The stink had grown intolerable to my inhumanly keen sense of smell. By the time I was done it was so late that I knew Denise was asleep. I let her sleep. To my surprise, I actually cared about her being well rested and alert when we talked. The feeling was similar to the guilt in that it seemed out of place for a monster.

The next day, I dropped out of the sky and touched down quietly on the neighbor's roof across the street from my house. Most of the neighbors were still at work so I wasn't worried about being seen. It was late enough in the season to be dark by the time they got home. I wore stolen dark gray sweat pants, running shoes and a hooded sweatshirt to blend in with the shadows once the sun went down.

A half hour later Denise drove around the corner. The garage door went up, she drove in, and the garage door went down. Ten minutes later Tim's Mustang pulled up and parked at the curb in front of my house. He climbed out and walked up my driveway. I beat back a surge of jealous rage that made my hunger flare.

It took all I had to keep myself from launching from the rooftop and tearing his heart out. My mind conjured all kinds of scenarios for why he would visit Denise. Each one gnawed away at my self-restraint. If he had produced a key to my front door he would have been dead before he got it into the lock. Luckily for him, he rang the doorbell.

When Denise opened the door the sight of her made me gasp. I was shocked at how desperately I missed her. My vampire eyes picked up miniscule details about her that I'd never noticed. Every one of them added character and made her more beautiful than she was the last time I saw her. If I still had a heartbeat it would have been racing. If I still had tears they would have been streaming down my face.

"How you doing, Kitty?" Tim asked.

I didn't see or scent any lust between them. Tim's mind only betrayed the concern of a friend. Denise was mired in melancholy, thinking about me, missing me as much as I missed her. There were no romantic thoughts about one another. My jealousy subsided, and with it, my hunger.

Denise sighed. "How do you think I'm doing?"

She turned to allow Tim to enter and then closed and locked the door. I leapt from the roof, sailed across the street, and landed soundlessly on my roof. I heard them go into the living the room. Tim sat on the couch, Denise in the recliner.

"My husband told me he was turning into a vampire and then took off. You came over the next day and confirmed it. How the hell am I supposed to be doing?"

"It's a lot to digest," Tim acknowledged. "I refused to believe in vampires until I saw them with my own eyes."

Denise sighed. "How could God let evil like that exist?"

"I'm not the expert on God, Kitty," Tim admitted. "But we have one on the way. Some people are coming that can answer a lot more questions than I can."

"What people?" Denise asked.

The doorbell rang. Denise rose and walked to the door. When she opened it she saw two older men. One was tall, thin, and dressed in a Catholic priest's garb. The other one was short, just south of overweight, and looked a little like TV's Columbo, trench coat and all.

"Let me guess," Denise said. "Father Burns and Detective Weller."

"We're sorry about your ordeal," Father Burns said sincerely. "If there is anything we can do to help you through this, please let us know."

Denise ushered Burns and Weller into the home. Weller stepped in and grabbed Denise gently by the shoulders. "I've been accused of being blunt and insensitive, so forgive me," he began, "but we don't have time to mince words. I know you're hurting but you have to face the fact that the man you married is gone."

Denise pulled away and slammed the door shut.

She turned to Father Burns. "Is this what you call helping me through this?"

"Denise, my friend may lack tact," Father Burns threw Weller an annoyed glance, "but he is telling the truth. Major's soul is gone. What now resides in his body is an aberration of nature. We have reason to believe he may return for you."

Denise gasped. "Why?"

"Because he's not going to want to be alone," Weller answered.

"He's *not* alone. According to him, he's running around with the bitch that made him. Excuse me, Father."

"No need," Father Burns said with a dismissive wave of his hand. "I know how upset you must be."

Weller spoke again. "He may be running around with her now but he loves you. It's been our experience that vampires…" Denise lowered her head at the mention of the word 'vampires.' Weller noticed but he went on. "They sometimes grow attached to people who were special to them before they changed. If he really loved you, and I'm sure he did, he'll want you to join him."

"I can't believe I'm listening to this," Denise said to no one in particular.

"Where's Ms. Williams?" Tim asked.

"She chose not to come," Father Burns answered.

"And we don't blame her," Weller added. "She's been through enough. The Padre and I, however, *had* to come."

"Had to?" Denise asked.

Father Burns nodded. "After Richard and Andre, Weller and I did more research, fearing that Andre and Richard weren't the only ones of their kind. Our research led us to a group called SHROUD. Society of Hallowed Reavers Of the Un-Dead."

Weller picked up the story. "It's a secret association dedicated to ridding the Earth of vampires. The group is as old as the vampire legends. It's not a large group, as you can imagine they have a hard time recruiting. Most people don't believe in vampires. Most of those that do are too frightened – or too sane – to hunt them. There are fewer than two hundred of us scattered around the globe."

"Us?" Tim broke in. "Have you two joined them?"

Father Burns shrugged. "How could we not? After witnessing Andre's evil and Richard's torture, I swore to do all I could to prevent it from happening again."

"Same here," Weller added. "Andre wanted to end the world as we know it. The thought that there could be more out there like him made it easy for me to retire from the force and join SHROUD."

"You think Major wants to do that?" Denise asked.

"As his wife you know him better than us," Father Burns said. "We're hoping you could help us by providing some insight into the way he thinks, things he might long for that he could never have attained before."

"Tim's known him longer than I have," Denise argued. "Can't you just work with him?"

"C'mon Kitty," Tim said. "I could never know him like you did. Mage and me were like brothers but I know how he felt about you. You were his life, his soul mate. He shared things with you that he would never share with me. We both know that."

"Stop talking in the past-tense!" Denise snapped. "He's not dead."

"He's undead," Weller said bluntly.

Denise cut her eyes at the retired detective but Tim spoke before she could respond.

"Don't let him get to you. He's an asshole by nature."

"Then why did you call him down here?"

"He didn't," Father Burns said. "We called him. We heard through our regional contacts that there were signs of activity in this area. It started with a man that was found dead on Gessner. The body was burned beyond recognition, as if someone was trying to hide evidence.

"The body didn't burn quite long enough, though. The medical examiner was just able to make out a set of bite marks on his neck. Later, cattle were found dead from as far north as Dallas to as far south as Galveston. All of the corpses had been partially eaten by what appeared to be a huge dog. However, some of the sites had far less blood than they should have based on the trauma to the bodies."

Weller said: "These are signs of a newly made vampire left to fend for himself. Experienced hunters either hide the body or burn it thoroughly. Even when they mutilate a victim badly enough to disguise the true manner of death, a significant lack of blood at the scene gives them away.

"Eventually the cattle stopped dying in that fashion. That means the killer either started hunting wild animals, or worse, he started to feed exclusively on people and learned to do a better job of covering his tracks."

Denisc shuddered.

"What ultimately spurred us to come down here," Father Burns continued, "was the trap-party down in Galveston.

Tim frowned. "Trap-party?"

"Trap-party," Father Burns repeated. "Vampires are known to throw what they call 'Frenzies' to lure humans into a large, enclosed group. Frenzies, as you can imagine, is short for *Feeding* Frenzies. They target vampire enthusiasts. Frenzy organizers are secretive. They leave clues in different places, including the Internet, that only a true enthusiast or actual vampires are likely to find."

"Right," Weller said. "Some younger hunters got the idea to throw fake Frenzies. The idea is to lure as many vampires as possible into an enclosed space that's rigged to kill them. We call them trap-parties for obvious reasons.

"At the recent trap-party in Galveston, seventy-two out of the seventy-three vampires in attendance were destroyed. The lone survivor, a male vampire, used some very disturbing and rare abilities to get out of there in one piece. We came to see if we could help find him."

"We called Tim to let him know we were on our way down here," Father Burns said. "That was when he told us about Major."

"You think the one that got away is Major?" Denise asked worriedly.

"Don't know," Weller admitted. "But we need to find him, whether it's Major or not." He turned to Tim. "You said he was turned by a woman named Su-Yin at a strip club."

"It's called The Dungeon. She dances there."

"That's where we'll start. Give us the address."

"I can take you there," Tim offered.

Father Burns declined. "It's far too dangerous. We can't investigate with untrained civilians."

"We went after Andre together," Tim reminded.

"I know," the priest acknowledged. "You shouldn't have been with us, then. SHROUD members do a great deal of research and training before going into the field. We've learned that vampires have different abilities. Some can even read minds. It's taken a couple of years but we've been trained to control our thoughts. You haven't."

"You can help us out in different ways, kid," Weller assured. "But not yet. Tonight we only observe and gather info. We can't risk getting our cover blown."

"This is crazy!" Denise blurted out.

Tim turned to her. She could see how sad he was. "We know you don't want to believe us, but after what Major told me and showed you…"

"Are you going to kill him?" Denise asked.

Father Burns answered. "It's my turn to be blunt, young lady. We *have* to. I understand if you don't want to help, but we need you. We need all the help we can get."

"No," Denise said with a quivering voice. "I can't."

"Then at least stay with us," Tim pled. "Weller wasn't kidding about Mage coming for you. He and Father Burns are crashing with me they're in Houston. Stay with us until we can make arrangements to get you out of the city."

"This is my home," Denise argued. "My family is here. You can't just ask me to leave."

"You won't be safe here as long Major exists," Father Burns cautioned.

Denise shook her head defiantly. "He wouldn't hurt me. I don't care what you say he is. He would never hurt me."

The way she said it almost made *me* believe it.

Weller chuckled darkly. "Some people don't believe in vampires until they get bitten. Listen, Denise, we're trying to help you. Don't you want to live?"

"What I want is you out of my apartment," Denise snapped, fed up with the madness. "All three of you."

Weller shook his head and left. Father Burns sighed and followed. Tim went to the door but turned back to Denise.

"If you won't help us Kitty, at least let us help you."

"I'll leave Houston if I have to, but I can't help you kill the man I love. I'm sorry if you can't understand that."

"I understand," Tim said. "All too well."

He loved Richard like a brother, but when push came to shove he agreed to at least try to do what had to be done. I was right there with him. It broke both of our hearts to help Weller and Father Burns hunt our friend. Now the three of them were about to start hunting me.

"I'll come crash with you guys tonight," Denise said. "But right now I need a little time to myself."

"You got it," Tim replied. "Just make sure you get to my place before sundown."

Tim left and closed the door. Denise locked it and stood there for a moment. She wiped a few tears from her cheek and went to wash up. Her head spun like a top during her forty-five minute shower. When she finished, she pulled the curtain back and almost screamed when she saw me sitting on the sink. Somehow she managed to stay silent. All she did was stare.

"Those guys gave you a lot of information," I said tenderly. "Your mind is racing right now."

"How do you know?" she questioned. "Were you here the whole time?"

I shrugged. "I was around."

"I never invited you in. Vampires aren't supposed to be able come into homes uninvited, right? And it's still daytime. I thought vampires couldn't survive in sunlight."

She was being sarcastic. Even though part of her accepted what was happening, she still couldn't, or wouldn't – consciously admit it to herself.

"This is still my house. I don't need an invitation. And you're right. Most vampires can't survive sunlight. The thing is, there are all kinds of vampires just like there are all kinds of people. But you don't really care about any of that, do you? You're wondering –"

"What do you want, Major?"

"I don't know. At first I thought I wanted to die. Now I know I don't. I'm leaving Houston for good but I wanted to see you first."

"So you can kill me? Or turn me?"

"Kitty, I didn't choose this. You have to believe that if I could make everything the way it was I'd do it in a second. But I can't. This is what I am now. A lot has changed but two things haven't: I love you, and you still love me."

"You didn't answer me, Major."

"Su-Yin is going to die tonight. If I can find that son of a bitch Pedro, he'll die, too. Once they're gone I'll be alone."

"I guess I have my answer. Weller was right."

Denise was composed on the outside but her heartbeat echoed in my ears at such a fast pace I was surprised she didn't faint. The smell of her fear combined with the aromatic soap in the lingering steam from the shower. The intoxicating, almost tangible fragrance aroused my hunger. Denise must have seen it in my eyes. She reached for a towel and covered her nakedness as if that could stop me.

I refused to let the hunger take over. Instead, I reined it in and started saying things I did not plan to say.

"I'm cursed to walk the earth forever and I want you to walk beside me. You're the only woman worthy to walk beside me. We could live like royalty, like gods."

"Or animals," Denise corrected. "We'd hunt like wolves but hide like rats. We'd have to murder people to live."

"Maybe not, Kitty. There may be a way to feed without killing. I've been thinking about it, and –"

Denise cut me off. "Are you listening to yourself? *I believe in God*, Major. You know I'm a Christian. How could you ask me to follow you into hell?"

"God?" I scoffed. My anger began to seethe. "He turned his back on me when Su-Yin bit me, so I've turned my back on Him." Crimson light flickered in my eyes. "Besides, I'm only *asking* you as a courtesy."

She'd been caught somewhere between patronizing and humoring me. The idea that I was actually a vampire was still too crazy for her believe. She had seen a little and heard more, but not enough to erase that last shred of hope that vampires weren't real and I was just a disturbed human. When she saw that blood-red glow in my eyes, though, I could see and feel all of her doubt drain away. She spoke, her voice was soft and emotional, but beneath the sadness I felt her defiance and resolve.

"If you force me to turn you'll be no better than Su-Yin."

She was right. I thought about the loathing I felt for my maker and the plans I'd made for her. Denise would feel that same loathing for me if I turned her against her will.

She continued. "If you ever loved me, if you really do still love me, you won't force me to turn."

I stood up straight and glared at her. My vampire implored me to take her. It would've been so easy.

"Leave Houston, Denise. Go far away from here and don't tell anyone where you're going. Don't tell Tim or your family. If you do, I'll read them and I'll find you. Pray to your precious God that you never see me again."

I faded into a mist that blended in with the dissipating steam of the shower. Denise, thinking I was gone, finally gave in to her fear. She stepped out of the shower, swooned and fainted. I was right there to catch her.

The smooth brown skin of her neck, glistening with moisture, and the natural scent of her flesh and blood caused my upper and lower fangs to extend involuntarily. I wanted to carry her to the bed to lay her down comfortably but I knew I wouldn't be able to fight the hunger that long, so I set her gently on the floor. If I had been able to cry, I would have. But I couldn't cry anymore, so I walked out of bathroom, out of the apartment and out of Denise's life.

The rest of the day was spent wandering the city and thinking. My body ached from lack of rest and the sun exacerbated my discomfort. I wanted to find a nice dark corner to sleep so that I could be rested and replenished for a night of hunting. But I couldn't do that. I had to think of a way to get to Su-Yin.

And then I remembered the trap.

Years earlier, Andre's companion – or servant, or whatever the hell Eric was – proved to Tim and me that Richard was a vampire and convinced us to help kill him. He showed us how to rig a spring-trap meant to launch a stake through Richard's heart. We set up the trap the way he instructed, not knowing that he had us rig it to make certain Richard wouldn't die. The pain and anger caused by the trap was supposed to push Richard over the edge and make him finally give in to his hunger. Eric's plan worked perfectly.

I believed I could use the same sort of trap for Su-Yin. It would have to be modified but I was confident I could do it. That memory was a painful one, so I could recall it to the slightest detail. I needed tools, so I found a hardware store that carried everything I needed. Once I filled a shopping cart with all the necessary tools and materials, I rolled it to the cashier and fished out the last couple of dollars I'd taken from Travis. A quick push into the minds of the cashier and the people standing near me made them think it was the exact amount needed to complete the purchase.

A man wearing a three quarter length wool coat was leaving the store just before me. They didn't have what he wanted so he was going back to his pickup truck empty-handed. He turned apprehensively as I came up beside him. The sun had set. My strength was at its peak. It was easy for me to do what I had to do next.

"I need a ride," I said as I eased into his mind. "Let me load this stuff in your truck. I need to make one stop and then you can drop me off somewhere."

He wanted to refuse but a subtle push made my wishes his. "You got it, stranger."

Twenty minutes later we were passing Su-Yin's home. I reached out with my mind to see if she was there. She wasn't. She could block me from reading her but she couldn't conceal her presence. She'd already left for her nightly hunt. I had the stranger stop there and help me unload the truck.

Like the last time I was there, I caught a fleeting sense of something near. It vanished the moment I made contact, as if it had never been there. The sense was so vague that I couldn't tell if it originated from inside or outside the house. Once it was gone I was sure the house was empty. There was no repulsive energy at her threshold. Perhaps her invitation for my earlier visit lasted in perpetuity.

It took a few hours to get everything set up. I hid several gallons of gasoline in an attic that looked like it had never been visited. When I was done I left her home. Su-Yin was not one of the vampires that could tolerate sunlight, so I had every intention of returning in the morning.

I released my involuntary chauffeur. He had a wife and children that were probably already starting to miss him. If he had come up missing there would've been an investigation. Too many people had seen me with him and the hardware store had video cameras. I let the man go home, but not before I fed.

I didn't bite him, though. If I had done that I would have had only three options afterward: kill him, which I'd already decided not to do; make him a thrall, which I still wasn't ready for; or let him turn and figure things out for himself. That might've attracted the same hunters that killed all those vampires in Galveston, which was out of the question, at least while I was still in town.

One of our stops had been to a medical supply store. I caught the clerk while she was closing up and "suggested" to her that she should let me in to pick up some free supplies. I used those supplies to help temporarily sate my hunger.

Instead of biting my chauffeur, I used a needle, syringe, and rubber tubing to siphon blood from a vein in his wrist. The metal, plastic, and rubber that the blood had to pass through ruined its taste. The outflow of blood was much slower than it was with a bite. None of that mattered. The job got done and the donor wasn't infected.

The potency of human blood is much greater than animal blood. My strength increased with each swallow. I was sorely tempted to drain him dry. In the end, the altered taste made it easier to resist the usual urge to gorge. The man watched with an expression of detached curiosity as I drank just enough to get my strength up but not enough to impair him. His safe return home was in my best interest.

I sent him on his way I strongly suggested that he drive back to the department store parking lot where we met. I told him to take a brief nap and forget everything he and I had done. If he did remember any of it, it would come to him like the hazy memory of a dream. Before I let him go, I took his coat. The cool autumn air didn't bother me but people were starting to look twice at the skinny guy walking around in a t-shirt in that weather.

To this day I'm still not sure how I knew that I could manipulate him that way. Su-Yin hadn't shown me. Hell, I don't even know if she could do it. There was nothing in the literature I read that would have taught me. I simply wanted it to be so I willed it to be, and I somehow knew it would be.

CHAPTER TEN

Before I knew it I was on a bus heading south. A sick nostalgia urged me back to The Dungeon. I had nothing but unpleasant memories of that place but I was drawn there anyway. My vampire fed on bad memories. They fortified the darkness within me and gave it the strength to overcome my resistance.

I could have flown there but I wanted to preserve my strength. Besides, I preferred to be near people. My hunger was temporarily sated so there was no fear of losing control, and scanning minds was an interesting way to pass the time. Humans' mundane concerns about jobs, money and loved ones; their petty jealousies and selfish fantasies, they were all my own personal brand of entertainment.

A seeing-eye dog led a blind man wearing dark glasses onto the bus. The bus driver knew the man and gave him a kind greeting. The dog got one whiff of me and got nervous. She looked around to find the source of the disturbing scent. When she found me at the back of the bus a tiny whimper escaped her mouth her hackles went up. Her reaction confused her master but the dog was well trained. Despite her fear, she dutifully led him to an unoccupied seat. I looked into her owner's mind and found the dog's name. He wondered why Abby was so apprehensive all of a sudden.

The blind man had another thought. He thought he felt an evil presence.

Without the distraction of sight his other senses were heightened, including his primal sixth sense. His head turned slowly in my direction. It seemed like he was staring right at me. His preoccupation with me was so keen that the people around me thought he was faking his blindness.

I whispered soothing thoughts into the minds of Abby and her master. Within moments the dog settled down. Her owner, however, would not be so easily pacified. He could tell that I was projecting and he was able to resist. The blind man reached up and groped for the string to ring the bell that would signal the driver to let him off at the next stop. His trembling hand couldn't find the string. No one else seemed to care so I reached up and pulled the string for him. The bus driver stopped as soon as he could and waited for the blind man and his dog to make his way to the exit.

The bus driver said, "This isn't your regular stop, Al."

"I know," Al answered. "Abby and I don't like this bus tonight. We'll get the next one." He turned in my direction one last time as Abby led him off the bus.

A young man sitting in front of me turned and noted: "Damn, man. Dogs and blind people don't seem to like you very much."

"That's because they can feel me," I answered softly.

"Feel you?" he asked.

"Yeah." I eased a coil of cold fear into him. "Leave me alone or I'll make *you* feel me too." He quickly turned away.

Ten minutes later I got off the bus, walked about two blocks and reached The Dungeon. I stood on the sidewalk in front of the club and scanned the minds inside and outside. Neither Pedro nor Su-Yin was around but a flicker of familiarity brushed against my consciousness. When I tried to clarify those thoughts, I picked up a flash of alarm and then they vanished as quickly as they appeared.

At first I thought it was another vampire or two but I quickly ruled that out. The vampire mind has a unique edge to it that I didn't detect just then, and I would have caught the distinctive scent of my kind. I walked toward the club and listened to my surroundings with my acute sense of hearing.

A person had to think about the words they spoke. Even if they were being duplicitous, they still had to form the lie within their mind before it reached their lips. I compared voices to thoughts. When I found a voice that coincided with a thought stream, I filtered out both. In a matter of seconds, only two voices were left.

Those two remaining voices stood out easily. The hunters down in Galveston had a distinctive thought pattern that made them stand out. The two whispering voices I'd filtered down to in The Dungeon were even more disconcerting because there were absolutely no thoughts behind them. It was like listening to a disembodied voice from another room. The voices also stood out because they were familiar.

"Did you feel that, Padre?" whispered Weller's voice.

"Yes, detective," Father Burns in the same low volume. "How could I not? There's a vampire near. It's reaching out to identify a likely victim."

"Think we'll be able to spot it?" Weller asked.

They were casing the club from a parked car across the street. I used the large group of people in front of the building to shield myself from their searching eyes. When I entered the club I stayed near the front wall and continued to eavesdrop on them. It was surprisingly easy to tune out all of the other voices and thoughts around me.

"I think it went into the club," Weller said. "Places like that are candy stores to a vamp."

"What do you propose we do?" Burns asked. "Going in there isn't wise. We'd be somewhat conspicuous."

"What else can we do?" Weller replied. "No one knows us here. They'll just think we're a couple of old weirdoes. What do we care?"

"I don't have to remind you that we're only here to observe, not engage."

"We should at least get a look at it, Padre, get a description to give to the youngsters."

"Fair point, old friend."

They walked across the street and to the front door of the club. A bouncer stopped them. I couldn't get into the minds of the priest and the retired detective but the bouncer was easy. I penetrated his mind and looked through his eyes.

"See this badge?" Weller said authoritatively. "Texas Ranger. We have business here."

Weller had switched out his Columbo-style trench coat for a denim duster and a felt, pinch-front cowboy hat. Blue jeans and leather cowboy boots completed the ensemble.

"What about your friend?" the bouncer asked.

Father Burns was not dressed his usual priestly garb, but he didn't go all out with the western gear the way Weller had. He wore a leather jacket with blue jeans and Timberland boots. It was weird to see him dressed in secular clothing.

"Here's my ID," Burns said, flashing a realistic badge. "HPD. Would you get out of our way now?"

Both men affected passable east Texas accents. Burns did a very good impersonation of a cop. I was impressed.

"OK, old dudes," the bouncer conceded. "Go on in."

I slipped into the shadows when the men came into the club. They went to the end of the bar and used their fake badges and ID's to convince two patrons to give up their barstools. Father Burns surveyed the dance floor. Weller's eyes were frozen on pictures hanging up behind the bar. Each picture was of a beautiful lady. Some were close-ups and others were full-body shots of half-naked or completely naked women.

The bartender walked over to the clearly out-of-place gentlemen. "What can I get you, officers?"

"Is it that obvious?" Burns asked.

"Oh, yeah. So, what are you drinking?"

"Nothing for me," Father Burns declined.

"Shiner here," Weller instructed, his eyes never leaving the pictures on the wall. "No mug."

"I see your partner's fascinated with our wall of fame," the bartender noted. He leaned toward Weller. "You see anything you like? If she's working tonight you may be able to get a complimentary lap dance. They do that for cops sometimes."

"I see a lot of things I like," Weller answered. "But I see one in particular. Take a look, Padre."

"Padre?" the bartender asked.

"It's a nickname," Burns said. "Mind your business." The bartender walked away as Burns turned to Weller. "As for you, detective, I don't have time to ogle nude –"

"Look," Weller interrupted. He pointed to a picture of Su-Yin. "Does she look familiar to you?"

Burns nodded. "Very."

Burns waved the bartender back. When he reached them Weller pointed to the picture. "Who is that looker?"

"That's Su-Yin. She used to work here."

"Used to?" Weller asked.

"Used to," the bartender echoed. "She hasn't been here for almost a week. She has a bad habit of showing up for work she feels like it but she's never been gone this long. I'm assuming she's not coming back."

"Do you think she's been fired?" Burns asked.

The bartender scoffed. "Hell no. For starters, she's banging the owner, which a lot of the girls do, but economics is the other reason. That broad brings in more regular customers than any of our other dancers. Don't ask me why. I mean, she's sexy as hell but we got ladies here who are a little prettier, bigger butts, bigger boobs, and better dancers. Still, they don't bring in half the money Su does."

"Maybe she does things that the rest of your girls won't," offered Weller.

"Possible, but what she does on her own time has nothing to do with The Dungeon," the bartender said defensively. "All the girls do in this establishment is dance."

"I'm sure that's all they do," Weller said with a smirk. "Can you can tell us where she lives?"

The bartender shrugged. "Don't know. I have her number but she hasn't answered for days. The owner might know where she is but he's missing too." The man leaned closer to the two older men. "Do you think they're dead?"

Burns gave him a sidelong glance. "What makes you ask that particular question?"

The bartender leaned away defensively. "Don't get any ideas, man. You're here asking questions, they're missing. It's a reasonable question under the circumstances."

"Where can we find the owner?" Weller asked.

The bartender reached in his pocket and pulled out a business card. "Pedro calls himself a music producer. We all know it's a front to get girls to 'audition' for him. He gave me this card to give to good-looking prospects. It has the address of a studio he supposedly owns."

"Thanks," Weller said as he took the card. He turned to Father Burns. "Padre, pay the man."

"Nah," the bartender refused. "Drinks are always on the house for Houston's finest. Rangers, too."

Weller put a hand on the priest's shoulder. "The least you can do is tip the man."

The priest reluctantly placed a five-dollar bill on the bar. "Why do I always have to tip?" Burns complained. "I don't even drink."

Weller shrugged and walked away. Father Burns grunted and followed. They left the club and went back to the car.

"Looks like we have a lead, Padre."

"Yes, but I'm troubled. That night..." Burns paused for a moment. They referred to the time Richard killed his father and himself as "that night." Any reference to those events still sent a chill up their spines.

Burns continued. "Richard said he made his first kill before he got to Andre's house."

"Now you're thinking it was Su-Yin?" Weller asked.

"That picture of Su-Yin looks a lot like the photo of Kim Cho, the stripper killed at that peep-show establishment. It was the same night. Andre or any other experienced vampire wouldn't have left a body to be found so easily. The police report noted the markings on the DOA's neck. Her body went missing from the morgue three nights later. The two attendants were found dead with their throats ripped out."

"So, Richard turned her," Weller allowed. "We find her and take her out like the rest of them." Weller was silent for a moment, thoughtful. "What are the chances Richard's victim, Tim, and Major would all end up in Houston at the same time, let alone meet?"

"With Andre as the catalyst for all of this," Burns said, "I don't think it's a coincidence. If Richard turned her and she turned Major, Major could be a Third."

"What the hell is a Third?"

"Detective, you really need to study more. They don't give us reading material for paperweights."

"You gonna answer my question or not?"

Father Burns sighed. "It's written that the third generation in the blood line of a human and vampire hybrid has unusual powers and apocalyptic potential. According to the texts, the flood that prompted Noah to build his arc was nothing compared to the destructive power of a Third."

"Ok, Padre, in English now."

"Richard was a half-breed, the first generation," Burns explained. "Kim Cho, or Su-Yin as she's known here, was Richard's first and probably only convert. That makes her the second generation. Major was her convert. That would make him the third generation...and possibly *a* Third."

"But she's been a vampire for years," Weller argued. "There's no telling how many people she's turned."

"I doubt there have been many, detective. You know that vampires are usually very selective about who they make."

Weller agreed. "They're competitive and territorial. They won't create potential rivals for prey. They'll make thralls to use as servants for a time but very seldom will they fully convert someone. Most of their victims are just food."

"We know Major was not just food for her," Burns reasoned. "If that were the case she would have killed him, not turn him. And the way he came to Tim and Denise indicates that he's more than a thrall. Thralls stick by their masters and are cut off entirely from their former lives."

Weller grunted. "She still could've turned others besides Major. If she did, one of them could be a Third."

"True," Burns started, and then recognition lifted one of the priest's eyebrows. "The creature at the Galveston trap-party...the 'unusual powers' he reportedly displayed."

The detective worriedly rubbed an open hand from his forehead to his chin and sighed. "The odds aren't starting to look good for us, are they? What is this you mentioned about apocalyptic potential?"

"According to some legends, a Third has an extreme amount of power. The most frightening of them is the ability to call the essence of destroyed vampires back from the spirit world and place them into human hosts, turning the humans into vampires without even biting them."

Weller frowned. "How many vampires have died over the years?"

Burns thought for a moment. "Thousands that we know of. SHROUD didn't start keeping a record of slain vampires until 480 AD. There's no telling how many died before then. There's also no way of knowing how many have been slain by people unaffiliated with SHROUD."

"You mean a Third could bring all of them back?" Weller was starting to get frightened.

"I don't know about all," Burns admitted, "but he could bring back more than enough."

"If he does turn out to be a Third, he can't be the first one. There has to have been others."

"There are rumors," Burns conceded. "It's said that one will rise every millennia. During the first millennia, Emperor Diocletian is suspected to have been a Third. There is debate between Genghis Khan and Adolph Hitler as this millennia's Third. According to the prophecies, a Third in the third millennia is believed to be the evil that ends the world as we know it and ushers in a new age."

"We're just a few years away from the next millennia's Third," Weller said needlessly. "You're saying it can make humans go the way of dinosaur?"

"Not quite. Vampires prefer human blood. Eradicating us destroys their preferred food source. In all likelihood we'd be like cattle or pigs...livestock. The legends call it the Culling."

"That was Andre's plan," Weller realized. "He wanted to use Richard to spawn a Third, to bring about the culling."

"Yes," Burns concurred. "Through control of the Third he could control the civilized world."

"We'd better haul ass, then," Weller declared. "This isn't just about Major anymore. If he's not the Third another of her victims might be. We have to find this Pedro guy."

The priest held up a hand to stay his anxious friend. "Let's wait until morning. He may be one of Su-Yin's converts. If we're to find him, let it be while the sun shines."

"I'm inclined to agree, Padre, but at the very least we can do some recon tonight. It'll save us time tomorrow."

Their words faded from my range as they drove away. I stood in the darkness near the street-side wall of the club, dumbfounded. Nothing I'd studied referenced anything about a Third. Even with all my new power, I couldn't believe I had that kind of potential. I'd never heard of emperor Diocletian, but being in the same category as Hitler or Genghis Khan was not cool.

If Father Burns were right, though, that would explain quite a bit. Both Su-Yin and Renee told me I was different. The hunters in Galveston knew there was something unique about me, something that made me more dangerous than other vampires.

I didn't have time to worry about it at that moment. It was time for more preparation. I had work to do in the morning as well.

CHAPTER ELEVEN

I dozed off in the sewers a few hours before sunup to get some rest before carrying out my plans. Exhaustion had obviously gotten the better of me because the morning and most of the afternoon came and went. When I woke up it was almost dusk. I emerged from a sewer grate when the coast was clear and took to the sky. The most critical part of my plan was getting to Su-Yin before the sun went down.

There was still a little daylight left as I stood in front of Su-Yin's home and sent out a few mental probes. She was there, as I knew she would be. She also sleeping, as I hoped she would be. I went quietly into the house.

There was a brief fear that I'd feel the home's energy and that it would repel me, but it didn't. She'd welcomed me into her home once so I assumed that invitation continued in perpetuity. What I did feel was that strange presence again. And again, I couldn't detect any thoughts or even the aura of another mind. Still, I was certain something else was in or near the house. I went in anyway and crept up to the attic.

I stalked silently across the wood-plank floor, running the fingers of my right hand along the matching wall. The attic was dark though the sun had not yet set because the windows were painted black. When I reached the door to the storage room I saw that the gasoline I put there was missing.

"Lose something?" Su-Yin asked from behind me. I didn't hear her coming and she hid her thoughts.

I tried to come up with an answer she would believe. Even though I'd learned to shield my thoughts, this was too obvious. There was no point in lying. Resolved, I turned and saw her standing in the doorway to the storage room. She wore a see-through white silk teddy with nothing underneath. Her lingerie and porcelain skin were in sublime contrast to the darkness of the room behind her.

Lust bloomed within me instantly. But it wasn't *my* lust. She was projecting again. This time I refused to give in to it. I glanced indifferently at her and said:

"I sure did."

"Trespassing is against the law, Major. Though I have to say, hiding the gas in my own house was a good idea. I hardly ever come up here."

"What gave me away?" I asked, genuinely curious.

"The scent, you dumbass, yours and the gasoline. They lingered downstairs long after you left. If you'd brought the gas in through the attic window I might've missed it."

I shrugged. "I'll keep that in mind."

"What did you plan to do to me, anyway?" Su-Yin demanded. "You were going to torch me while I slept?"

"Yeah."

She was taken aback by my honesty. Even without reading her mind I could see she was disappointed. I denied her the opportunity to catch me in a lie. That would've given her an excuse to rant and rave and feed her anger.

My curtness and matter-of-fact tone gave her a moment's pause. I was ready for her to explode anyway. Instead, she surprised me by mirroring my calmness.

"Try to take me out now," she challenged. "Or are you too afraid to fight like a man?"

"I wish I were a man. You took that away from me."

"Bullshit," she spat. "You love what you are, what I made you. And what you are, Major, is *mine*."

Her hand was around my neck before I could react. She was still faster than me. With a flick of her wrist she sent me flying into the hall.

"I made you," she snarled. "Thanks to me you have powers you could never dream of."

"That's where you're wrong, Su-Yin. I used to dream about these powers all the time. I had nightmares about them damn near every night. My best friend had these powers and I saw what they did to him."

"My maker was weak," Su-Yin said.

"No. We're the weak ones. Richard had the strength to fight this."

"Would you rather die?" she asked.

"I'm already dead."

"Then come to me," Su-Yin beckoned, her eyes ablaze with bright red fury. "I'll fucking bury you."

She tried to stay outwardly calm but it was a losing battle.

"You come to me, bitch." I leaned nonchalantly against the wall. It creaked and clicked under my weight.

She tried her best to bring out my rage by projecting violent fury. I wouldn't let her penetrate my mind and it pissed her off.

"What's wrong?" I taunted. "You've never had a man resist you before?" Su-Yin glared and kept projecting. I felt it and grinned. "I bet no man ever said no to you even before Richard turned you. Maybe I'm saying it now because you're not as sexy as you think you are."

Su-Yin visibly flinched at the verbal assault. To her, her looks were everything. They were the source of her pride, income, and self-worth. That didn't change when she became a vampire. If anything, it intensified her narcissism. Her upper lip curled back slowly and her fangs unsheathed.

"You ever stop to think maybe there was never anything special about the way you looked?" I pressed.

By then I could feel her wrath radiating from her like heat. She wasn't projecting anymore. Manipulating me was the furthest thing from her mind. She was just really, really pissed. So I pushed a little more.

"Maybe men flocked to you just because they knew you were an easy piece of ass."

She roared as I put my full weight on the floor plank beneath my right foot. A loud click sounded as she pounced.

A floor panel snapped up right in front me. A foot-long wooden stake protruded from the end of it. Su-Yin collided with it, impaling herself through the stomach. She stopped in mid flight and shrieked in pain and surprise. She looked down at the bloody mess of her mid-section, looked back up at me, and favored me with a frightening smile.

"Nice try, boy, but you missed my heart."

Her smile twisted back into a hellish snarl as she gripped the floor panel with both hands. Before she could free herself I removed my weight from the wall plank.

There was another loud click behind Su-Yin. She turned her head just in time to see one more spike-studded panel swing down from the ceiling. This spike sunk deep into the middle of her upper back and exploded from just below her neck. Dark, thick blood splashed onto my face.

Her glowing red eyes transformed into orbs so dark that their blackness was stark even in the dim attic. The corners of her mouth curled up at an impossible angle. Rows upon rows of scythe-like teeth pushed down from her blackened gums. She screamed and laughed again.

"YOU MISSED THE HEART AGAIN, YOU STUPID FUCK! DON'T YOU KNOW ANYTHING?"

"I *do* know." I pulled a sharpened 2x4 from my coat.

Her maniacal laughter stopped. Her obsidian eyes widened. She writhed between the two panels like a hooked fish, causing them to moan and crack.

Grasping the makeshift stake in both hands like a pole-vaulter, I threw myself at her and thrust it forward. The sharp tip plunged into her chest, through her ribs, and punctured her heart. She coughed up blood as she wrapped her arms around me and pulled me close. My chest struck the flat end of the 2x4 and drove it deeper into her. Her fingers extended into long skeletal claws that she dug deep into my back. The pain was excruciating and sensual at the same time.

The opposing sensations ignited my hunger and lust. I licked her blood from my lips and grew even more aroused. My manhood stiffened where it pressed against her pelvis and my fangs extended further.

I longed to penetrate her while drinking her blood. I went as far as unzipping my fly before my survival instinct screamed that I was doing exactly what she wanted. The exquisite pain she inflicted caused my resolve to weaken. Even through her maddening agony her own survival instinct made her project overwhelming lust.

It almost worked, too, but instead of ravaging her, I braced my palms on her shoulders and tried to push away. Her rage and pain and desperation made her stronger than ever and she was physically stronger than me to begin with. I had tasted human blood only a few times while she gorged every night. My strength was no match for hers. I slipped my forearm against her throat and was just barely able to keep my face and neck away from her snapping maw.

Her body jerked and wrenched furiously, causing mine to do the same within her death-grip. Blood pulsed from her punctured heart. Her contorted mouth sprayed me with foul-smelling gore. Soon the top and bottom planks snapped and we tumbled to the floor. I was so engrossed in the moment, in fighting against her physical assault and my growing lust, that I forgot how easily I could easily free myself.

I transformed into vapor and drifted away. Su-Yin's roar took on a note of frustration. I reincorporated in the room behind her and watched. The sight was disgusting and fascinating at the same time. Her terror of impending death and anger at my betrayal was so intense that their scents gushed from her every pore. A deep breath took in the aroma and flavor of it all.

For a moment I considered looking for something I could use to take her head and put her out of her misery. My vampire, on the other hand, urged me to stay back, to watch the spectacle and continue to drink in the dark emotions. My loathing of Su-Yin and the vengeance that I'd just exacted heightened my vampire instinct. It quickly overcame any human compassion I had left.

I opened all of my senses to her suffering and reveled in it. It was the ultimate rush, better than I ever got from feeding on a human. Her fear poured into me and made me stronger. Her rage gave me deeper pleasure than the most explosive orgasm I'd ever had.

I wondered if Richard felt this way when he destroyed his maker. Probably not. Rich was too soft, too emotional, too damned sad to take any pleasure from destroying Andre. I didn't have that problem. I couldn't even remember how sadness felt. What I felt was a deep sense of satisfaction watching her squirm on the floor. Unfortunately, though, she finally went still and my rush subsided.

She wasn't finished. I knew that from all of the research I'd done. Had I left her there like that Pedro would eventually have found her. If he removed the stakes and gave her enough blood she would recover. Once again my human reasoning told me to take her head and be done with it. And once again, the sadistic nature of my vampire took over.

I reached into my pocket and pulled out a box of wooden matches. There was no gas to fuel a fire but there was plenty of wood in the attic. I used one match to ignite the entire box and tossed the flaming box near Su-Yin. It seemed to me that a fire ignited on the floor an instant before the lit matchbox actually landed.

The flames spread quickly to Su-Yin's still body. She went up immediately, as if her skin was more flammable than her clothing. I patiently waited and watched while the fire did its work. To my surprise, her eyes suddenly popped opened and her mouth gaped wide in a silent scream. The accusing glare she shot at me was, for lack of a better word, unsettling.

And then her obsidian eyes burst from the intense heat. One last surge of her pain and terror washed over me and then there was nothing. She burned to ash right before my eyes. The body collapsed in on itself, bones and all, until only a barely recognizable outline of a human shape remained. I smiled.

The flames spread hungrily across the wooden floor and up the wood-paneled walls. That was my cue to get the hell out of there. When I exited her paint-blackened attic window I saw that dusk had come and gone. I had gotten off lucky. Had I waited any longer the night would have given Su-Yin enough strength to overcome my attack quickly.

And then another realization occurred to me. There was no longer the sense, however vague it had been, of another presence in the house. I reached out with my mind and found nothing but the consciousness of nearby vermin and other animals, curious about the fire or afraid of it. Some searched for prey while others hid from predators.

There was an apartment complex a little under half a mile away. The buildings that comprised the complex were all four-story structures. I identified the one that would provide the best view of the house. I wanted to watch it burn just as I'd watched Su-Yin burn. A few seconds later I crouched atop the chosen building and watched the fire consume the house. My eyes, ears, nose, and – most importantly – my mind were trained on the conflagration.

My senses were so jacked that I couldn't have gotten a clearer picture of what was happening if I'd been standing a few feet away. I watched partly because of simple, morbid fascination. But even more than that, I wanted to see if anything escaped the flames. I knew Su-Yin was dead – truly dead – before I left the house but I was still concerned about the other presence I'd felt earlier.

The house burned nicely as the minutes passed. If nothing emerged from the crumbling house by then I knew, it never would. I was all set to leave when I spotted a car driving towards the burning home. It was Tim's red Mustang. My first instinct was to reach out with my mind but I could clearly see Weller and Burns accompanying him in the passenger and back seat respectively.

I knew better than to try to "read" their minds. The priest and cop were sensitive to psychic intrusion and would know immediately that they were being observed. Instead of using my mind and alerting them to my presence the way I did outside the Dungeon, I amplified my hearing and sight.

Blood of the Third

"Tim, neither detective Weller nor I wanted to bring you here after sundown."

"Blame this Houston traffic," Tim replied. "It's bad enough without the wrecks and construction we ran into. Besides, shouldn't we all wait for backup? I remember you saying there were other hunters in this area."

Weller grunted. "They're on the way. We're just doing recon. Su-Yin will likely be out hunting by now. We don't need you here."

"I know," Tim replied. "You told me a hundred times on the way over. But, hey, your rental car broke down and you two don't know your way around Houston."

Father Burns sighed. "I find it a bit strange and, for you, a rather convenient coincidence that this 'car trouble' occurred when it did. You work on cars, Tim. Couldn't you have at least taken a look at it, perhaps fixed it for us?"

"Convenient coincidence," Weller scoffed. "It won't be convenient if he gets his ass killed."

"We didn't have time for that," Tim said. "I'll take a look at the car in the morning. I promise."

"If you live to see the morning," Weller groused. "What about Denise?"

"Kitty's safe at her church. The story you gave her pastor and the HPD about a stalker was enough to get the sanctuary open and guards posted there."

"The Chicago ordeal wasn't enough to scare you away from this kind of thing?" Father Burns asked.

"I'm scared to damn death. Under different circumstances I'd be going in the other direction, but this broad took away my best friend. I want in on the kill."

"Look," Father Burns said, pointing ahead. "There's a fire burning up there."

The car stopped a safe distance away from the inferno and the three men climbed out. They were armed to the teeth. Guns undoubtedly loaded with silver rounds hung from holsters against the hips of both Burns and Weller. Small metal crossbows hung near their waists from shoulder straps. Tim was armed with a crossbow as well. Leather bags about a foot long hung from their belts. The tops of their slender quivers were open to reveal the flat, notched ends of small stakes. The older men had wooden stakes in their quivers while Tim carried heavier silver bolts in his.

Father Burns held his long, silver staff. The bottom end tapered to a point and the upper end branched into a cross that encircled by a gilded wreath. Weller wore a silver chain around his neck with a silver crucifix hanging near his heart. Tim was Muslim and didn't wear Christian symbols.

He wore a cross when we went after Andre but back then he was Muslim in name only. The crazy thing was that the crucifix protected him. His true faith in Allah flowed through the talisman even though a Catholic priest had consecrated it.

The sad thing was that my crucifix didn't work for me even though I'd been baptized as a kid. That always made me a little jealous. It was probably the real reason Su-Yin picked me instead of Tim that fateful night.

But anyway, Tim grew more devout after that, so he didn't wear any Christian symbolism. He wore a thin silver chain that held a silver pendant of Allah. Even with the distance between us I could feel the power radiating from it when I focused on him.

Burns and Weller wore light trenches and Tim wore a light jacket. I was pretty sure they had all kinds of nice little dangerous toys hidden beneath their coats, especially the older men.

"This is the place?" Tim asked.

Burns peered at the blaze. "Yes, according to the address in Pedro's rolodex. It appears someone beat us here."

Tim had pulled ahead of the older men, who were in no particular hurry. He looked over his shoulder and asked: "What do you think happened here?"

"It could've been an accident," Weller answered. "But I don't think it was."

"Hunters, then?"

Father Burns frowned. "Not likely. We would have been informed if SHROUD hunters did this. I suppose it could've been unaffiliated and unprofessional hunters. Professionals of any type keep a much lower profile than this."

It didn't matter that the priest was right. I was offended at being called unprofessional.

"You think she's in there?" Tim asked.

"I hope so," Weller said. "What do you think, padre?"

"I think we have a long night ahead of us, detective. We should stay here until the fire is out. We'll use our SHROUD contacts in HPD to keep tabs on the investigation."

"No telling how long that could take," Tim pointed out.

"The kid's right, Padre. There has to be something we can do in the meantime."

"Well," Burns mused, "perhaps we could –"

His words were cut short and his eyes widened with horror. Before the other two could ask what was wrong, the priest struck out at Tim with the lower end of his staff and swept the young man's feet out from under him. Tim went down in a heap just as something huge and snarling darted from behind the Mustang and sailed through the empty space that Tim's head occupied a millisecond earlier.

The thing soared a few feet toward the burning house before it landed. It scrambled awkwardly for a few feet before it found its balance and turned to face the hunters. I looked into the creature's mind and found nothing there. Its thoughts, no, its awareness, was no more developed than that of a dumb animal. All it knew was hunger, and only flesh and blood would sate its appetite.

The light from the burning home allowed the men to see the creature in disturbing, orange-tinted detail. Tim looked on with dread while Weller and Burns stood mouth agape. There was a glint of recognition in their eyes.

"Thompson," they breathed in unison.

Thompson might have been human once but he damn sure wasn't anymore. He was in a disgusting state of un-death. His gray skin was as dry as dust and sloughed off in some places while in others it was covered with festering sores. The only clothing the creature wore was a pair of slacks so tattered that more flesh than cloth was visible.

His back was so severely humped that it caused his grossly oversized torso to pitch forward. He was bent so severely that he nearly walked on all fours. Long, bony arms ended in gnarled protracted fingers with knob-like knuckles that scraped the ground. Curled yellow claws extended from his fingertips. Long, misshapen bare feet brandished claws identical to the ones on his hands.

Ragged tufts of matted, filthy hair sprouted from his head in thick clumps in random spots on his scalp. Other parts of it were hairless, rotting patches of skin. The creature's nose and mouth joined to form a stunted canine snout with disproportionately wide nostrils. The mouth contained hellish bony scythes dripping with brownish slime protruding from black gums behind thin bluish lips.

His head tilted slightly, yellow eyes burning at the humans from beneath a sloping brow covered with thick, wiry hair. As he regarded the three men I picked up a weak flicker of recognition that was quickly replaced by a leer of primitive hunger. Thompson, as Weller and Burns called him, growled and then charged.

The hunters were ready. Weller's gun was out and Burns leveled his crossbow. They fired simultaneously and deftly. A silver bullet struck Thompson in the head and a wooden stake pierced his chest. The missiles did a little damage, but very little. They passed through him as if his body was made of mush. Other than a faint hiss and a bit of steam, the bullet had no visible effect on the creature. The force of the stake, however, knocked him back on his heels.

Thompson stumbled drunkenly backward while Father Burns reached into his coat. When Thompson gathered himself and charged again, Burns produced an aerosol can equipped with something that resembled a miniaturized version of a trigger-activated garden hose spray nozzle.

I realized what it was just before Burns launched a spray of fire from his mini-flame thrower. Fire engulfed the Thompson-monster. He emitted a high-pitched scream and started running around in circles. He then dropped to the ground and began to roll around in the damp grass.

Weller went into the right side of his coat and brought out a dart-gun. He took out the dart that was already loaded, dropped it in his pocket, and then fished out a different dart from an inner pocket on the opposite side of his coat. By that time the flames were all but extinguished and Thompson was struggling to his hands and knees. His once-gray skin was soot-colored and sizzling. Patches of blackened flesh bubbled up on different parts of his body. The stink of sour, burning flesh assaulted the hunters' noses.

This time the monster turned his attention to the least threatening of the three. Tim's crossbow was already loaded so he raised it and fired. The silver bolt made a crunching sound as it broke through scorch-hardened flesh but then passed right through the creature's smoldering torso with a soft squishing sound. Thompson stumbled a bit, regained his balance, and went at Tim a little more cautiously.

"Umm, can I get little fire, Father?" Tim called with a shaky voice as he fought back panic. He backpedaled and tried to knock another bolt with trembling hands.

"He's too close to you," Burns warned. "Put some space between you so I can get a clearer shot."

"I can't outrun this thing," Tim said as he finished loading his crossbow. "You've seen how it moves. He's only hesitating now because he's expecting another shot. If I turn and run I'm as good as caught."

Thompson growled and lurched forward. Tim launched his silver bolt. Thompson ducked the missile and leapt forward. Tim cried out as the creature barreled into him and bore them both to the ground. Thompson must have been heavier he looked. Tim was much bigger but the breath exploded from his body when Thompson's full weight came down on him.

Tim screamed and kicked in a full-blown panic as he worked his way free. It didn't occur to him that the monster was not biting and scratching and tearing at his flesh. Tim hustled to his feet and took several hurried steps back before he noticed that the monster was just lying there, face down and still. The feathered tail end of a dart protruded from the back of Thompson's neck. Tim calmed his nerves and hurried over to Weller's side. He put a hand of thanks on the older man's shoulder as detective Weller slipped his dart gun back into his inner pocket.

"What the hell is in that dart?" Tim asked breathlessly.

"A sedative, of a sort."

"You two know this guy?"

"He was our southwest regional contact," Weller said. "He should've been the one to call us down here. Protocol dictates that the lead hunter at the Galveston trap-party contact Thompson to tell him about the vampire that escaped. Thompson would then decide the next step. No one could reach Thompson, though, so we were contacted directly."

"What is Thompson now?" Tim asked as he finally regained his breath and composure.

"As far as we know," the priest began, "there are three levels of vampires. Wamphyri is the superior level."

Weller explained. "A Wamphyri is someone infected by a bite and in turn ingests that vampire's blood. Major is Wamphyri. They have free will and are very powerful. A knowledgeable vampire is very selective about who it turns into Wamphyri."

"That does *not* look like what we have here," Tim noted.

"You also have the thrall," Weller continued. "The thrall is infected by the bite of a vamp and then consummates the deal with the blood of a human. Thralls aren't as powerful as Wamphyri. They're compelled to honor their makers' wishes until the maker is destroyed or purposely sets it free. Until then it's the servant of the one who turned it.

"In the absence of a direct command from its master a thrall pretty much does what it wants. A freed thrall can create other thralls. If it bites a human and then shares its own blood before the new thrall tastes human blood, it can actually create a Wamphyri even though it can never become one itself."

That sounded a lot like Pedro. Su-Yin left him a thrall but turned me into Wamphyri. Did she see something in me that she didn't see in him? I'm sure she regretted the hell out of that decision while she burned.

"So now I know what it's not." Tim's frazzled nerves shortened his patience. "What the hell *is* it?"

"That," Father Burns concluded with a nod at Thompson, "was a putrid marionette."

"It sounds a lot spookier in Romanian," Weller said. "The padre has trouble with that language."

"As does the detective," Burns shot a look at Weller. "The name is fitting in any language. A putrid marionette is the product of a human that's been infected, but not by a bite or the blood of a vampire. It's infected by a vampire's flesh."

"Flesh?" Tim frowned.

"A vampire takes a sliver of its own skin and places it into a human, usually under a flap of skin or by a forced feeding. The flesh dissolves into the victim's blood stream."

Weller took up the explanation. "It breaks down into parasites that multiply over and over as they feed on the very life force of their host. The victim decomposes from the inside out while the parasitic organisms keep it animated.

"A putrid's body isn't dense enough to stop a bullet or a bolt. They pass through the creature instead of staying imbedded long enough to do any serious damage."

"The worst thing about the creature," Father Burns chimed in, "is that the host can feel him or herself breaking down. They feel the agony of stiffening joints, atrophying muscles, and contracting internal organs and they can't do a anything about it. They go mad from the pain long before their transformation is done.

"Once the change is complete they're basically paralyzed until their maker orders them to move. They're just barely aware but they can't so much as blink without being commanded to. It drives them mad."

"That's where 'marionette' part comes in," Tim realized.

"Paralysis without the numbness," Weller said. "Their masters can show it new levels of pain with just a thought if they choose. The putrid marionette can't even scream unless their master allows it. It can live in that state indefinitely if it's provided enough living flesh and blood to feed on. Otherwise it would waste away to dust and slime."

"Damn," Tim winced.

"That's a fate they usually reserve for people they particularly dislike," Burns confided. "Vampire hunters fall squarely into that category and SHROUD is certainly at the top of the list. Thompson was supposed to be observing them. He must have been discovered."

"He must've been sloppy," Weller corrected.

"It doesn't matter now," Burns said. "We can only pray for him. He's almost at peace."

"OK," Tim interrupted, "I got a serious problem with this 'almost' shit. Are we gonna finish this thing off or what?"

Weller shook his head. "It's not time yet."

"How long are you gonna wait?"

They heard the approaching sirens. Weller looked over his shoulder and gave Father Burns a worried glance.

"Padre, the pute's body changes our plan. There'll be too many questions if we stay. We have to finish this and go before the locals get here."

"You know we can't rush this," Burns admonished.

"What the hell do you mean we can't rush?" Tim demanded.

"This is a process," Burns explained. "Calm down."

"Thompson isn't finished yet," Tim said, speaking to the hunters slowly as if they were children. "Cops and firemen are on the way. *Damn* a process!"

Thompson's body jerked violently. Tim jumped straight up in the air and hurried several paces behind Weller.

"See! Look!" Tim pointed anxiously.

"Yes," Burns said with eerie calm. "Look."

Thompson's body began to convulse. Gurgling and choking sounds escaped his scorched lips. He actually looked like a puppet whose strings were controlled by an unseen puppet master in the throes of a seizure. The body jerked so hard that it popped up into the air, turned, and landed on its hands and knees.

Tim stared open-mouthed as Thompson hacked and heaved and spit up dark, chunky gore onto the grass. It hacked a few moments more, and just when Tim thought things were as bad as they could get, they got much worse. The tip of something gelatinous and flesh-colored inched out of the putrid marionette's gaping mouth.

The wet snap of breaking bone resounded over the crackling flames of the burning house as Thompson's lower jaw unhinged like a snake's. His mouth cracked open wide enough to allow the bulk of the thing within it to squeeze free. It fell into the grass with a splat. Thompson crumpled to the ground and went completely still.

I was fascinated. The thing Thompson spit up reminded me of a giant earthworm with both ends tapered to flat tips. There were no visible eyes or mouth or anything else to distinguish its head from its tail. Its skin was a thin, transparent film, like a moist sausage casing filled with yellowish liquid and fatty substances. A network of webbing made of stringy purple and green vessels wriggled around within that mess. The thing's roiling, slug-like movement was not controlled by the flesh on the outside but by the stuff on the inside.

Tim gagged and vomited almost as violently as Thompson spit up that disgusting mess.

Father Burns handed Weller his flame-thrower. Both men calmly walked over to the squirming thing. The priest stopped a few feet away from it and propped his tall staff against his chest. He reached into his pocket to pull out a pair of gloves and pulled them onto his hands. He lifted his staff with both hands and brought down its pointed tip into the middle of the foul body, pinning it to the ground.

Weller blasted it with fire and held the flames on it while the thing thrashed about helplessly. The staff heated up in Father Burns' hands but his gloves made it just bearable. The thing squealed and sizzled under the fire. I could smell it from my rooftop perch nearly a half a mile away. It smelled of scorched flesh, feces, and rot.

Less than a minute later the remains of the disgusting thing stopped moving. Burns finally pulled his hands away from the heated staff and let the firm earth hold it up. Weller continued to blaze away until the thing melted down to an oily, black, bubbling substance. When Weller stopped the fiery assault there wasn't much of it left, but what was left was rank.

A sickened expression contorted Tim's face. "It smells like roast pork and shit!" he said in disgusted awe. "I thought that thing dissolved inside of its host."

"It does," Weller confirmed. "But we hit him with a saline, silver nitrate and liquefied garlic solution. Its chemical makeup is unbearable to the parasitic microorganisms and causes them to retreat from the rest of the body and recombine inside the stomach. It then expels itself through either the gullet or the lower intestines."

"We were lucky," Burns assured. "You wouldn't want to see the other expulsion process."

"I didn't want to see *this* one!" Tim looked in the direction of the approaching sirens. "That's my lesson for tonight. Can we get the hell out of here?"

The three of them rushed into the Mustang and Tim gunned the engine. I continued to listen. The crackling flames, the sirens, and the sounds of the Mustang's revving engine were all tuned out so I could hear their words while they were still within my expanded range of hearing.

"You guys said putrid marionettes can't move a muscle without a command from their master," Tim reminded. "Does that mean his master is still around here somewhere?"

"Quite the contrary," Father Burns said. "The only time a marionette displays that level of savagery is when its master is no longer present to command it. When I say 'no longer present' I mean destroyed. After that, all it knows is hunger."

"That's good news," Weller added. "The vampire that turned him was likely in that house when it burned. This was Su-Yin's place. It stands to reason she's dead."

Thompson was the faint presence I sensed in and around Su-Yin's place. I couldn't hear his thoughts because he didn't have any. As primitive a creature as he was, he was adept at hiding his psychic impression. It was likely a defense mechanism, a way to hide itself from potential predators. I'd learned my lesson for the night, too.

Later that night I crouched atop the north ledge of the Chase Tower in downtown Houston. As I looked north and slightly west, I found that I could make out the green lights outlining the Bank of America Plaza in downtown Dallas. My mind drifted to other places and times as I tried to remember what it was like to be human. Many of those memories had already faded away.

I remembered that Rich, Tim and I had good times together but I couldn't remember specific events anymore. Detailed memories waned into simple emotions. I remembered us laughing but I couldn't remember what we laughed about. On the other hand, every argument or fight, even those in our childhood, could be recalled as vividly as if they happened earlier that day.

The vampire within me was phasing out memories that made me happy or sad while solidifying into crystalline clarity any memory that made me angry, envious or horny. Happiness and despair were weak emotions that sapped a vampire's strength and resolve. Negative emotions were strong and helped to forge a better killer. I was beginning to understand my "new" self more and more.

And I was hungry. Feeding primarily on livestock, wild game and the occasional human kept me alive but relatively weak. My hunger intensified when I looked down to watch people walking around on the street. Their thoughts floated up to me in random drifts of insignificance.

All of them were so completely clueless it was almost laughable. They had no idea how close they were to death. I instinctively focused on the smaller and weaker ones, the ones I knew I could take down with the least amount of effort. Children, the elderly, and the disabled were the most logical targets.

The healthy adults were so self-involved they wouldn't be much more trouble. By the time it would occur to them to fight back, I'd already be wolfing down their lifeblood. Most of them were completely preoccupied with thoughts about running late to their destinations. They anticipated meeting friends, spouses or lovers. I could smell their anger, their lust, their fear and despair. All of it stoked my hunger.

Perhaps I'd continue to target the homeless and hopeless. There were people down there who thought they had nothing to live for. Many of them knew there was no one who would know they were missing if they disappeared. Some of them had homes, apartments or even houses but they were loners, cut off from the world by choice or circumstance.

A few of them were predators. They weren't vampires, though they were just as hungry. Theirs, however, was a different kind of hunger: muggers looking for just enough money for a fix and willing to do anything to get it; psychos eager to spill blood for no other reason than to watch their victims bleed; rapists whose desire for sadistic carnal pleasure could only be satisfied by an unwilling partner.

They sized up potential victims the way I did, targeting the weak and the most vulnerable. I decided that if I gave in to the hunger that evening, *they* would be my targets. My vampire wanted to consume their negative emotions as it had consumed mine. I felt their misplaced rage, their perverted lust, and their inexplicable madness.

And then I felt something else. I shot to my feet and turned. Two men stood on the roof behind me. They approached from downwind of me and it wasn't by coincidence. One was a few inches taller than the other. Their postures were relaxed but their apprehension was palpable. Their thoughts were like white noise in my head. They were expertly blocking me from their minds and I knew at once they were vampires.

"You appear to have a lot on your mind, young one," the taller man said.

He spoke with a heavy Central American accent and distinct Aztecan features. The only anomaly to his otherwise obvious ethnicity was his skin complexion. It wasn't just fair. The man was downright pale, as if the sun had not touched him in ages. I was certain it hadn't.

My eyes narrowed as I studied him. I knew I'd never seen him before but there was something familiar about him…too familiar. Whatever it was teased the edges of my awareness. I couldn't tell if it was his scent, his posture, his voice or just his general bearing, but there was definitely something there.

"Who are you?" I challenged.

I tried to read their minds again and again I could not. Their emotions, however, were far less difficult to decipher. Their uneasiness grew by the second.

"We're travelers," the shorter one said. He had ashen, milk-white skin and an Eastern European accent. He was German, or maybe Austrian. "You're new, aren't you? You were very recently turned."

"What do you care?" I asked.

"Yes," the taller one agreed. "You are new. You still try to resist the urge to feed on humans. The scent of animal blood is strong on you."

"That makes you weak," the shorter one said as if I didn't already know. "Stronger vampires would try to destroy you, perhaps even feed on you."

I was still on edge from my encounter with Su-Yin and craved an outlet for my unfulfilled bloodlust. The two strangers became prey in my eyes as much as the humans I'd been assessing only moments before. I perceived their warning as a threat and responded by baring my fangs and claws and whispering:

"Try me."

Instead of rising to my challenge as I hoped, they retreated a few steps.

"We don't want any trouble," the taller one said quickly. "We are travelers, not warriors."

"You're hiding your thoughts," I said. "But I can tell you're afraid of me. Why?"

"If you do not know, you truly have much to learn," the European stated.

"So teach me," I demanded. "And you," I said to the tall one, "why are you so familiar to me?"

He raised an eyebrow. "Your senses are unusually acute for one so new," he observed.

"If the two of you really don't want any trouble," I snarled, "you'll answer my questions."

The tall one smiled and shrugged. "As you wish, angry one. M*e llamo Manuel Del Sol.*"

The shorter one nodded. "I am Bernhardt Steiner."

The names meant nothing to me. "That answers my first question. Now answer the last one."

"I seem familiar to you," Del Sol explained, "because you are of my bloodline."

Steiner was as surprised by the answer as I was. He looked at his taller companion curiously and then looked back at me.

"Bullshit," I denied.

"I assure you it is not bullshit," Del Sol insisted. "Tell me, did you know of the one who calls himself Andre?"

I didn't reply. I didn't have to. The mention of Andre's name by someone outside of my Chicago acquaintances alarmed me in a way that was impossible to conceal.

"Ah, I see that you *are* familiar with him," Del Sol noted. "I am his maker. Judging by what I sense in you, Andre's great ambition has been fruitful. Tell me, young man, has Andre survived to see his dream realized?"

"I don't know what you're talking about," I lied.

Del Sol scoffed. "Of course you do. I cannot read minds as I felt you trying to do to me. I can, however, read hearts."

"I don't know what you're talking about," I repeated.

"Either you know exactly what I'm talking about and don't want to admit it, which is an intelligent decision, I must admit; or you know *something* is different about you but you do not yet know what that something is."

"Regardless," Bernhardt chimed in. "Other vampires will sense your uniqueness. Some will fear you for it and seek to destroy you. Others will see opportunity and try to make use of you."

"Indeed," Del Sol concurred. "Some vampires hunt weaker ones merely for the sport of it. Your distinctiveness will give them even more of a reason. And then, of course, there is *La Secta de la Ascension*."

"That's the second time I've heard that name." I knew enough Spanish to recognize "*secta*" was some sort of group or cult. "What kind of group is it?"

"As the name implies," Del Sol began, "*La Secta de la Ascension* a group dedicated to the ascension of our kind. They work to ensure that our existence remains secret until the time comes when they feel we are ready to take our place as the dominant species on this planet."

The culling, I thought, recalling the conversation Weller and Father Burns had with Denise and Tim.

Bernhardt nodded. "They would surely employ you to accomplish their goals, whether you wanted to be in their employ or not."

"So if you wish to survive and remain free," Del Sol concluded, "your strength has to be at its peak. That means feeding on human blood exclusively."

"Why are you telling me this?" I asked. "Why give me all of this helpful information?"

Del Sol shrugged. "There was a time when I did not care one way or the other about *La Secta's* goals. I was, in fact, curious about how the world would look if they were successful. I have since learned that *La Secta* not only wants to enslave mankind. They would hold dominion over vampire kind, as well. I, for one, prefer the hunt. The idea of humans as so much cattle holds no appeal to me, and I certainly do not wish to exist under the yoke of despots."

Bernhardt reached into his pocket and pulled out a business card. "There are more of us out west." He held out the card to me. "Los Angeles and San Francisco are ideal places for us. We blend in easier there than we can almost anywhere else in the United States."

I took the card from him and turned around to look thoughtfully out on the city of Houston. Chicago was my home but it was no longer an option. Su-Yin warned me against L.A. and I took her warning seriously. I had the feeling San Francisco would be just as competitive. When I turned back to tell the strangers I wasn't going west, they were gone.

Printed upon the card they gave was: "Club Eternal Night – Party in Perpetual Darkness" along with an address. What the hell did I care about a dance club in California? I stared at the card and wished it would burn.

I nearly jumped when it ignited in my hand.

So what I thought I saw at Su-Yin's earlier that night was actually what had happened. The floor did ignite before the matches made contact with it, and I made it happen. I held the card by its corner and watched in amazement as it blazed, blackened and curled. I dropped it off the roof just before the flame touched my fingers. A stiff breeze carried the glowing ashes into the darkness.

When Weller and Burns spoke of the possibility of me being a Third I didn't want to believe it, but it was getting harder to deny. Other vampires had an instinctive fear of me, similar to the way one predator recognizes a superior predator. Su-Yin was afraid of me as well. She could veil her thoughts but not her scent.

There was always a bit of nervousness when we were together. Her outward appearance never revealed it but I could smell it. On some level she knew there was something different about me. She intuitively wanted to control me but not destroy me. She tried to use intimidation and seduction to keep me under her power. It wasn't until she realized she couldn't control me that she tried to kill me. That was pretty much the same scenario the travelers described.

Maybe I was a Third. Maybe I wasn't. It didn't matter. I had no interest in doing the things Weller and Burns said a Third had the potential to do.

Sunrise was an hour away and I was exhausted. I was tired of thinking, tired of fighting. There was only one thing I *did* want to do and I would have to be well rested to get it done. I wanted to find Pedro before he found me, and then snuff out his dark fire.

CHAPTER TWELVE

The sun was going down. I awoke from a restorative sleep in the back of a junk van in the middle of an auto salvage yard. The first thing I noticed was the sound of footsteps. Two youngsters crept around the yard looking for something to steal.

They inspected various discarded car and truck parts while I sat quietly in the van waiting for them to leave. The hunger was upon me but I didn't have a taste for these boys. Their thoughts were muddled. The sickening scent of crack cocaine and the sharp odors of marijuana, methamphetamine, and alcohol drifted around them like invisible clouds, assaulting my hypersensitive olfactory nerves.

I threw subtle mental warnings against them as they rummaged around. My intention was to project an irrational, unexplainable fear so that their natural survival instincts would turn them away. Unfortunately for them the drugs warped their common sense and dulled their instincts. Instead of scaring them away I heightened their curiosity.

"Say, Dub," one of them, named Tony, began. "What's the deal with that van over there?"

"Damn if I know," Dub answered. "But there could be something in there worth some cheddar."

"Let's check that shit out, then. We might be able to come up."

"We gotta do this quick, though, Tony."

"I know. It won't take long for that Rottie to finish them cheap steaks we gave him. He'll come looking for us soon."

The scavengers shuffled over to the van. Tony tried to open the back door but it was locked.

"Dub, get something to pry this bitch open, or bust out the window or something."

While Dub scrambled to find a tool, Tony continued to yank at the door. "Hurry up, Dub!"

He tried the handle again and then stopped when he noticed a shadow on the van door. Tony turned and saw a squat, husky figure in the fading light of the setting sun.

A massive canine crouched atop a rusty pickup truck. It's mouth twisted in an evil snarl and its golden eyes fixed on Tony. The young man's mind was too distorted for him to be afraid. Instead, he was amused.

"What the fuck? Yo, Dub! Come peep this!"

Dub turned from his search and his eyes widened when he saw the animal. "Damn, that's a scary mutt."

"That ain't no mutt," Tony corrected. "That's a big-ass wolf right there."

Dub shook his head. "Ain't no wolves in Texas – wait, hold up, man. That ain't no damn wolf. Look at them hands."

"You mean paws fool..." Tony laughed, squinted, and leaned forward. "Wait, what the..."

"That's right, Tony. Those are *hands*. That must be some kind of generic mutation or something."

"The word is genetic, dumb-ass, not generic. I'll kill it. I got a cousin in Hempstead that does taxidermy. That thing's gonna make a mean trophy."

"What the fuck is taxi...what you said?"

"He stuffs dead shit," Tony elucidated as he eased his hand toward the pistol tucked in the inner breast pocket of his shabby windbreaker. "Look close, Dub. I want you to see how good a shot I am."

Tony's fingertips touched his weapon. Corinne pounced. She was on him before he could clear the gun from his jacket. Tony screamed as the werewolf sunk its teeth into his wrist. The powerful bite crushed Tony's bones and her weight bore the beleaguered man to the ground. The back of his head smacked against the cracked pavement and his pistol went flying.

Dub yelped and looked frantically along the ground for a weapon. He found a long iron pipe, snatched it up, and sprinted to help his friend. Dub raised the weapon to strike as he passed the rear of my van. The back double-doors flew open and I reached out, caught the pipe in my right hand and Dub's shoulder in my left. I yanked him into the van with so much speed and force that he lost a shoe. I broke his neck before he could scream.

Tony lay on the ground dazed and struggling to catch his breath. Corinne trotted over to the discarded gun, scooped it into her jaws, and crushed it with one powerful bite.

Tony sat up and inspected his broken and bleeding wrist. "I must really be fucked up," he said to himself. "This don't even hurt."

He was thankful the attack was over but curious as to why it ended so abruptly. His substance-addled mind came to the conclusion that Dub somehow scared the wolf away.

"Dub! Dub! Where you at?"

There was movement at the edge of his peripheral vision. Tony had fallen near the driver side of the van and struggled to his feet to get a better look. He turned to see that the rear doors had been opened. White mist poured slowly out of the van and floated along the ground. Tony looked curiously at the mist but was distracted when he noticed his friend's gym shoe lying near the van.

"You better not be in there smoking without me, Dub!"

Tony peeked around one of the open doors and saw his friend lying motionless. Dub's eyes stared blankly at the roof of the van. His mouth was open wide and oozing spittle. He assumed Dub was just zoned out from whatever drug he'd been smoking. He laughed out loud.

"Let me get some of that shit, man!"

Dub didn't respond or move. Tony grabbed his partner's shoulders and pulled him to a sitting position. Dub's torso was upright but his head dangled at an impossible angle and flopped limply.

"Oh, shit!" Tony swore.

He dropped the lifeless body and ran as fast as he could. After several steps he looked down and saw a mist swirling around his feet even as he ran. He recognized it as the same mist that streamed from the back of the van

"I'm having a bad trip," he huffed as he ran faster.

Tony repeated that phrase over and over to convince himself it was true. He darted through a maze of rusted out, busted up vehicles and spare parts, but try as he might, he couldn't get away from the mist. Instead, it swirled higher up his legs. He tried to brush it away but when he swiped at the mist it clung to his hands. The icy tendrils gained substance until they felt like frigid ropes tightening around his legs. He fell forward and threw up both hands to brace for impact with the ground.

He never hit the ground.

The mist suspended him in midair. The more he struggled the tighter he was squeezed. He screamed but the impossibly tangible mist tightened around his neck to cut the sound short. Fingers of it snaked into his mouth and nose and then down his throat. Tony soon passed out from lack of oxygen.

I impressed myself. Everything I did was instinct, and I had no idea I could be so powerful in my vaporous form. I whisked Tony into the van and closed the door behind us. Dub was paralyzed from his broken neck and Tony was unconscious, but their hearts still beat.

That was not to be the case for much longer. I was going to let them pass unharmed but I changed my mind. The effort expended to warn them away only made me hungrier. As much as I loathed their foul scent and taste, I drank deeply from both of them.

If they'd heeded my not-so-subtle subliminal warnings they would have lived to toke or shoot up another day. Corrine could've killed them both but she hadn't, so it stood to reason she didn't intend to. It occurred to me that I could've tried to manipulate their memories the way I had my unwilling chauffer two days earlier, but he had been clear-headed. My projection of irrational fear didn't work on their intoxicated minds so I doubted an attempt to affect their memories would have.

And I was hungry. I didn't take enough blood to kill them. I only drank enough to temporarily quell the hunger until I could find a more palatable meal. When I was done, I checked their pockets. One of them had a credit card. It wasn't his, though. Dub might have been his nickname, but I doubted a man of Anglo descent would have the first name Elizabeth. I took what little cash they had and left the card. Credit cards were traceable.

That same old guilt returned as soon as I was done. Not only did I feel guilty about the men I'd just fed upon, I felt guilty about the very prospect of feeding on future human victims. I couldn't understand where the guilt came from. I'd accepted the fact that I was a predator. Vampires aren't supposed to feel bad about taking down prey.

Forcing myself to focus on something other than the guilt, I turned my attention to the best way to finish them off and the time that would be wasted concealing the bodies. Those concerns quickly faded when I sensed what was outside the van. I opened the rear doors and stepped into the night. Corinne was there, still in her wolf form.

"I didn't think we'd ever meet again."

Corinne answered with a low, familiar growl. She was eager to feed.

"I appreciate you letting me feed first. I know how you prefer to feed on live prey so I left them breathing for you."

As soon as I stepped out of her way, Corinne rushed into the van to commence her repast.

I briefly wondered if her appearance was a coincidence or if she had been tracking me. If she was tracking me, I'd see her again. As I flew away, the sound of tearing flesh, chomping teeth and breaking bones faded into the night.

The moon was full but hidden behind thick, murky clouds. I sat atop a roof in downtown Houston and wondered how I could find Pedro. He had to know by that time that his mistress was gone and would no doubt suspect me. I didn't have the slightest idea how to find him and I soon grew tired of contemplating him.

My thoughts wandered back to my own predicament. I'd lost count of the days and weeks that had passed since I was turned. The acceptance immortality made time irrelevant to me and I could feel my vampire continuing to strip away all concern for my former life.

The people, however, remained vividly in my memory. Especially Denise. The names, faces and voices of everyone I'd ever met could be recalled in an instant, but there was something different about my memories of them. Even though I remembered them all, they seemed like peripheral characters from a movie I'd seen long ago.

And then I thought about my parents. What did they think when they came home and I was gone? Neither one of them really believed I'd be there when they got home from work. They hoped, but they weren't naïve enough to expect it. They were convinced that I was a hype, a hopeless drug addict, and that I would do what hopeless addicts did. I'm sure they were surprised when they realized I didn't steal anything.

I was surprised I still thought about them at all. The visit to Chicago was supposed to give me some closure, yet their faces came back to my mind and stayed there no matter how I tried to push the memory away. Did I have to tell what happened to me? Was that the only way to get the closure that eluded me? There was no way I could tell them that. How could parents believe their son had become a vampire?

There was only one parent I knew of that could.

I decided to follow the advice Tim gave me on the night I was turned, to do what I couldn't force myself to do in person back in Chicago. I reached into my pocket, pulled out a prepaid mobile phone that I'd bought from an all-night convenience store earlier that evening, and called Camillia Williams. She answered the phone on the third ring.

There was something almost comforting about the familiar voice. Ms. Williams was a good friend to my parents and had been like a second mother to Tim and I. Now I planned to tell her something that I couldn't possibly tell my real mother.

"Hey, Ms. Williams, this is – "

"Major?" she finished. "I barely recognize your voice."

"I know it's been a long time, but…"

"That's not what I mean," Camillia interrupted. "You sound *different*. Is everything all right?"

The question made me chuckle. A low feral growl rumbled just beneath the muffled laughter. The sound did not get past Camillia.

"Oh no," she breathed. "Not you, too, Major."

"You've been talking to Weller and Burns, haven't you?"

"Yes, but not about you," Camillia answered. "They haven't called me since they left for Texas. They told me there was activity in Houston but I didn't know they were talking about you."

"So how did you know?" I was genuinely curious.

"There's an edge in your voice," Camillia explained. "I've heard it before. I heard it from Andre and I heard it from my baby. That's not something I can forget."

"I didn't want this happen, Ms. Williams. I didn't choose this for myself."

"Your mom told me you paid her and your dad a visit a few days ago. They were worried about you being strung out on drugs."

"They were half-right, I guess. I am strung out."

"Did you come to my house?"

That caught me by surprise. The way she said it sounded more like a statement than a question. I thought about her looking my way while I spied on her from the hospital roof.

"Did you see me Ms. Williams? Did you…sense me?"

There was a pause before she answered. "Weller and Burns helped me learn to be more aware. I felt someone brush against my mind but I had no idea who. I never would've guessed it was you. Why didn't you say anything? Why didn't you come close enough to talk to me?"

"I don't know." That was a lie. I thought about the lust and hunger I felt when I watched her through agent Mitchell's eyes. If I'd gotten close enough to speak to her, I wouldn't have been able to resist the urge to feed.

"What do you plan to do, Major?"

"Live." I chuckled. "Damn, I guess that's kind of a contradiction since I'm the walking dead now. 'Exist' might be a better word."

"You may have other choices," Camillia said calmly.

"What choices?" I snarled. "I made my first kill a long time ago. There's no turning back for me now."

"That's not what I'm talking about, Major."

"Are you talking about the choice Richard made? Are you saying I should kill myself?" I laughed loudly. The sharp intake of breath I heard on the other end of the line let me know that my laugh frightened her.

"Sorry, Ms. Williams. I don't have that kind of strength."

"You may have other choices," she echoed. "Please remember that."

"I don't know what you're talking about."

"Major, do you know why Richard was so important to Andre?"

"Yeah, I know why. Do you?"

"Of course. I'm not in SHROUD but I've done a lot of research over the years. I've had a lot of conversations with Weller and Burns. I'm familiar with the legends."

"So…do you buy that 'Third' crap?"

"I don't know what to believe, but I'm not about to dismiss anything. I've seen too much to do that."

"So how does it feel to have babysat the boy that grows up to bring about the apocalypse?"

"This isn't a joke!" Camillia chided. "Even if there's the slightest bit of truth to the legend, you don't have to bring it to fruition."

"I agree, but I didn't call to talk about vampire lore."

"Why did you call?"

"What else did my mom say about me?"

"She asked if I'd talked to you recently. They were worried sick. They were on the verge of filing a missing person's report before you showed up at their door and they couldn't understand why Denise hadn't already. I couldn't either, until now."

"I don't want them to worry anymore," I said softly.

"You care," Camillia noted.

"My parents have to be told something."

"What would you have me say?"

"It doesn't matter. Tell them I died. Tell them whatever it takes to make them stop worrying."

"There's still some humanity in you, Major." Camillia's voice held a shadow of hope. "If there wasn't, your parents wouldn't matter to you. You have to hold on to that."

"I don't know how I can." I ended the call.

Su-Yin was gone. I had no idea where Pedro was. There was only me. I wanted so badly for Denise to join me. I could've made her my thrall but I didn't want a thrall. They were just followers without any free will. A companion was what I needed, which meant I couldn't turn Denise against her will. She had to want it or she would have the same hatred for me that I had for Su-Yin.

Of course, I could project the desire into her. The problem with that was it would only be temporary. She would eventually figure out that it was a false desire and resent me even more. The only true companion would be one that willingly chose to be a vampire.

Amara.

The thought came to me in an instant. She was incredibly attractive with an innocence that made her even more desirable. The mere thought of corrupting her purity stoked my hunger. When I first started to turn, I looked into her mind and found there was already an attraction there. I also saw that she would dedicate herself mind, body, and soul to the man she chose. If she accepted me she would make the perfect companion.

A cool, late autumn nighttime wind carried me to Amara's apartment. The city rushed by beneath me as I sailed a half mile above it. She lived just outside the city in a small subdivision separated from Houston by wooded areas and pastureland. It was a long, beautiful journey.

I was surprised I even noticed the pleasant panorama. Up until then my flights were strictly practical. They were the fastest way to get from point A to B and the best way to survey potential prey without being spotted. I'd never cared about or even noticed the view. Noticing a woman's beauty is one thing. That's basic lust, an emotion that the darkness within me feeds upon readily. The appreciation of a cityscape's aesthetics was something else entirely. It was fun, which was impractical and useless…utterly human.

Yet I couldn't deny I was starting to enjoy it. It wasn't just the flying either. What had started out as a dreaded curse started to feel more like a gift. The augmented senses, the strength, speed, mindreading, the ability to morph into vapor; all of it was growing on me in major way (no pun intended).

How could Richard have rejected this kind of power? To this day I have no idea if he was able to do all of the things I can but what I'd seen him do was impressive. It scared the hell out of me back then, but I was human back then. Looking back at it from my new perspective I'd started to forget what made it such a problem.

Sure, the hunger was admittedly bothersome if I didn't sate it soon enough. I still couldn't understand why I felt so guilty when I killed. And of course, there were the hunters, but I was determined to find a way to deal with those inconveniences. Ultimately, none of those things bothered me as much as the prospect of a solitary existence for the rest of my unnatural life. As awesome as my new abilities were, they weren't quite enough. I had to share this experience with someone who would appreciate it.

A ride that would have taken over twenty minutes by car took less than six the way I traveled. I lurked in the shadows outside of Amm's home for a few minutes. I needed time to come up with a way to tell her about the gift I intended to share with her. The obvious answer came to me like a bolt from the sky. I would let my vampire guide me.

I knocked on her door and waited, listening to her thoughts before she reached the door. She wondered who it was. She didn't appreciate unannounced guests. *Whoever it is*, she thought, *is about to get told the hell off.*

She snatched the door open and locked eyes with me. Her irritation turned instantly to pleasant surprise that she skillfully hid with an angry facade.

"What are you doing here?" She demanded.

I only stared.

She raised an eyebrow. "Have you gone deaf?"

"I was thinking about you, Amm."

"Well you've seen me," she snapped. "In my pajamas, with no makeup, and my hair all jacked up."

"And you're as beautiful as ever." I said it while I pushed the thought into her mind. It had more effect that way.

Her mouth twitched in a brief smile that I would've missed if I'd blinked. She swept it away quickly but a blush had already formed on her cheeks.

"I don't think your wife would like you being over here."

"Do you like me being over here?" I asked.

"Of course not," she snapped again. "You're married. I don't get down get like that. I hope you didn't think I did."

"I knew you didn't," I assured. "But Denise and I aren't exactly together now."

Her interest was piqued, and again, she didn't let it show. "Am I supposed to be the rebound chick? I don't think so."

"Nothing like that," I lied. "I just wanted to see you. I just wanted to talk."

She was persistent. "It would be a bad idea for you to come in."

The banter became tiresome to me.

"Just think about it for a second."

I started to project subtle thoughts and stronger emotions. The action was instinctive, reflexive. I didn't even realize I was doing it at first. It would have been easy for me to make her do whatever I wanted her to do, and it was very tempting. That, however, was not what I wanted.

I forced myself to stop. It was important that I didn't force her. I would do my best to verbally persuade her but every choice had to be hers. Even though I stopped projecting, I couldn't stop myself from listening to the faint whisper of her thoughts as she assessed the situation.

I made it overtly clear that I was attracted to her. It was just as clear to her that I knew she was attracted to me. None of that mattered. There was simply no way she would consider having a relationship with a married man, no matter how much she wanted to. She told herself that she would be polite and talk to me for five minutes, but then I would be out of there.

"You've got five minutes, Major, then you're outta here."

I stepped into the apartment. She closed and locked the door behind me. Her roommate, dressed in a sheer, skimpy nightgown, walked into the foyer.

"Amm, what the hell is going..." she stopped short when she recognized me. "Ooooohhhh," she teased. "Girl, I hope you know what you're doing."

"I'm not doing anything, Shannon," Amm assured.

"Whatever," Shannon mumbled. I caught a brief image in her mind of the three of us in a ménage à trois. The image stirred my lust, which in turn stirred my hunger.

"Now everyone is gonna know you were here," Amm complained after Shannon left the room. "That girl can't keep her mouth closed for anything. You should leave."

"Come with me," I bade.

Amm almost laughed, but then she saw – and I made sure she felt – how serious I was.

"What do you mean?" she asked.

"I can't explain it with words. Come here."

My vampire called to her in low, intense waves. I projected my will involuntarily. My hunger overcame my patience and pulled her to me stronger than it had in the break room that day, in my infancy as a vampire.

I whispered the thought *kiss me*. She hesitated. I said it aloud as I sent the thought along with a wave of lust. She glided to me on her tiny, bare, perfect feet and put her arms around me. I felt my canine teeth elongating the moment our lips met.

And then I stepped back. That was not the way I wanted it. She wasn't supposed to be food but I couldn't stop myself from exerting my will over her. Amm turned away and walked nervously into the living room. I followed her closely. She stopped and turned to me.

"What are you doing to me, Major?"

"Will you come with me?" I asked.

"Why can't I say no?" she asked.

"You don't want to say no," I answered for her. "You trust me. You know I'll make sure no harm ever comes to you. You feel safe with me."

She nodded. "I do."

"So come."

"This isn't right..." she persisted.

It turned out her will was stronger than I thought. I could feel her resisting me.

"But you want to come with me, anyway. Don't you?"

I exerted even more of my will and pushed, or more accurately, I pulled her to me. There were no more words. She only nodded. Her pouty lips parted slightly and those big, beautiful, gray-brown eyes stared deeply into mine. She was amazed at how deep and dark my eyes had become. She was compelled.

In the shadowy corners of her mind I heard her subconscious warning her of grave danger. I did all I could to muffle those thoughts. I had her, but it was more me than her.

My vampire continued to slink its way to the fore of my consciousness. All it wanted was to feed but I wanted more. I wasn't an animal, at least not yet. I wouldn't let the hunger control me. It took a monstrous effort...yeah, *monstrous*, but I was able to beat back my vampire's influence. The decision had to be all hers.

"I want *you* to choose, Amm. I won't choose for you." I touched her cheek gently. "Relax. Let me show something. When I'm done, I'll let you decide for yourself if you want to leave with me or not."

I started to project again. This time, though, I didn't call upon the rudimentary thoughts or primal urges that even the simplest of my kind can summon. I pushed fully formed thoughts and images into Amm's mind.

I showed her the power she would have, the immortality. Her youthful beauty would be eternal. The potential abilities to fly, morph, and enter the minds of others at some level were all revealed to her. She was allowed to look through my mind's eye as I recalled the many spectacular, superhuman exploits that I'd performed as well as Andre, Richard, Su-Yin and Pedro.

Amara was astounded by what she saw. The intrigue of my world was too much for her deny. I wasn't satisfied, though. I had only shown her the things that I thought were cool. Her decision couldn't be based on half-truths. She had to know the entire story.

I let her feel the hellish pain of the hunger, the danger that sunlight would pose. It wasn't deadly to me but there was no guarantee she would have the same tolerance. She saw the murdering she would have to commit in order to live. She saw in vivid detail the looks of terror and confusion on the faces of my victims as their lives slowly ebbed away.

Fear began to accelerate her heartbeat.

I showed her the cold, competitive nature of our kind. I made her understand that would always have to be on guard against vampires that would see her as a threat to their own food source. I revealed to her that most of us are pure killers, and some would hunt weaker vampires for sport.

And then I showed her the human hunters. She had to understand that people, contrary to the beliefs of Su-Yin and Pedro, were not just cattle or game. I wanted Amm to know that some of our prey would stalk us as vigorously as we stalked them. I played back the Galveston trap-party exactly how I saw it. Amm got to see vampires burned to ash in ultraviolet light and holy water. She saw those that were not immediately reduced to ash being hacked to pieces.

I stepped back and gazed into her eyes. The projecting stopped and I released her from my influence. She was so overwhelmed that she stumbled backward and sat breathlessly on the sofa. She stared up at me for a long time as she caught her breath. Her expression was a combination of horror, curiosity, and, strangest of all, excitement.

"You've seen what to expect, Amm. You've seen and felt the things that I have in my short experience, both good and bad. We'd live a powerful, endless existence. The tradeoff is an eternity of darkness, mistrust, and murder.

"It's true isn't it?" she asked. "It's all true. My God."

She didn't bother to ask me how I felt about it because she already knew. I'd projected my feelings to her along with the images: pain, fear, fury, and unspeakable pleasure.

Amm understood completely what she would have to give up for this gift and curse. She was willing to make that trade...eager, even. Her face beamed with a stunning and devious smile.

"I want it," she breathed. "Take me. Make me like you."

To her, the price was small in comparison to eternal beauty and unfathomable power. She stood, glided to me, and slipped her arms around my waist. Her lips parted and she pressed them against mine. I wasn't projecting anymore so her actions were all her own. She was nervous but her fear gave way to desire. Even her subconscious mind, which had been screaming in horror only seconds ago, was intrigued. I couldn't believe she wanted it that much.

Her eagerness was unsettling. Something as dark and irreversible as living death did not even faze her and that gave me pause. All of the ugly images I showed her meant nothing in face of all that power. The visions awakened something inside of her. Beneath her beauty and innocence hid a ruthless ambition that wasn't evident until she saw the possibilities that came with being a vampire.

What kind of vampire would she be? I needed someone like Denise, a soul mate, someone with whom I could spend an eternity. Would Amara be someone like that? Or would she be like Su-Yin? The more I looked at her, read her thoughts and emotions, the more I realized that the latter would likely be the case.

Instinct told me that this one was not the one to turn. She would make a pleasing meal and an even better thrall. I smelled it in the purity and sweetness of her blood. She would not, however, make a good eternal companion.

Her roommate stepped into the living room.

"You two still just *talking*?" she teased. "Why don't you just get your freak on and get it over with?"

As I turned to respond there was an inward explosion of glass behind me. I turned in time to see a huge gray wolf sailing through the window at an impossible speed.

Pedro was on me before I could react, ripping and tearing at my throat and chest. He was all teeth and claws and stench as he mauled me. Fangs punctured my throat. Giant razor-tipped paws shredded the flesh of my torso and broke my ribs. The wolf drew back and thrust his head forward again to plunge its snout straight through my chest.

I tried to block his attack as best I could but it didn't do much good. Pedro's teeth cracked through my sternum and pierced the lining of my heart. A rib punctured one of my lungs. My vision started to waver. It was a struggle to stay conscious while Pedro continued to rip and tear.

The women screamed and ran to the back of the apartment. Pedro, satisfied I was incapacitated, decided he wasn't going to leave any witnesses. He bounded after the women to stop them so he could come back and finish me.

I couldn't believe how careless I'd been. Pedro had probably been tracking me for days. I was so transfixed with Amm that he was able to hide his thoughts from me. His hunting experience allowed him to move with such stealth that I couldn't detect him until he struck.

All of my energy was now focused on staying conscious and healing my heart and lungs. I could still hear Pedro, however, doing his work. As my vampire worked furiously to mend my torn flesh, my mind reached out. Pedro was preoccupied with the women and knew I was helpless so he made no attempt to block me. I was able to look through his eyes and what I saw was terrible.

Pedro closed in on Shannon and bit a large chunk out of her right thigh, ripping out muscles and tendons and severing her femoral artery. She crumpled to the floor writhing and moaning in agony. He then morphed into human form to continue after Amm. She reached the back door and opened it but Pedro was too fast. He threw his body against the door and slammed it shut. Amm staggered backward and tried to turn but Pedro was on her. He grabbed her by the shoulder, yanked her to his chest, and sank his fangs into her neck.

He didn't waste much time. He drank enough to render her unconscious but not enough to stop her heart. She would be infected when she awoke. Shannon would bleed out, but Pedro had bitten her, so the wound would turn her as well. Pedro wanted thralls. He surveyed his handiwork for a moment and then came back to the living room.

I'd struggled to my knees by the time he returned but I was too weak to do anything else. My chest burned from my injuries but was nothing I couldn't handle. I'd been in constant pain of one sort or another from the moment I was turned. It was part of my life now. I'd long ago accepted the fact that the existence of a vampire was one of constant pain and hunger.

Pedro walked toward me, his fangs bared in a self-satisfied smile. I saw myself through his eyes...I looked like death. Blood soaked my shirt and neck. Countless bleeding scars riddled my face. My red eyes glowed weakly in the dimly lit room.

"Go ahead and read me," Pedro said confidently. "I don't care. You know what's next, anyway."

He was right. The only problem was he couldn't decide whether to kill me quickly or torture me slowly. His vampire, as well as his own ego, wanted to taste more of my fear. My pain was intoxicating to him, but his anger and impatience urged him to kill me quickly.

"You took Su-Yin away from me," he accused. "The fire didn't burn your scent away."

"I freed you from that sadistic bitch." I choked out the words and still managed to sound defiant. "You should be thanking me."

"Thanking you?" Pedro spat. "She was all I had, you fucking cockroach. She was all I wanted."

He opened himself to me so I could see the depth of his feelings for her. He'd fallen in love with Su-Yin the moment he laid eyes on her. She never once had to project any emotions to get him under her control. He put himself there.

Pedro didn't care that she was a vampire. When she revealed to him what she really was, he begged her to turn him so that he could serve her forever. It was pathetic. I might have felt sorry for the poor son of a bitch if he hadn't just torn me apart and was all set to finish the job.

Pedro was too big, too strong, and too experienced. He let his vampire instincts guide him and they were sharper than my own, fledgling instincts. His physical strength was hopelessly greater than mine, of course, because all he drank was human blood. The only edge I had was my mind, so if he wanted to torture me I would encourage him to do it. I needed all the time I could get to think of something.

"Better kill me quick," I dared. "You don't want me to recover. Su-Yin was afraid of me for a reason."

I felt him lean more toward slow torture. "You should be afraid of me, too," I warned. "But then again, you're too stupid to be afraid."

Challenging him to finish me quickly would provoke him to take even more time to draw out my suffering. Pedro wasn't dumb, though. He knew exactly what I was doing and he didn't care. He was so arrogant and confident that he believed there was nothing I could do to save myself even if he did let me regain my strength.

He delivered a kick that sent me sailing across the room. I hit the wall so hard I cracked it and dropped to my back. Pedro was standing over me the instant I hit the floor.

"Look at what you've done," I coughed, spattering black blood on the floor. "You've turned two women you know nothing about."

"You might be right," Pedro growled. "Maybe I *should* thank you. Su-Yin never would let me make a thrall for myself. Now I'm my own master with *two* of them."

"You turned them against their will," I reminded him. "Your mind's not strong enough to control them forever. When they break free of your will they'll get their revenge."

He lifted me by my belt and flung me across the room again. I bounced off of the far wall and again he was there before I fell to the floor.

"They'll be gone long before then. I'll keep them around until I get tired of fucking them and then I'll get rid of them and make two or three more thralls." He got two handfuls of my shirt and hoisted me into the air. "But first, I will finally take your head."

His nose and mouth merged and stretched into a hideous hairless canine muzzle. It was disgusting. My vampire worked so hard to heal me that I was too spent to dissolve into the mist that saved me the last time he attacked me.

Pedro growled and bared his teeth. He grabbed my head, plunging his claws through my flesh all the way into my skull, and snatched my head back hard enough to crack my neck. Shocking pain blinded me. His maw unhinged to display several rows of curved, dripping fangs.

When he tilted his head to the side to snap my head clean off with one bite, my vampire shifted its focus from healing to frantic defense. I lifted my hands in time to catch the snapping jaws before they could slam completely shut. His teeth drove through the palms of my hands like scorching spikes and still managed to puncture the skin of my neck.

Fortunately, I caught them before they could build up enough momentum to sever my hands and my head. Pedro removed his hands my head and dug his twisted claws into my sides. The fresh agony weakened me, allowing Pedro to successfully close his mouth tighter around my neck.

I knew from the start that I couldn't stop him with physical strength. Even though I'd stalled him for a moment, it wasn't even close to the amount of time I needed to heal. As I faded, my vampire brought to mind the night I killed Su-Yin, when I burned her. I recalled what happened on the rooftop after talking to Bernhardt and Del Sol, when I burned the business card. This time, I wanted Pedro to burn.

And Pedro burned. Energy born of desperation built up in my chest, surged through my bloody fingertips and into his muscular jaws where it erupted into fire.

The beast howled in surprise and pain and dropped me to the floor. He slapped at his face in an effort to smother the flames and only succeeded in igniting his hands. The flames on his face rushed to the inside of his mouth and down his throat. The flames on his hands spread to his wrists and then to his forearms and elbows. I entered his mind so that I could feed off of his pain and panic as he choked on the steam of his own smoldering esophagus.

Something in me snapped. Pedro's anguish and dread excited my vampire. He ceased be my attacker and became my prey. A perverse hunger raged within me, a different type of hunger than I'd felt before. It was not the hunger triggered by the vampire's need for sustenance. This feeling was more like an addict's craving for the drug of his choice.

The drug of choice in this case was Pedro's suffering and I instinctively knew how to appease that yearning. I had to teach him what torture really was. Even as he burned, I pounced on him and drove my fangs into his neck, but I was not trying to take his head the way he tried to take mine. His blood was what I wanted. I drank ravenously while Pedro fought madly. We fell to the floor in a tangle of limbs. His neck was locked firmly in my mouth and I was not letting go. He tore at the few patches of flesh that had not already been ripped open by his earlier assault but it did him no good.

I opened myself to every bit of his agony. I felt his body wasting away with the loss of his blood. His skin started drying out and his muscles began to wither. As his blood left him, his hunger grew. The ache in his belly burned more painfully than the fire that consumed his head and arms. Hunger usually strengthens us, but not that time. His black blood was spurting away too quickly.

Fear and desperation and hopelessness spiked the taste. Much of the sour fluid evaporated into fumes as soon as it touched the inner surfaces of my mouth. I inhaled deeply to keep any of it from escaping. The blood that did make its way past my tongue evaporated in my throat and esophagus. It warmed me to my core in a way that reminded me of overproof liquor.

The warmth intensified into searing heat. It felt like liquid fire in my veins. The burn, however, was more invigorating to me than painful. My vision spun madly and I grew light-headed. A strange euphoria swept through me. Pedro's blood was the most disgusting thing I'd ever tasted but it gave me a rush that human blood never could.

Pedro finally stopped fighting and went still. With a nudge of my will, the flames died out on his hands, arms, and ruined face. I stopped drinking an instant before his mind went blank. And then *I* took *his* head. In true death, Pedro's flesh and bones had gone so frail and desiccated that it was a simple feat for me to twist his head until the crinkly skin at the base of his neck tore like paper. His cervical spine snapped like an old twig. His head came off easily.

With Pedro's death, Amm and Shannon became human again. Their injuries, however, were far too severe for them to survive. They'd already bled out so they passed quickly and quietly into death.

The severed head in my hands began to morph. The long snout receded. The sharp teeth that were bared in an evil snarl shrank and blunted at the tips. The fresh scars healed. Moments later I was holding a human head. With a thought, I re-ignited it and dropped it on Pedro's chest. The fire quickly spread to the body and onto the floor of the living room. It would soon engulf the entire apartment.

Sirens blared in the distance. The other tenants of the small apartment building had called the police when all the noise started. They smelled the smoke and were filing out of their apartments. I leapt through the broken window in an attempt to fly away and I discovered to my dismay that I was still too weak to fly. I crashed headfirst to the ground. Pedro's blood intoxicated me but it hadn't fortified me.

I remembered seeing Shannon's car keys hanging from a nail in the kitchen so I rose to my feet and staggered drunkenly back into the apartment. It didn't take long to find them and stumble back out into the night. Amm and Shannon's first floor neighbors stood outside the building and watched me. The people on the second floor saw me as they made their way down the outside stairs.

I had to feed but there were too many people around. They eyed me with fear and suspicion. There was no way I could fight them off if they defended my victim. Police car and fire truck sirens were close enough for everyone to hear. I staggered to Shannon's car and sped away.

CHAPTER THIRTEEN

The high I had from Pedro's blood came down fast but I remained terribly dizzy. It was all I could do to keep the car on the road. The hunger was ravaging my insides. My vision was blurred and distorted by the flashing red and blue lights of police cars and fire trucks behind me. Beneath the sirens, I heard witnesses telling the police of my flight from the burning apartment. Two police cars called for backup and sped after me while the other officers remained to interview the witnesses.

I swerved all over the road. The police quickly gained on me so I floored the gas pedal. In my semiconscious state I lost control of the car as I approached a small bridge crossing over a shallow creek. I missed the bridge completely and the car plunged twenty feet down into pitch-black water. The creek bottom was soft mud and the car sank slowly into it. It took four panicked blows from my left elbow to knock out the driver side window. Murky water poured into the car but it didn't stop my desperate escape from the vehicle.

I'd struggled out of the car by the time the police arrived. The creek was as deep as my chest at its deepest point so I waded closer to the shore where the water was not as deep. I moved away from the ruined car as fast as my weak legs would carry me. The police shone their high-powered flashlights but I ducked beneath the surface of the murky water before they could spot me.

Their search was relentless. I pressed myself against the creek bottom and held my breath for a long as I could, until I thought my burning lungs would burst. I finally came to the point where I would either have to break the surface to take a breath or drown. By that point, with the pain and the hunger rendering me nearly unconscious, I no longer cared what happened to me.

Denise came to my mind again. She'd be better off with me gone. Hell, *everyone* would be better off with me gone. I opened my mouth and inhaled the muddy water.

And nothing happened. I felt the cold water and dirt and algae fill my lungs and clog my throat. It felt uncomfortable, indescribably weird, but I didn't choke. That was how I learned that while vampires breathe, we don't *have* to. It's an involuntary action that comes more from muscle memory than necessity. I would've laughed if I hadn't been in so much pain.

With slow, careful movements, I pressed myself face down into the creek floor and belly-crawled away from the search area. My enfeebled condition actually worked in my favor. I wanted to move faster but my waning strength wouldn't allow it. That sluggish movement is probably the only reason I didn't disturb the water enough for them see me moving beneath the surface of the shallow creek.

Eventually the sounds of police activity at the bridge faded. I crawled to the creek bank, vomited up the mud I'd swallowed, inhaled deeply, and started crawling again. The flashing lights from the police cars and the probing, conical beams from their flashlights dimmed and finally disappeared as I crept through the darkness along the banks of the winding creek.

I was able to snatch up a frog here and a water snake there in order to feed. Their cold blood tasted awful but provided just enough energy for me to keep moving until I caught the scent of cattle on the wind. It came from somewhere ahead of me. My hunger spurred me on.

The creek cut through a pasture and it wasn't long before I spotted the herd. I climbed out of the creek and stayed low as I crept upon the unsuspecting cattle and zeroed in on a target. It was important that I be as quiet as possible. There was still too much distance between the old bull and me. If the animals spotted me and fled, I wouldn't be able to sustain a long chase. I had to get as close as possible before I struck.

I stalked the animal the way a hungry lion stalks its prey. Being careful to stay downwind, I moved to within ten feet and gathered myself to pounce. The bull sensed me and turned to flee as I leapt at him, but he wouldn't be able to elude me. His wide neck was just within reach when I heard something whistle through the air.

A wooden stake sailed past my ear and something else hit me in the lower back. It pierced my flesh with a shuddering force that sent searing pain all through me. The force of it drove me to the ground a few feet short of the fleeing bull. The blood-coated tip of a silver spike protruded from my stomach. Steam rose from the sizzling blood.

I roared furiously as I pulled the silver bolt out of my midsection. My hands hissed and smoldered from contact with the silver. I turned in the direction from which the missiles had come and there stood Father Burns and Detective Weller. Both of them wore night vision goggles and were armed with small, modified crossbows.

"We can't let you regain your strength, Major," The priest said. "You know that."

"You missed the heart," I snarled.

Weller grunted: "We won't miss again."

He and Burns hastily reloaded their weapons. The pain from the silver bolt, my anger, and hunger-fueled desperation gave me newfound strength. I didn't know how long it would last so I attacked. I was too weak to fly but I could still move inhumanly fast on foot. The men, however, were able to reload and launch their crossbows before I reached them.

I snatched Burns' silver spike out of the air and used it to shatter Weller's wooden one before it could hit me and then I threw the silver spike back at Burns. He tried to dodge it but he was not quite successful. The bolt grazed his shoulder and knocked him down.

His shoulder bled and the smell of it drove me even harder. I was within five yards of them when Weller reached into his jacket and pulled out a shiny metal cross. The sight of it burned my eyes. An invisible force stopped me in my tracks and drove me away from the cop and clergyman. I backed up a few steps and stopped.

I averted my eyes and asked, "How did you find me?"

Weller answered. "Tim knew about your attraction to Amara. We were already coming this way when we heard about the fire on the police band. We figured if you didn't feed on the people in that apartment, the closest supply of livestock would be the most logical place to find you."

"SHROUD has taught you well, eh? They taught you two to mask your thoughts, and to use all of those neat little weapons?"

"Stop asking questions you already know the answer to," Weller snapped.

"You should've hung back and let the younger SHROUD agents come after me. You're both too old. You're weak, slow and stupid."

Weller chuckled darkly. "Look who's talking. You can barely stand. You've obviously been beaten to within an inch of your life and you're starving. You're the one that's weak and slow, and if you think we're falling for your bluff, you're the stupid one. You're biding time, kid, and so are we."

While Weller and I were talking, Burns had torn away his ripped sleeve and produced a small packet. He opened it to reveal some kind of medicated patch that he attached to his shoulder wound. I couldn't look into the priest's mind but I tasted his pain in the humid nighttime air.

"You gotta put down that crucifix to reload," I noted. "If you do, you're a dead man. Burns can't reload because he only has one working arm."

Burns used that one working arm to pull out a gun and open fire. I spun aside bullets that zipped past so close I could smell the hot silver, dropped to one knee and touched the damp grass. A trail of flames leapt up and sped toward my attackers. Both men jumped away from the flame just as it exploded into a ball of fire on the spot where they had been standing. The brightness of the flames temporarily blinded them through their night vision goggles and I used the distraction to turn and run. Father Burns blindly emptied his revolver through the flames.

A lucky shot lodged into one of my kidneys. I stumbled but I refused to fall. I heard the sizzle and smelled the smoke from the silver bullet burning inside me. The pain was debilitating. My vampire's frantic determination to survive was the only thing that kept me going. I'd escaped into the woods surrounding the pasture by the time Weller and Burns reached the other side of my wall of fire.

Burns' pain and blood loss diminished his concentration. That allowed me to get into his mind and look through his eyes. He watched Tim drive across the pasture in his Mustang, stop near them, and jump out of the car.

"Where'd he go?"

"We told you to stay on the main road," Weller scolded.

"I heard the shots and saw the light from the fire," Tim explained. "I thought you guys might need some help."

"He's running," Burns said. "He knows he's too weak to best men that know how to fight him."

Weller looked at the dying flames. "That last move looked pretty strong to me."

"And it took a lot out of him," Burns noted. "Probably most of whatever strength he had left. He's too weak to fight. He'll keep running."

"He might be on his last legs but he's still faster than Burns and me," Weller pointed out. "We'll never find him in those woods."

Tim studied the surrounding trees. "Maybe I can."

Weller glared at Tim. "Don't be stupid, man."

"I agree with the detective," Burns added. "In his weakened state, your young legs may be able to carry you fast enough to catch him, but what would you do then?"

"We can't help," Weller added. "I have to get the padre medical treatment for that gash in his shoulder."

Tim set his jaw stubbornly. "I have to."

"You are *not* trained for this," Burns warned.

"We can't let him get away. Look, I have these," Tim reached into his shirt to pull out his silver pendant of Allah.

He pulled up his sleeves to reveal a string of prayer beads wrapped around each wrist. He pulled out the same revolver he used when we went after Richard and Andre years earlier: his .44 Magnum Colt Anaconda. "It's loaded with silver. I copped the ammo from your bag at my place."

Weller grinned at the spectacle. The priest didn't.

"No," Burns commanded. "Come with us to the hospital. We have to come up with another plan."

Tim pocketed his revolver, scooped up Burns' crossbow and slung its strap over his shoulder. He took the quiver that hung from Burns' belt and attached it to his own. Lastly, he removed Burns' night-vision goggles and slipped them over his head. "You won't be needing these," he said.

Weller grabbed Tim firmly by the shoulder. "What the hell are you doing? Diminished or not, Major is still a vampire and you have no training."

"We may never get a chance like this again," Tim argued. "Maybe I can do some damage if he's as weak as you say."

"And if not?" Weller challenged. "You'll be dead or turned. The padre and I don't want to have to hunt you, too."

"I have to do this, Weller. Richard could only find peace when he took his own life. Major's will isn't that strong."

A tear crept down Tim's cheeks as he spoke. My best friend was hurting but he was determined to end my pain. He snatched away from Weller and walked away from the smoldering grass. Using Burns' night goggles to find a trail of my blood, he followed it into the woods.

"Damn," Weller swore. "How stupid is that guy?"

"Very," Burns agreed. "And he's just as brave."

Weller helped Burns into Tim's car. "Yeah? Well...the cemetery is full of brave, stupid people."

"Ask God to walk with him," Burns advised.

"I'm way ahead of you, padre."

The thoughts of Weller and Burns went quiet from my dwindling consciousness and the growing distance between us. I tried to zero in on Tim's location but I couldn't. It was a struggle just to stay on my feet. Thorny bushes tore at my flesh and low-hanging branches pummeled me as I moved clumsily through the dense woods. Thick tree roots snaking along the forest floor tripped me again and again but each time I managed to struggle to my feet.

The hunger was burning a hole in my stomach. My breath came in searing, ragged gasps. I had no idea which direction I was running. My vision, though, as murky as it was from pain and hunger, still penetrated the darkness easily.

I'd lost track of Tim but I knew he was on my trail. He was prepared for me and I was in no condition to fight. I needed to feed but there was no time to search for blood. My plan was to scoop something up from the ground or out of a tree, anything to feed on easily and give myself a bit of strength. I looked around for any form of life but there was none within my reach. The reason was clear. The nocturnal animals that usually flourished in this area sensed my presence, my hunger, and gave me a wide berth.

A moment later I realized I wasn't the only thing they gave a wide berth. A presence made itself known. It was a mental probe, an obvious one. Another vampire was coming and it wanted me to know it. It bored into my mind and filled my hazy consciousness with dread. It wouldn't let me probe it back. I couldn't tell which direction it came from and I couldn't pick up any coherent thoughts. All it allowed me to know was that it was coming, fast, and that it would end me.

The presence was so close I looked over my shoulder for it as I hobbled through the trees and brush. I was looking over my right shoulder and promptly tripped. My body spun as I collapsed, just as a whirling silver disk buzzed past. It sliced deeply into the back of my right arm and traced a fiery gash across my back as it whizzed by and sunk into a broad tree trunk. The impact spun me like a top until I slammed face-first to the ground. Had I not already been turning when it hit, it would have caught me flush and cut me in half.

I rolled over with a grunt and scanned my surroundings. The first thing I saw was instrument that put me down. What I thought was a disk was actually a throwing star as large as a man's hand. It was forged from pure silver. I could tell from the way it burned and cauterized the wound when it cut across my back.

A figure crouched in a high branch in the distance. It was a man, with long, straight black hair, clad in a cloak the same color as the surrounding shadows. Black gloves protected his hands from the silver of the throwing star he had just flung.

At first glance he reminded me of Manuel Del Sol: pronounced Aztecan features with pale skin that looked almost gray in the cloud-filtered moonlight, but that was as far as the similarities went. This stranger's face was long and gaunt, with sunken cheeks, pointed chin, and eyes far too big and spaced too far apart for his narrow face. The crimson vampire gleam those eyes were fixed on me. He glared down at me like a bird of prey eyeing an injured field mouse.

Are you *the legacy of Sam the slave?* he projected.

He sensed my confusion.

He called himself Andre but he will always be Sam the slave to us. I felt his amusement as he pushed more words into my head. *I was sent to monitor a potential threat and I find the most pitiful excuse for a vampire I've ever seen. Sam's labors were for less than nothing. Don't worry, cabrón. I will put you out of your misery.*

A fresh wave of pain washed over me, causing me to wince and blink. And then the vampire was gone, thoughts, scent, and all, as if he'd never been there. He was completely hidden from me. That meant he was coming for me. I pushed to my feet, turned and trudged away.

Agony pulsed through me with every clumsy step but I used it to stoke my panic, which in turn kept my legs moving. The exquisite pain also cleared my head. It clarified my senses enough to notice the blur of a silver garrote as it dropped over my head. It constricted before I could grab it. The razor-thin wire stung as it sliced my skin and burned into my neck.

Instinct kicked in. I burst into mist an instant before the garrote could take my head off. The mist dispersed until I was all but invisible. In my weakened state, I couldn't hope to hold that form for more than a few seconds.

I traveled as far and as fast as I could, which, under the circumstances, means I didn't go very far. The mist gathered and I materialized thirty yards away in a sitting position at the base of a tree. He saw me the moment I reappeared. Baring his fangs in a terrible smile, he leapt down from the tree with a powerful leap that covered more than half the distance between us.

His descent abruptly halted while his feet were still inches above the ground. The toe-tips of his shoes barely stirred the grass as he floated toward me. I never thought I'd see my end come for me that way, with me paralyzed by pain and exhaustion and the projected will of another vampire.

His freakish eyes dominated my vision. They seemed to grow impossibly larger as he came closer.

An icy breeze blew across the space between us. The wind caused his hair and his cloak to flutter to his right. He didn't even bother to brush away the strands of hair that blew across his face. They didn't seem to bother the hypnotic gaze that had locked me in place.

He was less than ten yards away from me when a massive figure streaked in from his right, upwind, so fast that it was only a blur. It engulfed him with a bone-jarring thud and swept him into a stand of trees and out of view. If I had blinked at that moment I would have missed it.

Whatever took him both shocked and hurt him enough to shatter his mental barricade. The pain and surprise distorted his thoughts so much that I could only make out a few words:

He fallado, Secta! Lo siento!

I had no idea what that meant but the word *Secta* stood out. It sounded familiar but my mind was too clouded at the time to recall where and when I'd last heard it.

His mind went silent after that, and he wasn't blocking me anymore. He was dead. All I sensed from the thing that took him was hunger and malice. I didn't know what it was or if it was coming after me next and I wasn't waiting around to find out. I pivoted on my backside, clawed at the tree behind me, pulled myself to my feet and resumed my escape.

My vampire was too malnourished to stop the flow of black blood from my countless lacerations. It wasn't long before my senses began to betray me. My vision, which had earlier pierced the darkness as if it were sunlight, faltered. The woods rushed by in a dark blur yet everything still seemed to move in slow motion. Of course, *I* was the only thing moving in relatively slow motion.

Every vein and artery in my body began to spasm. The blood moving through me burned like acid. I started running headlong into shrubbery. Somehow, though, I kept climbing to my feet. I hobbled on until I crashed into a tree trunk and went down once more. After struggling to my feet again, I could only take a few more steps before I crumpled facedown to the dank forest floor, clawing at the dirt and writhing in agony. That time I knew I wasn't getting back up.

The sound of my own wheezing echoed in my ears. Each breath made a moist whistling sound as air escaped through the bloody slit in my windpipe. And then my whole body went into paralysis. I hoped to go numb but I would have no such luck. The pain from the hunger and my injuries consumed me.

I gathered just enough strength to roll over onto my back. The clouds had dissipated enough to reveal the full moon in all its glory. The sight was breathtaking. A dark halo, so dark purple that it almost looked pitch black, surrounded the brilliant orb. Outside of the halo the sky was a slightly brighter shade of purple. The stars gleamed brilliantly.

All of my senses locked on to the captivating view. My deteriorating mind, slipping into a hallucinatory state, began to assign sounds to the sights. The twinkling starlight called to me with the soothing voice of wind chimes. The moon sang a mournful yet peaceful song of a woman's sorrowful moan. I managed a smile. If I was going to die, at least I would be lost in this beautiful night.

The sound of a footfall made me turn my head slowly to the side. I looked for Tim to step out of the darkness, his weapons poised to end me once and for all. To my surprise – and dismay – it was the last person I expected to see.

*Denise...*my mind whispered. My mouth and throat were too damaged to form the words.

Tears streamed down her cheeks. The sad moans I attributed to the moon were her actually sobs. The wind chimes were really the sounds of thin silver chains dangling from her neck and wrists. Small silver crucifixes hung from each one of them.

Moonlight reflected off of the silver talismans and caused the moisture in my eyes to smolder. In her right hand she gripped a long wooden stake.

Protection? I projected the question to her because I was too weak to talk. *From Weller and Burns?*

She nodded yes. "In case you came back for me."

She was close enough for me to look through her eyes. I saw myself and instantly wished I hadn't. My skin was closer to gray than brown and was as furrowed as crumpled paper. My mouth and nose were contorted into a hideous half-human, half-canine snout. The fierce red glow of what was once my vampire eyes had dwindled to tiny red pinpoints of light barely visible at the core of black orbs set deeply beneath a mess of thick, matted, wiry eyebrows. Brown, twisted fangs dangled from black gums and yellow slime oozed from the corners of my mouth.

Why'd they let you come? I never wanted you to see me...like this.

"They don't know I'm here."

How...how did you find me?

"I don't know," She answered through sniffles. "I felt you. It was like you were calling to me."

I thought about all of the times she'd come to my mind that night. Was I projecting to her without realizing it? I managed one more disturbing, sad little smile.

Maybe I was.

"I love you Major," Denise wept. "I always will."

I know. That's why I want you to be the one to end my suffering.

Denise nodded again. "I will." She wiped the tears away, knelt over me, and raised her wooden stake.

The memory of our wedding came back to me for the first time since I was turned. Our vow to each other replayed itself in my mind, our vow to stay together for the rest of our lives and, God willing, in the afterlife as well. That vow apparently didn't extend to an *un*life of vampirism. I used the last of my strength to voice one more request.

"Kitty...promise to remember me the way I was...the way I was before..."

"I promise, baby."

She brought the stake down with all of her might.

The IR goggles Tim wore allowed him to follow the blood trail easily. He didn't move as quickly as he would have liked because he thought it was best not to move too fast. Haste might cause him to lose his focus and he didn't want to run into an ambush.

He was full of guilt for what had to be done but he was determined to do it. Memories of Richard assailed him relentlessly. He felt partially responsible for what happened to Richard. When Eric, Andre's servant, first revealed that Richard was a vampire, Tim scoffed. He later felt that if he'd been more open-minded he might have been able to do something to stop Richard before the night Su-Yin was turned. If he had, he wouldn't be hunting his remaining best friend years later.

The blood trail finally ended, prompting Tim to look for a body. He found a large wooden stake protruding from the ground right where the blood trail ended, but that was all.

"What the hell?"

Dawn breaking so Tim removed the goggles and kept searching. He scanned the trees and surrounding brush to no avail. The sound of a breaking twig made him turn and fire the crossbow. The silver bolt found nothing but a tree trunk. Tim reloaded quickly and waited.

He saw movement out of the corner of his right eye. He turned and fired the crossbow again, and again there was nothing there but a tree. Leaves rustled behind him so he pulled his revolver from his belt, pivoted and fired several shots. Again, nothing was there. He reached for his quiver.

"Don't," I growled.

Tim turned again and brought up the pistol, but then he stopped himself from firing. I stood five yards away with Denise's still form cradled in my arms. My color had returned and Tim could tell I was stronger.

I tried to keep looking into his mind but I couldn't anymore. His thoughts changed once he was sure of my location. I could tell it wasn't a conscious action. His mind didn't get cloudy like a vampire's nor did it turn into the deliberate, rhythmic drone of a hunter controlling his thoughts. It alternated between moments of coherent thought and complete emptiness, like someone continuously turning the volume of radio up and down. I didn't understand it and I didn't like it.

"I'll drop Denise and have your bloody heart in my hand before she hits the ground," I lied. I was barely strong enough to stand and hold Denise at the same time, but he wouldn't know I was bluffing.

Tim glared at me. "You're bluffing. I could always tell when you were bluffing. I can *still* tell. Besides, I can see how weak you are. You're shaking."

I smiled. "Ok, then. Look over your right shoulder."

The incredulous look Tim gave me was almost comical.

I insisted. "If you can see how weak I am you should know I can't get to you in the time it'll take you to spare a quick glance."

The rustle of leaves and the sound of a low, rumbling growl was too much for Tim to ignore. Leaving his gun aimed at me, he looked over his shoulder and almost shit himself. A shaggy, dark-furred wolf stood less than five yards away. Even on all fours it was almost as tall as Tim. He glanced down at the beast's forepaws and saw that they were not *paws* at all, but humanoid hands tipped with evil claws.

Black blood from the wolf's recent meal dripped from its long, narrow snout. She had gotten as much meat as she could from the other vampire's bones but she was not sated. Tim saw her hunger as clearly as I did.

"If I drop Denise, my *friend* over there will be on you before she hits the ground, and you know there's no way in hell you'll turn that gun on her before she gets to you. Tell me if I'm bluffing this time."

Tim turned slowly back to me, too afraid to speak. I still couldn't read him but an obvious question was in eyes.

"Remember when we asked Eric about werewolves?" I asked. "Well, there you go."

Tim's gun and crossbow fell to the ground.

"So, you joined the hunt?" I asked needlessly. "You're worried about what they told you, about me being a potential 'Third.' You blame yourself for it."

Tim's eyes narrowed. "Are you reading my mind?"

"I don't have to," I said, purposely not answering his question. "You're helping them put me out of my misery."

"I know you won't do what Richard did. You can't."

"Of course I can't, Tim. But I don't want to do what they say a Third has the potential to do. I just want to live."

Tim scoffed. "That ship has sailed, hasn't it?"

I chuckled, it sounded more like a growl.

Tim looked down at Denise.

"Kitty's not dead," I promised. "You'd be surprised at how close she came to taking *me* out, though."

Denise sighed, looked up at me and said in a tired whisper: "The sun hurts my eyes."

"You turned her," Tim accused. A look of disgust twisted his features. "You're not afraid she'll burn when the sun comes all the way up?"

Denise shifted, turning toward Tim and opening her hand. A hypodermic needle, a short length of tube, and a syringe slipped out of her hand and fell to the ground.

Tim looked at the medical gear and back up at us. "You didn't bite her. Is that why you're still so weak?"

"I didn't want to infect her. I only took enough to get functional. I'm trying to find another way to feed, to exist."

"What happens next?" Tim asked. "You kill me?"

I shook my head. "No."

"Why?" Tim asked, genuinely curious.

"Because you're the brother I never had."

Tim scoffed. "We were the brothers Richard never had. That didn't stop him from trying to kill us, so forgive me if I don't believe you."

I shrugged. "You don't have to."

"You're gonna let me just walk away?"

"One condition: Richard was content to leave us alone until we went after him. The same goes for me. We're cool as far as I'm concerned.

"But if you hunt me...I'll hunt you back."

Tim stared at me for a long time before he spoke. "You don't have to worry about me. I want no parts of any of you. I can't speak for Weller and Father Burns, though."

"I'll deal with them when the time comes. I'm worried about you right now. I want you to promise me."

"You got my promise, Major. If I never see you again it'll be too damned soon."

I tried again to look into his mind and couldn't. But I knew Tim. I could look into his eyes and see that he was sincere. I smiled. "Now let me show you a cool little trick."

That made Tim nervous. He stepped back and reached for a bolt in his quiver as he watched me transform. A hungry growl from the massive wolf stayed his hand.

Even though I couldn't hear his thoughts, I could look through his eyes without any trouble. That made me a little more comfortable. Through his eyes I saw my body waver as if he were looking at me through superheated air. He stared in terrified fascination at Denise being suspended impossibly in the cold fog that had been my body a moment before.

She floated gently to the ground as the mist receded and then disappeared into the fading shadows of dawn. He looked to where the wolf had been and saw that she was gone, too.

My mind continued to look back to where Tim stood. He sank to a sitting position and buried his head in his hands.

By the time the morning sun crept higher in the sky and burned away the natural mists of dawn, Tim still sat there, staring at the wooden stake and the shadow it cast. He heard movement in the surrounding woods and looked up to see detective Weller step into view. Weller looked at the stake in the ground and the silver bolts in the nearby trees.

"Are you all right?" Weller asked suspiciously.

"I'm not a vampire, if that's what you mean, but hell no. I'm not all right. Major was here."

"I'm worried about Denise," Weller said. "I called the church. They said she's not..." He noticed her lying unconscious near the tree line.

Tim looked up at Weller. "That's because she came looking for her husband...and she found him."

"No," Weller breathed.

"Don't worry. He didn't turn her."

Weller sighed with relief. "She's a sweet girl. I'm glad we don't have to take her out, too."

"Don't include me in that 'we,' police man. My vampire hunting days are over."

"Really? After tonight I thought you might want to train with us and –"

Tim cut him off. "I'm finished! Don't you get it? I've lost the two best friends I've ever had to this shit. And Major had a werewolf with him. A freaking *werewolf*! I can't be a part of this craziness!"

Weller was temporarily dumbstruck. SHROUD never mentioned anything about werewolves. He took a moment to process this new information and eventually came to a conclusion. Vampires exist. Why not werewolves?

"That's all the more reason for you to fight these curses against mankind," Father Burns said. "We need your youth, your strength. With the right training, you could…"

"No. I'm done. I just want to put this behind me."

Weller slowly shook his head, almost in pity. "That's impossible, kid."

Tim disagreed. "It's damn sure worth a try."

"And then Corinne and I came west," Major concluded.

He sat on the floor, propped against the bottom of a leather couch with Corinne lying against his chest. His first impression of her was that she was distant and fiercely independent. Once she and Major decided to travel together she proved to be affectionate and fiercely passionate.

A man and a woman, Johnny and Roxanne, were lying a few feet away. All four of them were undressed except for their panties and briefs. The rest of their clothes were piled in a heap across the room. The other couple's tan, sweaty skin glistened in the light of a blazing fireplace.

Major continued. "We haven't checked out the Eternal Night club yet. We've only been here a few weeks and I'd like us to get our bearings before we start mingling with our own kind."

"Damn, Major," Roxanne said as she wiped away a moist blonde tress stuck to her forehead. "You have one hell of an imagination!"

"*Hell* yes," Johnny agreed. "You should write that down, man. Publish a novel or screenplay or something."

Corinne smiled.

"Oh," Major chuckled. "You think I made all that up?"

They didn't reply right away. Major's serious expression and the strange look in Corinne's golden eyes distracted them. Johnny and Roxanne paused for a moment and then laughed nervously.

"You almost had us there–" was all Roxanne could manage before Major was on her. Her attempted scream became a muffled gurgle when he grabbed her throat.

Johnny was momentarily frozen in terror. He reached for Major in a hopeless attempt to pull him away from his girlfriend. His wrist was snatched away by a hand with long claws where human fingernails should have been. Corinne pulled him around with a grip that fractured his wrist.

"He's busy," she growled.

Johnny turned and saw Corinne smiling at him with a mouthful of wolf-like teeth. A burst of fear-enhanced strength allowed him to snatch away. He jumped to his feet and sprinted out the front door, all the while screaming for help. Terror carried him down the stairs and out of the two-story apartment building in a matter of seconds. He reached his car, pulled the door open, reached for the ignition, and then he remembered...

"Looking for these?" Corinne asked from the back seat with a low, sexy growl. Johnny's car keys dangled teasingly from one of her claws. He screamed and bolted out of the car.

Corinne didn't even bother with the car door. She crashed through the side rear window and clamped her twisted fingers onto Johnny's shoulders. She snatched the doomed man headfirst back into the car through the broken window. Her arms and legs wrapped around him with a grip almost tight enough to crush his bones.

Johnny murmured in pain and dread as the breath was forced from his lungs. Corinne plunged her long, pointed canines into his right deltoid and tore off a bloody chunk of muscle, squirming with pleasure as she chewed and gulped down his flesh. She squeezed Johnny even tighter between her arms and legs, causing his joints to pop and his bones to snap. He soon lost consciousness from a lack of oxygen. Corinne released him and stretched luxuriously in the back, preparing herself for a leisurely repast.

A strong hand darted through the broken rear window, took Corinne by the throat and yanked her out of the car. Major lifted her above the ground until their eyes were level. He held a large, full, plastic garbage bag over his shoulder with his other hand. Corinne sniffed. Roxanne was in the bag. She was merely unconscious, not dead.

"What are you doing?" Major demanded.

"Eating," Corinne whispered through bloody lips with an annoyed expression on her face.

She grabbed the back of his head roughly and pulled him to her. She snaked her elongated canine tongue into his mouth and kissed him savagely, smearing Johnny's blood all over his lips and chin. Major kissed back for a moment before thrusting her against the car.

"Are you *trying* to get us caught? You don't ever let prey run this far. Anyone could've heard the screams. Someone could be watching us right now!"

Corinne raised an eyebrow. "You picked this building and neighborhood because both are abandoned. If someone was near we would've heard them or smelled them, or both."

She was right, of course. In fact, Roxanne was in the bag for convenience, not concealment. Major had learned that the flopping limbs of an unconscious person or a corpse could make them a bit awkward to carry.

"That doesn't matter, Corinne. You were supposed do your thing in the room while I fed through my syringe."

"You ever get tired of sipping through a straw?"

Major dropped Corinne and sighed. Of course he got tired of consuming blood that way, but he'd long since explained to her why he did it. It was easier to avoid notice if they hunted couples and left one of them alive and without teeth marks that would alert vampire hunters. The wound he drew their blood through would be dismissed as an injection of whatever drug Major managed score before the hunt.

Though they were less concerned about police than hunters, it could only help to misdirect them. Instead of a double-homicide or missing persons' investigation, police would investigate the survivor. With the survivor's memory of the attack erased there would be no plausible alibi and no one would know Major and Corinne had been with them. He never told Corinne how guilty he felt when he killed humans and he never intended to tell her. She would consider that a weakness and Major knew that would prove dangerous.

Major wondered if Denise would have given him this much trouble if he had turned her. If he had done so against her will, he knew the answer. He wondered what she was doing, how she was feeling, until he noticed his companion giving him a curious look. She wondered why he had such a faraway look in his eye. Major donned a mask of annoyance.

"Look, if you just *have* to play with your food, don't do it out in the open like this. Can you do that much for me?"

Corinne huffed. "I ain't immortal like you. I plan to have as much fun as I can before I die."

"Just be careful. We can't risk attracting attention."

Corinne dismissed his concern with a wave of a tiny, deadly hand. "I'm not worried. I know I'm safe with you."

Major pulled Roxanne's prone form out of the bag and tossed her down the block, well past the front of the car and several yards past a light pole. She landed roughly on the street, breaking bones and shredding skin against concrete. The toss would likely result in a concussion but she would live, and the additional trauma would serve his purpose.

The smell of fresh blood tempted him to feed again but he controlled it. It would take too long to rig up the syringe and tubing. Biting her was not an option. He turned and gave Corinne a nod.

"You're up."

She gave him pouty look. "Can I eat just a little more?"

"If you'd stayed in the room like you were supposed to instead of 'having fun' with your little chase, you could've fed to your heart's content. Now it's wild game or raw meat from a supermarket; punishment for breaking our rules."

Your rules, Corinne groused internally. She didn't know Major could read her mind. He doubted she would even care. She almost always said exactly what was on her mind. Nonetheless, he had a natural – or *preter*natural – compulsion to keep some aspects of himself secret.

Corinne was not happy but she performed her role as expected. She traveled with Major because he allowed her to feed on humans, her preferred prey, with a minimal chance of getting caught. He had a talent for covering their tracks.

She walked around to the driver's door while Major walked around to the back of the car. Corinne opened the car door, leaned in, and punched out the driver's side of the windshield. Four well-placed blows made a hole big enough for a human to pass through. She put the key in the ignition, started the car, and shifted it into neutral.

While she was doing that, Major rested the sole of his right foot against the car's rear bumper. Corrine gave him a thumbs-up and leaned away from the car, signaling Major to give it a hard push. The car sped directly into the light pole and struck it with a deafening crash. With a wave of Major's hand, a blaze erupted inside the vehicle.

Within moments the entire car was awash with flames. Roxanne appeared to be the injured survivor of an automobile accident. Johnny would be burned enough to conceal the gouge in his shoulder.

Major and Corrine disappeared into the night.

EPILOGUE

Tim was pissed. It had been a terrible night. There was no way his date was still waiting for him. They were supposed to meet at a club on the southeast side of Houston. Tim was unfamiliar with that part of town and he ended up taking a wrong turn somewhere and got lost. The kindest word he could think of to describe the neighborhood in which he found himself was "seedy."

"I have to get a Garmin or TomTom," Tim grumbled to himself as he parked his car outside a convenience store.

He went in to ask directions. The store was empty other than the clerk, who seemed to be even less knowledgeable about the area than Tim. He left the store frustrated and grew even more so when he discovered his car was gone.

"Shit!" He swore. He reached for the flip phone clipped to his belt then remembered it was in his car attached to its charger. "Shit, shit!"

The pay phone outside the store was of order and the convenience store clerk would not let him use the phone behind the counter. The clerk refused apologetically from behind bulletproof glass. Tim argued, begged, and bribed but the cashier was adamant.

He had to find another pay phone. The sun had already set and he had to walk through the unfamiliar and foreboding neighborhood. After one block the neighborhood went eerily quiet and dark. There was only one functional streetlight on the corner and none for the next few blocks.

The surrounding buildings were boarded up. There were no people on the street. Tim got a bad vibe from that direction. As he turned around to go back the way he came, he caught a glimpse of an overly affectionate couple in the inky shadows in the space between two buildings.

Slightly embarrassed, Tim looked away and kept walking, fully intending to mind his own business. After a few steps, the sound of the man's chuckle floated to him from around the building. Something about the voice made the small hairs on the back of his neck stand on end. The sound was both familiar and disturbing but he could not quite identify the reason. And then he stopped cold.

Tim walked backwards to where he had seen the couple and saw that they were still there. The residual illumination from the streetlight on the corner provided just enough light for Tim to see a man pinning a woman to the wall while kissing her. But then Tim realized he was not kissing a "her." He was kissing a "*him*," a small, thin, teenage boy dressed in tight cutoff jeans and a fitted tank top.

The kiss was deep and passionate and strange. While the teen's head and mouth moved intensely, the rest of his body was rigid. His hands were on the taller man's shoulders but not in a passionate way. It was as if he wanted to push the other off but could not find the strength. His posture was unnatural and all too familiar. Tim saw that posture years earlier in a Chicago park when Richard was kissing a girl.

That was after Richard had become a vampire. The girl was his victim.

Tim watched the man's mouth move from the teen's lips to his neck, allowing him to see the face of the young victim. It was expressionless at first, and then the teen winced and his blank expression morphed to one of surprise and pain. The taller man looked up at Tim and smiled with blood-smeared lips. There was a red glow in his eyes.

"You enjoying the show?" he growled.

Tim stepped toward them. The vampire was pleasantly surprised when the newcomer was not frightened away. Good Samaritans made easy meals.

"Leave him alone," Tim commanded.

"Or what?" the tall man asked as he released the teen. The youngster slumped against the wall and slid to the ground. The stranger started toward Tim. "You don't have the slightest idea what you just walked into."

"Yeah, I do," Tim assured as he pulled his .44 Magnum from a shoulder holster concealed beneath his windbreaker. He aimed it at the approaching predator.

"What do you plan to do with that?" the killer challenged as they neared one another.

Tim could feel the fear the vampire projected. His natural urge to turn and run was already strong and the vampire magnified it to an unnatural degree. He wanted Tim to run. He wanted the excitement of the chase, even a short-lived one. Tim knew it was happening and the attempted manipulation made him as angry and as determined as he was afraid. He kept the gun raised and kept moving forward.

"You gonna shoot me?" the vampire taunted. His red eyes glowed sharper as he smiled wider. The streetlights gleamed off of his fangs. "Shoot me, bitch!"

Tim had his conceal and carry license and had been to shooting ranges but was not a great shot. The distance between them closed enough that it did not matter. He could not miss if the vampire did not move, and he knew the vampire would not move.

The creature obviously could not read minds. Somehow Tim could feel when Major tried to poke around in his thoughts. Tim did not feel any kind of psychic intrusion from this vampire so he knew he had that one advantage. If the vampire could read Tim's mind, there was no way he would have kept advancing in such a deliberate, arrogant manner.

Tim fired three shots. Two of the shots hit the man's chest and one found his throat. Tim watched as the vampire stumbled backward several paces. It only took seconds for the stranger to regain his balance. He looked at Tim and laughed hysterically. His laughter was cut short when steam began to seep from the bullet wounds. The malevolent arrogance in his countenance twisted into fear and surprise. He clutched his chest and neck and doubled over in pain.

When he looked up again his once-human face was a mask of bestial fury and agonized confusion. Tim stepped forward and pressed the nose of the gun against the vampire's forehead.

"Silver bullets, bitch."

He pulled the trigger and blew the vampire's brains out the back of his head. Black blood and gore spattered against the wall. The vampire teetered from left to right before collapsing next to his victim.

Tim knew full well that the job was not finished. "Gotta take the head," he muttered to himself. "Pierce the heart and take the head."

He looked around for something to use and noticed a sign stuck in a small patch of grass near the street. The sign was a scribbled-upon poster board nailed to a long wooden post that had been shoved into the soil. He holstered the gun, ran to the sign and tore off the poster. It took two heavy tugs before the two-by-four came free. The end of the wood that had been pushed into the grass was cut into a point.

"Perfect," Tim said.

The vampire was still lying on the ground squirming in pain from his steaming and sizzling wounds. Tim hurried back to his attacker and raised the wooden post. Out of the corner of his eye, he saw something streaking toward him. Someone hurtled into him and drove him to the ground. Tim dropped the two-by-four and rolled along the ground with his assailant. He rolled to his back, got a grip a pair of narrow shoulders, and shoved the attacker away.

Tim rolled to his feet and saw the cross-dressing teen facing him. The boy's eyes held a dim red glow and tiny fangs were barely visible when he growled.

"Damn," Tim swore. "You turned quick."

He reached into the top of his shirt and produced the silver Allah pendant that hung from a silver chain around his neck. The teen screeched and turned to run.

"Can't let you do that," Tim said as he pulled his gun and shot the boy in his thigh.

The teen stumbled to the ground. Tim ran to the discarded strip of wood, scooped it up, and continued to the older fallen vampire. The monster had risen to his hands and knees and was struggling to stand. Tim stood over him and thrust the sharpened wood into the vampire's back. The pointed tip punched into his heart and came out through his chest. The vampire whimpered and crumpled to the ground.

"Now you have to take the head," advised an unfamiliar voice from the sidewalk.

Tim turned to see two strange men in long coats standing several feet away. One was a black with a shaved head. He stood a couple of inches shorter than Tim. The other was blonde and a couple of inches taller. The black man had a foot on the youngster's chest holding him firmly on the ground. Tim pulled his gun and leveled it at the newcomers.

"Who's next?" Tim challenged.

"We're not vampires," said the black man.

They opened their jackets and held out their arms to reveal their necks, wrists and black-clad torsos. They were adorned with rosaries and crucifixes. Their long coats concealed gun holsters and small, streamlined crossbows hanging from their belts. Both had straps fitted around their right thighs with quivers hanging from them. The quivers contained several nine-inch spikes of silver and wood.

"We're hunters."

"Do you have something to take his head?" Tim asked as he lowered his gun.

The blonde nodded before reaching into his pants pocket and producing a loop of fine metal wire. Tim assumed correctly that it was a silver garrote. The blonde man walked past Tim and over to the impaled vampire.

"Are you guys SHROUD?" Tim asked.

The man holding down the teen looked somewhat surprised. "What do you know about SHROUD?" he queried.

"A little," Tim said. "I know you guys are some sort of vampire-hunting organization."

"*How* do you know about SHROUD?" the other demanded as he applied more pressure to the struggling teen.

Tim watched the blonde loop a couple of coils around the vampire's neck. With one deft pull, the silver wire sliced and burned cleanly through the vampire's flesh and bone.

The creature's head went rolling away from its body. Tim skipped away as the severed head rolled past his feet. The head continued on toward the other hunter. The man moved his foot from the now-still teen to stop the severed head. He produced a rolled-up black sack from an inner pocket of his long coat. The head was quickly scooped up and placed into the sack.

"You guys are serious, huh?" Tim asked.

"I asked you how you knew about SHROUD," the hunter reminded.

"Weller and Burns," Tim said. "Burns is a priest and Weller's a retired cop. They're from Chicago."

"Why do you hunt without aid from SHROUD?" the black man asked.

"I don't hunt."

"You carry silver bullets," the blonde noted. "You act as if you've done this before."

Tim shrugged. "I've hunted before, but I'm not a hunter."

Just then a third man joined them. He was gray-haired, noticeably older than the other two. He carried a wide roll of fabric. When he unrolled it, Tim saw that it was a body bag.

"He must be Tim," the older man said as he placed the open sack at the feet of the headless body. He and the blonde quickly pulled the sack over the corpse. The older man explained while he worked.

"The priest and detective spoke highly of him in reports of their Houston operation a year ago. The two of you were completing your training at the time." Once he and the other man got the entire body in the sack, he pulled the drawstring to cinch it closed.

"They tried to recruit him but he declined."

The black hunter tightened the sack containing the head then tied the drawstring to his belt. He then went over and lifted one end of the body bag while the blonde hoisted the other end. They carried the body out to the street.

The older man turned to Tim. "We're riding in a fairly large SUV, Tim. You're welcome to ride with us."

Tim looked at the other with an expression of suspicion. "I don't think we're going in the same direction."

The older man noticed the apprehension. "Don't worry. I'm not going to give you a recruitment speech. If you don't have a car, we can drop you off wherever you're going."

Tim glanced at his watch. "Well, I had a date tonight but that's pretty much shot to hell. I guess I could use a ride to the police station. My ride got lifted and I have to file a report. From there I can get a cab home."

"No problem," the older man said. "By the way, my name is Peter. Peter O'Riley." He extended his hand.

"Nice to meet you, Peter Peter O'Riley." Tim shook the proffered hand. "One condition, though. I am *not* riding in the back with the headless horseman."

"Of course not," grinned Peter.

"What about him?" Tim asked. He pointed to the unconscious teen.

"His maker died before he tasted blood," Peter said in a matter-of-fact tone. "He'll have a nasty wound in his leg but he'll live and remain human. He'll probably think the little he saw tonight was some sort of drug-induced hallucination."

"But he has a bullet hole in his leg," Tim pointed out.

"We'll let him worry about that," Peter replied as he turned and headed back to the street.

"You're just going to leave him here?" Tim asked. The teen began to stir as he slowly regained consciousness.

"Do *you* want to take him home?" Peter asked.

"Good point." Tim followed Peter to the SUV.

The older man climbed into the driver seat while Tim got in the front passenger seat. The other two SHROUD hunters sat in the back watching over the still corpse.

"Let me ask you something," Peter requested.

"No recruiting," Tim reminded. "You promised."

"Just curiosity," Peter assured. "With the first-hand knowledge you have of these monsters, how can you not aid us in their extermination?"

"You just answered your own question," Tim answered. "My first-hand knowledge of them is exactly what keeps me away. My involvement back then was personal. People I cared about were mixed up in it. They're all gone now.

"Richard and Major were my best friends. My 'first-hand' experience was the loss of them both. I don't want to lose anyone else, myself included. The more space I can put between myself and those bloodsuckers, the better."

"You weren't putting space between yourself and them this evening," noted the blonde.

"Tonight was different. I wasn't hunting, though."

"You couldn't ignore what you recognized to be a vampire attack," Peter said. "After what you've seen, how could you? That's a hunter's instinct."

"That's a human's instinct," Tim argued. "No way was I gonna let that kid just get..." Tim paused. "Hold up, how long were you watching?" he asked.

"We've been following that particular vamp for about a week," said the other man in the back.

"So you saw everything," Tim accused, bewildered. "You just watched him take that kid into that alley. Did it matter to you that he was going to kill or turn that poor bastard?"

"Our mission this evening was to watch him," Peter explained. "We had no plans to engage him. Our hope was that he would lead us to others of his kind. We suspect there's a coven forming in the area."

"What about the kid?" Tim asked.

"This particular vampire has killed all of his victims," Peter said. "If he had left *this* one undead, we would have dealt with him."

"Either way that kid was done for," Tim said in disbelief. "What kind of shit is that?"

"War shit," the black man snapped. "Make no mistake, this is a war. Wars have casualties."

"That's another reason not to join SHROUD. I'm not a soldier. I don't any part of your war."

They rode the rest of the way in silence until they arrived at the police station. Tim opened the SUV door and started to leave. Peter put a hand on Tim's shoulder and gave him a grave look.

"Young man," he started, "You're part of this war whether you choose to be or not. Your experience means you're sensitive now."

Tim sighed. "What does that mean?"

"You know the signs," Peter explained. "You know what to look for, even if you're not consciously looking. Vampires are all over the place and you'll be able to spot them."

"What's your point?"

"Do you know how to mask your thoughts?" Peter inquired. Tim only stared. The elder hunter continued. "If you spot one that happens to be a mind-reader, one of two things will happen: It'll read you and know you recognize it or it will realize that you're blocking your thoughts and take you for a hunter. The wrong facial expression can tip off a vampire that can't read minds. All of these things will make you a target."

Tim nodded. "Thanks for the heads-up. I'll burn those bridges when I get to them."

"You'll never be at peace again," Peter warned.

Tim climbed out of the vehicle and closed the door. As the SUV pulled away, Tim prayed it carried away his last experience with vampires and vampire hunters…and freaking *werewolves*.

END